KT-423-601

THE TEMPLAR

1097 and crusading fervour is sweeping Europe. The Infidels have seized Jerusalem, and an outraged Pope Urban II has called for the Kingdom of Western Europe to reclaim the Holy Land in the name of Christendom. The response is overwhelming: thousands flock to join up, eager to undertake the greatest pilgrimage of all.

Hugh de Payens, his younger sister Eleanor and his close friend Godefroi of St Omer are no exception. Caught up in the great swirl of events, they join Count Raymond of Toulouse's army, preparing for an epic journey that will take them across Europe, through glittering Byzantium to Jerusalem.

There's a fever of excitement amongst Hugh and the other crusaders as they embark on their travels. But that's before they know the depth of the hardships, treachery, trickery and bloodshed they will have to endure. Can they, and their dedication to the cause, survive?

THE TEMPLAR

Paul Doherty

WINDSOR
PARAGON

First published 2007
by Headline Publishing Group
This Large Print edition published 2008
by BBC Audiobooks Ltd
by arrangement with
Headline Publishing Group

Hardcover ISBN: 978 1 405 68718 8
Softcover   ISBN: 978 1 405 68719 5

Copyright © 2007 Paul Doherty

The right of Paul Doherty to be identified as the
Author of the Work has been asserted by him in
accordance with the Copyright, Designs and
Patents Act 1988

All rights reserved.

All characters in this publication are fictitious and
any resemblance to real persons, living or dead, is
purely coincidental

British Library Cataloguing in Publication Data available

Printed and bound in Great Britain by
CPI Antony Rowe, Chippenham, Wiltshire

Angela Francescotti dedicates
this book to her lovely granddaughter
Lucia Maria Francescotti

FIFE COUNCIL LIBRARIES	
811888	
BBC AUDIOBOOKS	4. 6. 08
	£18.99
LP	

Main Historical Characters

POPES

Urban II (1098–99):
launched the First Crusade at Clermont in 1095.

LEADING FRANKS

Adhémar of Le Puy:
Bishop of Le Puy in southern France and papal
legate on the Crusade.

Raymond of Toulouse:
Count of Toulouse and Lord of St Gilles. Leader
of the southern French Crusaders (Provençals).

Bohemond of Taranto:
Leader of the southern Italian Norman Crusaders.

Godfrey of Bouillon:
Leader of a contingent of Crusaders from
Lotharingia and Germany.

Robert of Normandy:
son of William the Conqueror and Duke of
Normandy; leading figure amongst the northern
French Crusaders.

Robert of Flanders:
Count of Flanders; leading figure amongst the
northern French Crusaders.

Stephen of Blois:
Count of Blois; leading figure amongst the
northern French Crusaders.

Hugh of Vermandois: (Hugh of Paris)
Count of Vermandois in northern France and
brother of King Philip I of France.

Tancred of Hauteville:
Bohemond of Taranto's nephew.

Baldwin of Boulogne:
Count of Boulogne; Godfrey of Bouillon's
ambitious brother.

Peter the Hermit:
charismatic preacher and leader of the People's
Crusade.

Peter Bartholomew:
Provençal visionary who 'discovered' the Holy
Lance at Antioch.

Hugh de Payens, Godefroi of St Omer
friends, French knights on the First Crusade
who later founded the Templar Order.

Raymond Pilet:
Provençal captain in Raymond of Toulouse's army.

Walter de Sans-Avoir:
Lord of Boissy.

William the Carpenter:
French captain, noted for his cruelty.

BYZANTINES AND ARMENIANS

Alexius I Comnenus:
Emperor of Constantinople (1081–1118); founder of the great Comneni dynasty.

Manuel Boutoumites:
Greek envoy who ended the Siege of Nicaea.

Tacticius:
Greek general who accompanied the Franks to Antioch.

Thoros:
Armenian ruler of the city of Edessa; adoptive father of Baldwin of Boulogne, who killed him.

Firuz:
Armenian officer of Antioch, who betrayed the city.

MUSLIMS

Kilij Arslan: ('Sword of the Spirit')
Seljuk Turkish Sultan of Rhum in Asia Minor.

Yaghi Siyan:
Governor of the city of Antioch.

Ridwan of Aleppo:
Siljuk ruler of the Syrian city of Aleppo; led
Muslim relief force to Antioch.

Atabeg Khebogha:
Emir of Mosul and renowned general; Leader of a
massive Muslim army to relieve Antioch.

Iftikhar:
Fatimid Governor of Jerusalem.

Author's Note

The Templar is based not only on primary documents but on numerous accounts of people who actually travelled from Europe to take Jerusalem in July 1099. I have, at all times, tried to follow the tone of these accounts and the language they themselves use. A note at the end also comments on this extraordinary venture, which seared world history and had such long-term effects. The various crusading armies moved from France, Italy and Germany to Constantinople, then across to what is now modern Turkey, turning south into Syria and Palestine. The journey of the main army under Raymond of Toulouse was quite simple—across northern Italy, then following Via Egnetia along the Adriatic and into Greece. The main historical characters are listed, and their actions are based on the evidence of eyewitnesses. I have also kept to the simple division between two conflicting cultures in the Middle Ages. In the world of Islam, the term 'Frank' was used to describe any westerner. In turn, most Europeans were unaware of the different sects in Islam and generally used the terms 'Turk' or 'Saracen' to describe their opponents.

Prologue

Regis Regum rectissimi prope est dies domini.
(The day of the Lord, of the most righteous King,
is close at hand.)

The *Dies Irae* of St Columba

The monk lifted his cowled head and peered through the lancet window overlooking the wild heathland of Melrose. Harvest time was close, but his task was only just beginning here in the stair tower of this ancient fortified manor house. He stared round the chamber at the neatly stacked ledgers, indentures, chronicles, letters and memoranda: these had all been collected from the libraries of the Order of the Temple and brought here in the summer of Our Lord 1314.

'Everything we could steal or buy,' the old woman murmured as she rested on her cane, staring through the small oriel window. She didn't even bother to turn round.

'*Consummatum est*—it is finished. Brother Anselm, you've heard the news?'

The young Cistercian monk coughed and nodded. He realised why he was here. He had been sworn to secrecy on the great leather-bound, gold-embossed Book of the Gospels chained to its lectern in the centre of the room.

1

'Nineteenth March past,' the old woman whispered. 'Jacques de Molay, Grand Master of the Temple, and Geoffrey de Charny, Preceptor of Normandy, burnt at night fastened to a stake on the Île-de-France. Innocent they were . . .' She hobbled over to Brother Anselm and smiled down at him.

'Father Abbot,' she leaned over and girlishly stroked the monk's smooth cheek, 'has released you from all duties.' She waved round. 'To form this into one seamless cloak. A chronicle of the Order of the Temple from its origins to the end.' She grasped Anselm's wrist; the grip was surprisingly strong, despite her apparent frailty. Her light grey eyes held his.

'You are my kinsman Benedict; you have the sacred blood of the de Payens, the founders of that order.'

'*Domina*, how shall I write it?'

'As a chronicle,' the old woman replied. She turned and walked over to the neatly stacked manuscripts. 'As if you were there, Brother. Be like the prophet Ezekiel in the Valley of the Dead: breathe life, blood and flesh into these dry bones.'

Part 1

The Parish Church of St Nectaire in the Auvergne. The Eve of the Feast of St Ignatius of Antioch, 16 October 1096

Dies irae et vindicatae tenebrarum et nebulae.
(A day of anger and of vengeance, of darkness and thick clouds.)

The *Dies Irae* of St Columba

Duelling eagles had been seen fighting above the black curtain of trees, whilst in the night sky javelin threatened javelin beneath crossed swords. Blazing marriage torches had turned funereal. Winds started lightning bolts out of the clouds, which terrorised the people with their slanting flames. Comets scored the sky. Summers burned white-hot. Winter came in sheets of ice. Satan was seen everywhere. In that remote and unknown part of the great ocean called the Sea of Darkness, which teemed with monsters, devils could be seen rising from the midst of the waters, the fierce black band of the Prince of Demons, an awesome warning of what was about to happen. The time of confrontation had arrived.

The words of the Holy Father, Pope Urban II, had been released like darts the previous November. Jerusalem had to be liberated from the Turks. It was God's will. Men, women and children began arming for war. They brought out shields,

3

the paint peeling, their frames bare, javelins with their points forced back, swords, daggers and spears all blackened or rusting. Forges were fired in villages and hamlets, the hammering and pounding going on deep into the night. Flames leapt up against scorch-marked walls as the weapons of war were sharpened and refined ready to cull a bloody harvest. Horses were brought in, hooves and mouths checked. Sumpter ponies were trotted across icy meadows and carefully inspected. The Frankish world was about to move, to journey to Jerusalem and free the Lord's Holy Places from Turkish hands. The people of the west hastened to fulfil the prophecies and portents as the skies clouded over with steel during the day and were riven at night by the clash of mythical weaponry. Masses were chanted, candles and tapers lit before the ghostly statues of a myriad of saintly protectors. Aves, Pater Nosters and Glorias were recited. Sins were shriven, penances accepted. Men, women and children took the cross, lying face down in a thousand freezing naves with the winter mist boiling along the mildewed flagstones beneath them whilst the carved face of their tortured Saviour stared down at them from the rood screen.

The great lords mortgaged their estates, pledged their revenues to the cross, begged pardon for sins and took the money offered by the good brothers of St Benedict to turn their ploughshares into swords and sickles into spears. Husbands swore fidelity towards their wives and loyalty to their kin as they drew up their last wills and testaments. Jerusalem called! Christ's fief beckoned! God's warriors were to free it from the hands of the Turks. *Deus vult!* God wills it! The cry echoed like a trumpet blast through the lands of the Franks. God's will would be done! Nevertheless, the cross-bearers also dreamed of jade-green seas, of courtyards as wide as summer fields, of horses with manes the colour of the whitest wheat, of marbled porticoes, precious cloths of camlet, damask and brocade, of jewels as large as carbuncles, of warm, golden days well away from the cold, dank air of the forests or the gloomy mist-haunted woods of the west. The fire of expectation flared through the lands of the Franks; the flames of faith, hope and charity glowed alongside those of ambition, greed and lust. God's will must be done in these last days. Men claimed the Apocalypse was imminent, the sudden rapture of the Day of Judgement, which was about to be sprung on every man like a trap. Nobody must be found wanting!

Nothing had been the same since the previous autumn, when a misty haze hung heavy over fields black and bare after the harvest had been gathered in. The grey walls of Clermont had become a shrine drawing in the caped churchmen with their glittering crosses, and the lords, their banners and gonfalons of red, gold and lily-white snapping in the breeze. On a purple dais, a curly-bearded cleric, shoulders weighed down by a pure white gold-embroidered pallium, delivered God's message. Pope Urban II added his own summons. 'I speak to you who are present here,' he began in a ringing voice. 'I announce it to those who are absent that Christ has ordained this. From the borders of Jerusalem to the city of Constantinople, terrible tidings have gone forth. A certain race has emerged from the Kingdom of the Persians, a barbarous people who have invaded the lands of the Christians of the east and depopulated them by fire, steel and ravage. Such invaders, Turks and Arabs, have advanced through the empire of Constantinople as far as the Middle Sea and as far as the straits which are called the Arm of St George. The empire of Constantinople is now mutilated. Until this present year the empire has been our defence; now it is in dire need. These Turks have driven away many Christian captives to their own country. They have torn down the churches of God or used them for their own rites. What more can I say to you? Listen now, these pillagers pollute the altars with the filth of their bodies. They circumcise Christians and pour the blood of the circumcision upon our altars or into baths and fonts. They use our churches now withdrawn from the service of God to stable their horses. Yes, these churches are served not by holy men; only the Turks may use them. Even now the Turks are torturing Christians, binding them and filling them with arrows or making them kneel, bending their heads so their swordsmen can cut through their necks with the single blow of a naked sword. What shall I say about the rape of women? To speak of that is worse than to be silent. You in France have heard the murmur of agonies from beyond the borders of Iberia! The time may well come when you will see your own wives violated and your children driven before you as slaves out of the land.

'Reflect also on those fellow Christians who have travelled the seas as pilgrims. If they carry money, they are forced to pay taxes and tribute every day at the gates of cities and the entrances to churches. If they are accused of anything, they are forced to buy their freedom again, and as for those who have no money but trust in Lady Poverty, what of them? They are searched. They even have the calluses cut from their bare heels to see if they have sewn something there. They are given poison to drink until they vomit and burst their bowels to show if they have swallowed coins. More often their stomachs are cut open to be searched; their intestines pulled forward and slit so that what is hidden may be revealed. Who can relate this without sorrow? These are your blood brothers, children of Christ and sons of the Church. On who else will fall the task of vengeance and justice unless on you who have won such glory in arms? You have the courage and the fitness of body to humble the hand lifted against you.'

Urban, his voice thrilling with passion, now turned his anger on his listeners. 'You are girded knights, yet you are arrogant with pride! You turn on your brothers with fury, cutting down one then the other. Is this the service of Christ? Let us hold to the truth! To our shame: this is not our way of life! Orphaners of children, despoilers of widows, slayers of men! You reek of sacrilege! You are murderers awaiting the payment of blood-guilt. You flock to battle like vultures that glimpse a corpse from afar. This is hideous! If you would save your souls, lay down the guilt of such knighthood and come to the defence of Christ. All you who carry on feuds, go to war against the Turks! You who have become thieves become soldiers, fight the just war, labour for the everlasting reward! Let no obstacle turn you aside;

7

arrange your affairs, gather together supplies, enter upon this journey when winter is ended. God will guide you . . .'

Urban paused, leaning against the dais. He watched the assembled mass. Men burst into tears, faces in their hands, women turned away, and then the cry came. *'Deus vult!'* The shout rose to a roar as men drew sword and dagger in a clash of steel, bellowing their war cry to the skies. Urban lifted his hands and motioned for silence.

'Where two or three are gathered together in my name, there am I in the midst of them,' he intoned. 'Unless the Lord God had been in your minds, you would not have cried *"Deus vult!"* So I say to you, God himself has drawn this cry from you. Let that be your battle cry when you go out against the enemy. Let this war cry be shouted: God wills it! Moreover, whoever shall offer himself upon the journey must make a vow, and wear a sign of the cross on his head or his breast. The old and sick should not go, nor those unfit to bear arms. Women should not set out upon this holy pilgrimage without husbands, brothers or guardians, for such are a hindrance rather than an aid. Let the rich help the poor. Do not let possessions detain you, nor the love you have for children, parents or homes. Remember what the Gospel says: "You must forsake all to follow Christ." So go forth upon your path to the Holy Sepulchre, wrest that land from the invaders and keep it for yourselves, a land that flows with milk and honey! Jerusalem, fruitful above all other lands, where the Lord lived and died for us. In His Holy Sepulchre kneel and give thanks for your faith. Go, and fear not. Your possessions here will

8

be safely guarded, whilst you will take from your enemy even greater treasures. Why fear death in a land where Christ laid down his life for you? If any should lose their lives, even on the journey by sea or land in this battle against the Turks, their sins will be forgiven. I grant this to all who go, by the power invested in me by God. Do not fear torture or pain, for that is the crown of martyrdom. The way will be short, the reward everlasting. Yes, I speak with the voice of a prophet. Take up your arms; it is better to fall in battle than see the sorrow of your people and the desecration of the Holy Places . . .'

And so the summons went out. Adhémar, bishop of nearby Le Puy, Urban's envoy, was appointed to take the Voice of God and turn it into the Voice of the People. Urban was of Cluny, and his black-robed Benedictine brethren also carried the message out into the fields, villages and cities. They painted a picture of heavenly delight awaiting all who took the cross: Jerusalem, the eternal city, guarded by lofty towers, with foundations of precious stones, protected by gates brighter than the stars; even its battlements glowed with pure crystal. Inside, the streets were paved with gold and silver, its palaces of gleaming marble, lapis lazuli and precious gems. Crystal waters spurted through golden-mouthed fountains and silver-edged pipes to water health-giving trees, fragrant flowers and medicinal herbs. During a cruel winter, with the meat smelling rancid, the fruit and vegetables turning black and rotting, the bread rock-hard, not to mention the prospect of worse to come, the vision of such a heavenly city was more powerful than any psalm or hymn. Young

9

men left horse and plough to prostrate themselves before the rood screen of their church. Two slivers of red cloth, sewn in the form of a cross, were clasped on their shoulders. A few days later they would stand in the same stone-flagged, hollow-sounding nave to receive the purse and staff, symbols of being a pilgrim as well as a cross-bearer.

Winter passed bleak and hard. Berries and roots became the staple of life, whilst the soft breads, fresh meats and plump fruits of summer grew to be only a distant memory. Many more began to envy the *crucesignati*, or cross-bearers. The prospect of bathing in the warm waters of the Jordan, of walking amongst a paradise of fruit trees and feasting on sweet, tender meats and the softest manna was almost as tantalising as that of everlasting life. Such dreams warmed the freezing cold of winter in draughty rooms filled with peat-smoke, which curled and cured the stale meat hanging from rafters or shoved into crevices above the hearth. *God wills it*. The message went out, seeping through the rain-soaked villages and frost-imprisoned hamlets with their rutted tracks, stinking animal pens and dingy houses. The cross, two slivers of red cloth, would transform all this.

God wills it—the refrain was taken up in halls and solars where the smoke-darkened tapestries ruffled and flapped against limestone walls in a vain attempt to keep out the sneaky icy draughts. *Deus vult*. A glorious path had been opened to salvation in this world and redemption in the next. Why, men wondered, wait for spring to break the hard soil, to stare up at the clouds and pray desperately for good weather? Why not journey

10

east to the marvels of Jerusalem, destroy God's enemies, seize back the Holy Places and win the Lord's friendship for all eternity? No more hardship, no more war between neighbours, no more back-breaking work on the land or perilous journeys from one place to another as darkness descended and the wood-mists swirled. Other glories beckoned: the gold, silver and precious stones that adorned the fabulous cities of the Byzantines. Conversion to the call was swift. Even professional men of war hurried to take the oath. They too prostrated themselves before the altars of a thousand churches. They pledged their estates wherever they could, settled debts, made peace with enemies, drew up wills and turned to the business in hand. How many spears, how many arrows were needed? What armour? How many pack horses? They drew in others as former opponents invoked the Truce of God, which meant that a warrior dedicated to the cross was sacred— and that included his property and family.

The great lords were also lured, amongst these Raymond, the sixty-year-old Count of Toulouse, Lord St Gilles, or Sanctus Aegidius, to whom he had a special devotion. Raymond became a fervent cross-bearer. Small and wiry, his hard head shaved close as well as his grey beard and moustache, he had a warrior's face. Some said he had lost an eye fighting the infidel in Iberia. Others claimed he had been on pilgrimage to Jerusalem and had his eye plucked out for refusing to pay the tax the Turks levied on all who wished to worship in the Holy Sepulchre. These same people whispered how Raymond kept the eye in a special pouch and had pledged vengeance for it. Raymond of

11

Toulouse mortgaged his estates, settled his debts, took the oath and sent out his messengers. The Provençals, the count's subjects, listened and marvelled at the portents that accompanied his proclamations. One night the moon turned blood-red. A shepherd saw a mighty city in the air. A star appeared and advanced by leaps and bounds towards the east. Torches of fire swept the sky. A sword of wonderful length was suspended from heaven and hosts of stars fell, each one representing the death of an infidel. Springs ceased to give water and spouted blood instead, indicating how the blood of their enemies was about to flow. Twins were born joined to each other; could that mean that east and west were to be united? The cross was seen everywhere. The stars themselves were congregating into one gigantic cross. A priest reported that the heavens had opened before his eyes and a huge cross had been displayed before him. Another priest maintained he had seen a vision of a knight and a Turk in combat in the sky. After a desperate battle, the infidel had been thrown from his horse and killed by the knight, who delivered his fatal blow with a cross. A sure sign that heaven was with them. God wills it!

Better still, they argued in taverns and alehouses, life would improve. They would be liberated from tilling the harsh fields in endless, grinding monotony. The journey to Jerusalem was an escape not only from evil-smelling dark alleyways and damp hovels but from the strictures of life. Women dressed in men's clothing and flourished spears with warlike threats. Priests, caught up in the frenzy, assumed the cross without consulting their bishops. Monks emerged from monasteries; some of them had not seen outside life since their youth and yet their abbots could not restrain them. Those who engaged in the sacred cause were, by papal decree, exempt from all taxation and relieved from duties if their lord did not take the cross. Debtors could not be held to account as long as they were a cross-bearer. No legal suit could be started against one who wore the sacred sign, whilst the cross was protection against almost any criminal action. Prisoners were released on the understanding that they would fight the Turks. Robbers who had been a terror to their neighbourhood for years were received into the peace with open arms. No man was so sin-laden that he could not be purged by merely assuming the cross and carrying out his vow. Women urged husbands, lovers and sons to enlist in the sacred cause. The man who held back was looked upon as a traitor to Christ and a coward to his community. Women's garments were sent to him. Men and women burned and cut the sign of the cross on their own bodies and even branded their children, including infants at the breast, with the all-important symbol. A priest appeared with a cross burned deep on his forehead and confirmed it had been accorded to him by heaven.

Nowhere did the word of God move so deeply as in the village of St Nectaire, close to Clermont where Urban had preached. It was a wild countryside dotted with extinct volcanoes now covered by craters full of wild flowers and grassy clumps, its limestone gorges washed by turbulent streams. A landscape of contrasting colours like the different shades of dark on a pigeon's wing.

The hymn to the Crusade had blown strong and clear here. The tensions of life would be released, all dissolved in the glorious journey to Jerusalem, which according to some was only five hundred miles away, or was it five thousand?

On the eve of the Feast of St Ignatius of Antioch, the Year of Our Lord's Incarnation 1096, the people of the manor of St Nectaire met in the chilly nave of their parish church. All assembled. Folk memory, as well as the records of the time, clearly establishes that, as does the chronicle written by Eleanor de Payens. They took the oath. They prostrated themselves on the freezing-cold floor of that haunted, sombre nave so recently polluted by spilt blood, its sanctuary violated as the witch Anstritha had been dragged out screaming to be hanged above a roaring fire. Those who had witnessed that, even participated in such a violent act, now tried to forget it as they concentrated on their own secret sins reeking of evil, their souls full of an insatiable hunger for absolution. The villagers of St Nectaire took the cross, the staff and the wallet. Jerusalem beckoned. They would exult when their feet trod the sacred streets behind its holy walls and heaven-built gates. Satan would be no more. The Lord of Hosts would encamp with them. They chanted the lines of the psalm:

One thing I have asked of the Lord,
For this, I long.
To live in the house of the Lord all the days of
  my life.
To savour the sweetness of the Lord.
And behold His Holy Temple . . .

14

Once this finished in a resounding 'Amen', Father Alberic asked them, as they sat on the rough benches before the rood screen, to look on the ravaged face of their crucified Christ, reflect on their sins and seek absolution. One by one they were to move across to the shriving pew where Father Alberic, in his dusty black gown, sat in the mercy chair to listen, exhort and bestow absolution.

The place of penance was in a shadowy transept concealed behind a squat, drum-like pillar. One candle of pure beeswax, a pledge by Hugh de Payens, glowed invitingly; its dancing flame illuminated the vivid wall-painting nearby: a scene from the Apocalypse, Satan's persecution of the elect, a river of torment that the Lord of Hell vomited against the Church. The widow Eleanor de Payens was the first to cross to this shadowy place of repentance and absolution. She had followed her brother from the green fields of Compiègne on the left bank of the Seine outside Paris: like him she had taken the cross and so must be shriven. Eleanor's graceful, strong face was shrouded by a veil, her skin unpainted, her bright grey eyes clearly troubled, her full lips slightly parted, firm chin jutting forward. She found confession difficult; she always did. She knelt before the shriving pew, whispered her list of petty sins, then paused, head down.

'And?' Father Alberic whispered. There was always an 'and'.

'Father, I am a widow. My husband Odo . . .' Eleanor paused, 'he fell one night and killed himself.'

'I have heard of this.'

15

'But not the full truth, Father. He was deep in his cups. I encouraged him in that.'

'Why?'

'To keep him from me, but he came searching. At Compiègne,' Eleanor continued in a rush, 'in our castle, a tower built of stone with a wooden hall alongside, my chambers lie high in the turret.' She took a deep breath. 'He came up, Father. I was alone. His mouth was full of foul oaths, his heart bubbling with malice, his belly swilling with cheap wine. I met him on the stairwell. We fought. I pushed him, Father, he fell, striking his head against the walls, the sharp stone steps . . .'

'You were defending yourself?'

'Father, I was pleased to see him fall.' Eleanor could say no more. She could not confess those last sins, her secret pleasure at Odo's death, those long hours she stayed in her chamber, neglectful about what had happened to him.

However, Father Alberic was nodding understandingly, hand already going up, lips mouthing the 'Absolvo te'.

Eleanor left the shriving pew. She had leaned so tensely against the mercy chair that her arms and wrists ached. Alberic had said that her penance would be her pilgrimage. She crossed the nave and knelt in the Lady Chapel, staring up at the carved face of the Virgin. Eleanor closed her eyes and once again whispered the Confiteor.

'I confess to almighty God, and to you my brothers and sisters, that I have sinned exceedingly . . .'

Would she, Eleanor wondered, gain peace and absolution in Outremer? Would she kneel in the Holy Sepulchre and ask forgiveness? Or would

16

Odo's angry, hate-filled face, full of fury at his own impotence, come like a shadow of the night to haunt her? No one knew the full truth, not even her beloved brother Hugh, or his close comrade Godefroi of St Omer, to whom she was so attracted. Was that also a sin, her secret thoughts and desires? Little wonder she was determined to journey to Jerusalem. She had brushed aside her brother's objections, whilst meeting Godefroi of St Omer was only further encouragement to take the cross. Moreover, to stay in that rain-washed manor at Compiègne, alone and vulnerable, waiting for the ghosts to return . . . Eleanor caught herself and sighed. Her pilgrimage was certainly not for selfless reasons. She chewed her lip and wondered about her brother's . . .

At the mercy chair, Hugh de Payens was also seeking absolution, for the drunkenness that followed his wife's death in childbirth, his consolation with the occasional whore, and above all, his constant absorption with the tourney or the mêlée, his need, even hunger, for a life of fighting. If he could only sweep this up, purify it and place his sword at the feet of the Lord and Holy Mother Church . . . Father Alberic heard him out. The priest was glad Hugh was their leader. He was an accomplished knight, skilled in war and swordplay, who had purified himself through service in Iberia against the infidels. A fanatic? Alberic wondered. Hugh's face was lean; his dark eyes, thin lips and slightly hooked nose gave him a rather cruel, predatory look. He was tall and slim, with the long, powerful arms of a swordsman, a soul looking for a song, Alberic concluded as he raised his hand in absolution. Yes, the priest was glad Hugh de

17

Payens was to be the leader of their company as well as an ally in Alberic's own secret search for the truth.

The same applied to Godefroi of St Omer, who came next. In contrast to Hugh, Godefroi was a rather stout, short young man with a smooth, smiling face beneath a mop of flaxen hair. His clear blue eyes gazed out on the world like those of a confused child. Godefroi of St Omer, the only beloved son of his parents, gave the impression that nothing in life was too serious. As he began to list his sins, Alberic realised that Godefroi, his manor lord with advowson to this church, was like a forest pool: a placid surface hiding a veritable tangle beneath. Despite his looks and easygoing ways, Godefroi had also taken part in the *chevauchées* into Iberia. Fired by the *Chanson de Roland*, the epic deeds of Charlemagne and his paladins, he had fought the infidels along the rocky gorges of the mountain passes. Nonetheless, he had become a deeply troubled man, a knight who now realised war was not glory. He talked of dark, despairing days, freezing cold in the mountains. How the rain and hail slashed down, smashing tents, spreading infection amongst the horses and rotting the already mouldering pork and the weevil-infested biscuits. How the rain had turned their shirts of mail to heavy rust. He also described massacres on dusty plains, wells and river beds being choked with corpses. Godefroi had returned from such wars wondering what all that had to do with the love of Christ. He asked the same question now and received the usual answer: God's will! Urban had preached this and the Church upheld it. After all, hadn't God in the Old

18

Testament raised David the warrior to defend his people? Moreover, in the New Testament, Christ had told Peter to simply put up his sword, not throw it away. Father Alberic quietly congratulated himself on this clever piece of casuistry, taught to him by a canon lawyer from Avranches. He was about to administer absolution when Godefroi's head came up, and he stared full and frank at the priest.

'And there's Anstritha, Father. She was involved in our secret quest. Her death troubles us.'

'Our quest remains. They claim she was a witch.'

'Who sought refuge in our church.'

'I could not help her,' Alberic hissed, 'nor could any of you. The Lady Eleanor and the Lord Hugh were visiting Clermont. You were with them. It happened so swiftly, her blood does not stain our hands.'

Godefroi nodded, rose and walked away. Alberic put his face in his hands as if in prayer, a sign to the next penitent that he was not yet ready.

And to whom do I confess? the priest wondered. Memories swirled back like prophets of doom. Old enemies bearing old sins. The battle line at Senlac buckling. The mailed horsemen milling in, faces hidden behind conical helmets and broad nose-guards. The Fighting Man, the battle standard of Wessex, drooping like a wounded bird in the wind. The screams of blood-splattered men, his own heart giving way. The ring of faith around Harold Godwinson tearing and splintering like a tree struck by lightning; his own courage ebbing like wine from a cracked cup.

'Coward!'

The word still lashed Alberic's soul, as it did

19

when he tramped the roads with Brother Norbert. Anstritha was simply a fresh cut to an old wound. A clever woman, skilled in simples and herbs, she was a woman of secrets who had followed the same path as Alberic, Norbert, Hugh and Godefroi, searching for the truth. Perhaps she could have been better protected? Yet she had certainly been marked down for death. Villagers, hooded and visored, taking advantage of their manor lord's absence, had attacked her in her shabby house on the outskirts of the village. God knows the reason! A child had died. Food was scare. The signs had been seen. A victim was needed, and Anstritha became the scapegoat. She had fled to this church, begging for Alberic's help. He was going to give it, God knows he was! He was terrified. Anstritha even might name him as an accomplice in her secret business. He had hurried back into the sacristy, but the corpse door had been forced and the mob surged in. Alberic had hid in the narrow, incense-filled enclosure whilst the mob had dragged Anstritha out and hanged her from a makeshift gallows above a fire. Eventually she had stopped screaming. The Lord Godefroi had returned the following week, but despite his anger and that of Lord Hugh, the culprits escaped unscathed.

A loud cough made Father Alberic take his hands away. Robert the Reeve, anger incarnate, was waiting, his choleric face twisted in impatience. The priest secretly wondered if Robert had had a hand in poor Anstritha's death, yet he doubted the reeve would confess to that. After all, in the eyes of many villagers, Anstritha was a witch, deserving of death, a righteous act pleasing to

20

God. Behind Robert waited the rest: Imogene, the pretty, dark-haired widow whom the Lady Eleanor had agreed to take with her on pilgrimage as a helpmate and companion; Fulcher the blacksmith; Peter Bartholomew, the young hunchback who saw visions in the dark, wet woods; and behind him a score of others, including Alberic's close friend Norbert the Benedictine monk. Norbert, however, would not be kneeling at the mercy chair. He crouched at the foot of a pillar while the rest milled around. They were impatient for the priest to finish so they could feast on the bread, wine and tasty meats laid out on trestle tables, garlands of wild flowers woven around the jugs and flagons. Tonight they would celebrate, and within the week they would join Raymond of Toulouse, Count of St Gilles, in his march on Jerusalem. For now, however, the shriving continued, though the harsh whispers were drowned by the rising hum of conversation. Hungry eyes drifted to the heaped platters, and people wondered if their horses and pack ponies stabled in God's Acre outside were safe. At last Father Alberic finished. He climbed into the crude wooden pulpit and they all gathered around.

'The Lord is a man of war,' Alberic intoned from the Book of Exodus, 'and so must ye . . .'

Father Alberic's tongue changed from the words and phrases of the *langue d'oc*, the speech of the south, to those of the *langue d'oïl* of the north, as he described the exploits of the great warriors of God in the Old Testament. Eleanor, leaning against a pillar, jumped as the priest's talk was cut short by the church door slamming shut. She whirled round and stared at the man garbed in a black cotehardie that fell over leggings of the same colour, his stout ox-hide boots jingling with spurs. He wore a white tunic beneath the black, which peeped out between the creases of his robe. The sword belt slung over his shoulder carried a sheath, a knife and a short stabbing sword. Eleanor's first impression was that the stranger was the devil come to dispute with them: that saturnine face under the close-cropped hair and those clever eyes, which, despite the poor light, reflected the mockery in his soul.

'I am Beltran.' He spoke the *langue d'oc* like a troubadour. He glanced impishly at Eleanor. 'I am a poet, a soldier, but above all, the emissary of His Excellency Raymond, Count of Toulouse, *fidelis miles Christi et Papae*, faithful soldier of both the Lord Christ and the Pope.' He brandished a small scroll tied with a red ribbon. 'I am here at Count Raymond's behest to lead you.'

'We have a leader.' Eleanor pointed to her brother.

'Then I will be his adviser.' Beltran's face broke into a smile. 'I also bring you a copy of the Count's personal banner.'

'We have taken an oath to God,' Godefroi declared hotly. 'We hold nothing in fief or knight service to any lord.'

'No, no,' Beltran replied merrily. 'The Count offers you protection under his banner.' He undid his jerkin and brought out the blue and gold pennant of the Lords of St Gilles. 'I must also check your supplies and stores. So,' he held up his hand, 'by what name shall ye be called?'

'The Poor Brethren of the Temple,' retorted Hugh, walking forward. 'We took the idea from the psalm about living in the Lord's house all the days of our lives.'

'Yes, I know it.' Beltran let the banner ripple towards Hugh, who caught it and held it up. The nave rang with cheers. Swords, daggers, spears and axes were raised to shouts of *'Deus vult, Jerusalem!'* and 'Toulouse, Toulouse!' Father Alberic shrugged and came down from his pulpit, and Hugh ordered the feasting to begin.

The following morning the Poor Brethren of the Temple left a little later than had been decided, the sun already high above the grassy slopes and black volcanic rock of the surrounding countryside. The cause of the delay was the sudden death of Robert the Reeve, who had apparently staggered out, deep in his cups, and drowned trying to cross a stream. A most unfortunate mishap. God knows, there was a footbridge nearby, whilst nobody could explain why Robert was stumbling around God's Acre in the dark. Nevertheless, they found him floating face down, dead as wood. Father Alberic murmured the words of absolution and they buried Robert quickly beneath the ancient yew trees. Imogene the widow remarked how the reeve was already in the new Jerusalem. Father Alberic heard this and quietly prayed it was so, for, if any man needed God's mercy, then surely it was Robert the Reeve.

Part 2

Sclavonia: The Feast of St Lucy, 13 December 1096

Diesque mirabilium tonitruorum fortium.
(A day of marvels, of mighty thundering.)

The *Dies Irae* of St Columba

'I will wash my hands among the innocent and encompass thy altar, oh Lord. I have loved, oh Lord, the beauty of thy house and the place where thy glory dwelleth.'

Eleanor de Payens murmured the verse from the psalm at the entrance to her goat-skin tent. She stared out at the bank of mist swirling round, muffling sound and blurring the glow of camp fire, candle and lantern horn. Somewhere in the camp, a child cried. Eleanor shivered; it sounded like the echo of her baby's first and only cry as he slipped in blood from her womb. She could still feel his warmth, his little face shrivelled like a plum, the blinking eyes, the tip of that tongue hungry for her breast.

'The Lord giveth and the Lord taketh away,' Eleanor murmured. She crossed herself; the hard wood of the crucifix on her Ave beads knocked the tip of her nose, which was already cold and sore. 'And the same for noses.' She grinned to herself, always averse to self-pity, and went back to sit on the small chest that served as a stool. She extended her mittened fingers over the chafing dish, a mix of

24

charcoal and dried twigs, and stared across at Imogene sitting on a leather pannier. The widow woman was dressed like a nun in black veil and robe, her olive-skinned features and raven-like hair almost hidden beneath a grimy wimple. Her fingernails were bitten to the quick and she sat with hands extended over the heat, eyes closed, lips moving soundlessly. Beside her, as always, was that carved wooden box, its lid sealed, the top embossed with three crosses and the IHS monogram representing Jesus' Passion above the words *'Deus vult'*. Imogene, who shared Eleanor's tent, had assured her that that casket contained the heart of her husband, which she hoped to bury in some holy place in Jerusalem. Eleanor was not convinced. Imogene had a great deal to hide, but there again, Eleanor conceded, so did many of their fellow pilgrims, including her own brother.

'How long, sister?' Imogene was now staring full at her, eyes watchful. Had she, Eleanor reflected, realised that she shared a tent with a light sleeper? As the poet said: 'The truth always comes in dreams.'

'How long what?' Eleanor smiled.

Imogene shivered. Eleanor rose, went across and tightened the tent flap closer.

'We have been journeying for weeks.' Imogene pulled the threadbare shawl closer about her shoulders. 'These mountains . . .' Her voice trembled.

Eleanor nodded understandingly. As she had scribbled in her chronicle, they had left the grass-filled glades of the Auvergne and travelled north before turning east. Ahead of them the blue and gold banner of St Gilles flapped above the grizzled

25

head of Raymond of Toulouse. Behind him, in the dark robes of a monk, rode the shaven-faced Adhémar, Bishop of Le Puy, the Pope's legate in all matters of the cross-bearing. At first anyone would have thought they had reached Jerusalem as they marched joyously through the sun-warmed valleys. The trees still proclaimed the glories of summer, even though the silver and gold of autumn was beginning to appear. The Count rode his swift destrier ornamented with the gilded leather harness of Cordova, decorated with deep stitching and small gold and silver discs. The crowds surged out to greet such magnificence, scattering green leaves and scented petals along the dusty trackway. Garlands of flowers were looped over the weapons and harness of Christ's warriors, bowls of fruit thrust into their hands together with red stone jugs filled with the rich wines of the south or honey mead so sweet on the tongue. Church steeples trembled with the booming of bells. People clamoured to join them, including wiry mountaineers who would act as their guides through the Alpine passes. Farmers, yeomen, tinkers and traders, ribalds and counterfeit men swelled the throng to somewhere between fifteen and twenty thousand souls. Count Raymond took them all in to form new companies. Eleanor soon noticed how the Count remembered Hugh and Godefroi's participation in the *chevauchées* in Iberia: their company, now publicly known as the Poor Brethren of the Temple, was singled out for special favour, whilst its captains sat high in Raymond's councils.

'They say we should have marched south through Italy,' Imogene murmured.

26

Eleanor broke from her reverie. The sounds of the camp had grown louder: the blowing of horns, the shouts of huntsmen returning with fresh meat.

'My brother says no. Count Raymond believes the mountain passes down into the Lombard plain would not be passable, whilst a sea voyage from southern Italy to Greece always threatens danger.'

Imogene nodded understanding, though Eleanor suspected she had meagre knowledge of maps. Indeed, Eleanor herself had swiftly realised how little she knew of the world outside Compiègne or the Auvergne. Everything and everyone was strange and hostile until proved otherwise. The journey had only reinforced this. The Franks were taking their own ways with them, highly suspicious of everything new. If a stranger could bless themselves or intone the Ave Maria then that was better than any letter or writ. If they failed to, fingers crept to sword and dagger hilt. Distances and new kingdoms were only miles to travel on their way to Jerusalem, which lay at the centre of the world, however the maps portrayed it. Hugh and Godefroi had borrowed copies of such maps. They had shown Eleanor how Count Raymond had decided to march east across Italy, around the northern coastline of the Adriatic then south through Sclavonia to Dyrrachium in the kingdom of the Greeks. The journey was proving difficult enough, Eleanor decided to break the cold distance between herself and Imogene.

'At night you talk in your sleep about Robert the Reeve.'

'And what else?' Imogene asked quickly.

A horn brayed. Eleanor heard Beltran calling the Poor Brethren of the Temple to a *colloquium* before their standard. She was glad to evade Imogene's question, and quickly grabbed her hooded cloak. Imogene did likewise, and they left the tent. Eleanor summoned a boy, one of the mountaineers now attached to their company, to guard their possessions. Once satisfied, they hurried through the mist across the frost-hardened ground, trying to avoid the puddles of horse urine, the dirt of men, horses and dogs. On its perch at the mouth of a tent, a huge hawk screeched and stretched, claws moving to the jingle of its jesse-bells. Eleanor wondered how long such a creature could survive this cold. The frost stung her eyes, nose and mouth. The mist curled, a thick white vapour cutting off the light and obscuring all around them.

At last they reached the meeting place between the tents and the horse lines, a stretch of frozen grass now lit and warmed by scattered roaring fires, flames crackling greedily at the dry thorn and bracken. In the centre of this ring of fire stood a cart from which the Poor Brethren's banner floated on a pole. Beltran, Hugh and Godefroi standing behind him, grasped the side rails of the cart and gestured at them to draw closer. They did, though Eleanor, like the rest, also tried to position herself to catch some warmth from the fires. Beltran blew on a hunting horn, stilling the clamour. He had a powerful voice and had quickly assumed the role of being their herald and news-bringer. He stood silently for a while, then delivered his message like an actor in a play or a troubadour reciting a poem. Hugh and Godefroi looked very grim; Eleanor caught her brother's eye, but he simply shook his head and glanced

28

away. At first, the news was good.

'Other armies of cross-bearers,' Beltran declared, 'are moving east. Indeed, some are already approaching Constantinople. The Franks of the west are on the move accompanied by wondrous signs,' he added. 'Mysterious flocks of birds have been seen forming in the sky, pointing to the east, whilst some talk of a sacred goose that will lead them to Jerusalem.' Beltran paused as the crowd laughed and shook their heads. He then pressed ahead with his other news. He described how the men of northern France and Germany had been eager for standards to tramp behind. Some of the great princes of Europe had emerged to lead them. Godfrey of Bouillon was such a man, a true warrior. He and his two brothers, Baldwin and Eustace of Boulogne, who owned swathes of estates across northern France and the Rhineland, would also join them in Constantinople. Philip I of France had been eager to go but could not because he had been excommunicated for his infatuation with another man's wife. Instead Philip had sent his brother, Hugh of Paris, with two other warriors, Baldwin of Hainault and Stephen of Blois. These had been joined by the red-haired, green-eyed Robert of Normandy, nicknamed 'Short-breeches', brother of Rufus, the Red King of England, both sons of the Great Conqueror. These lords had collected as many men as they could and taken to the roads, escorted by their households, their greyhounds, lurchers and falconers running alongside them, a glorious cavalcade journeying to Jerusalem. More news was flowing in. How Bohemond of Taranto, the Norman adventurer from southern Italy, also intended to march with his war-like nephew Tancred. God was surely with them!

'Nor is it just the lords,' Beltran explained after a brief pause. 'The People's Army, under its leader Peter the Hermit and his lieutenant Walter, Lord of Boissy Sans-Avoir, nicknamed "Walter Sans-Avoir"—Walter Without Anything—have already clashed with the Turks—though with disastrous results. Peter's message is simple,' Beltran hastily explained. 'We must take the road to the Holy Sepulchre, rescue Christ's fief and rule over it ourselves. Such a land, flowing with milk and honey, was given by God to the children of Israel. Now we have inherited it ourselves, we must seize it from our enemies. We must take possession of their treasuries and either return home victorious or go to eternal glory blessed and purpled with our own blood . . .'

Beltran paused. People began shouting questions about Peter. Beltran replied that little was known about the hermit. Peter had possibly been born near Amiens. A poor man, he dressed only in a grey woollen robe with a hood pulled over his head. He rode a mule, his bare feet hanging down loose as he preached the taking of the cross. The hermit was dark of face, burnt black by the sun; he ate and drank nothing except a little fish, bread and some wine. According to Beltran, he was a passionate preacher whose tongue had been blistered by the Holy Spirit, a brilliant orator who, despite his shabby appearance, could persuade the most beautiful and noble women to lay their treasures at his feet. They even cut off hair from his donkey as sacred relics, and regarded Peter's bath water as a holy elixir. Beltran paused to slurp

30

noisily from a goblet of wine. Eleanor wondered if their herald was quietly mocking this common preacher who had stirred up so many to follow the cross. She glanced at Hugh; he stood, arms crossed, staring down at the wooden slats of the cart.

Beltran continued. According to one story, Peter had visited the Holy Sepulchre to witness first hand the violence of their enemies. Whilst in Jerusalem, he had also fallen into a trance and experienced a vision of the Lord Jesus, who had told him, 'You will receive a letter for your mission from heaven bearing the seal of a cross.' Peter claimed to hold such a heavenly letter, which was how he had swept through the Frankish kingdoms, exhorting all to follow the cross—not just the lords, but the forgotten and dispossessed. According to Beltran, orange-wigged whores, bejewelled pimps, catamites, counterfeits, cripples, vagabonds, adulterers, soul-killers, fornicators, perjurers and outlaws surged from the dank slums of the towns to mingle with his army of artisans, labourers, knights from Picardy, axe-men from Swabia and swordsmen from Cologne. Again Beltran paused to drink, smacking his lips in relish. Eleanor's stomach clenched. Beltran was a cynical soul. He was openly scoffing at those poor cross-bearers, and she suspected the story he was telling would end not in triumph but disaster. Beltran, however, now had them all spellbound and they drew closer. The herald described how the great People's Army, almost sixteen thousand souls, had surged across Germany threatening the Jews, extorting monies from these unfortunates before they assembled to hear Mass in hedge-Latin and chant their popular hymns. Peter's horde had then left Germany, following the Danube through the kingdom of Hungary, watched from afar by the Hungarian king's sheepskin-coated scouts on their swift ponies. The Hungarians, Beltran declared, were wise to be cautious. Coloman, their king, was wary of this long column of carts and horses and the unruly throng streaming across his kingdom beneath a host of crosses and tattered, brilliant banners.

The People's Army had expected to travel safely and securely, but whilst crossing the Danube, they were attacked by Patzinacks, Turkish mercenaries, mounted archers from the steppes hired by Alexius Comnenus, Emperor of Constantinople, to serve as police along his borders. A bitter battle ensued, during which German knights on a fleet of rafts attacked a flotilla of Patzinacks and beat them off. They captured some of these mercenaries and brought them before Peter. He immediately ordered their decapitation along the banks of the Danube and left their severed heads tied to the branches of trees as a warning to the rest.

Peter and his army, Beltran explained, then crossed the Danube into Alexius' territories and reached the city of Nish. Here the imperial governor promised them supplies and safe conduct to Constantinople. However, when some of the more fiery of Peter's lieutenants discovered that their advance guard under Walter Sans-Avoir had been badly cut up in a forest fight, they turned back to burn and pillage the suburbs of Nish. Imperial police shadowing the People's Army lost patience, and a furious woodland battle ensued. During this savage mêlée, thousands of Peter's followers simply disappeared. Afterwards, the cross-bearers continued their march, escorted by fierce mounted archers, who shepherded them as dogs would sheep. However, if any of the marchers wandered off the beaten track, these dogs became wolves, taking heads and fastening the grisly trophies to their saddle horns.

At last, Beltran declared triumphantly, the People's Army reached Constantinople. The cunning Emperor Alexius had them camped on the eastern side of the city near the Golden Gate and sent out carts heaped with supplies to feed them. Peter's horde, relaxed and refreshed, immediately turned their attention to the wealth of Alexius' city. The many thieves and vagabonds amongst them could not resist the temptation to loot; they even climbed on to church roofs stripping off the lead to sell to city merchants. The Emperor decided to move them across the straits known as the Arm of St George into Anatolia, the kingdom of the Sultan of Rhum, Kilij Arsan, who called himself 'the Sword of the Spirit'. Here the People's Army rejoined their advance guard under Walter Sans-Avoir who had taken up residence in a deserted fortress near Civetot.

Summer was ending in a golden glow, continued Beltran like a true troubadour; the harvest was ripening, fat-bellied cattle and sheep grazed in the meadows. The People's Army, bereft of Peter, who had stayed in Constantinople, began to have itchy feet and even itchier fingers. Foraging turned into plundering and reaping into rapine as they explored the paths through fertile valleys and well-stocked meadows. Although they did not know it— Beltran held a hand up—they were being closely

33

watched by Seljuk scouts, who soon noticed how disorganised and ill-led the People's Army had become. The Seljuks waited. The cross-bearers, hungry for plunder, planned a harrying *chevauchée*, a raid up to the walls of Nicea. They elected a mercenary, Rainald of Bruges, as their leader, and debouched on to the plains, unaware that they were being shadowed by the Seljuks on their nimble ponies, fierce warriors with their long plaited hair, necklaces and earrings; across their chests were lacquered armour plates, whilst from their saddle horns hung quivers and sturdy horn bows. These watched the cross-bearers and bided their time. Rainald led them to Xerigardon, a deserted fortress. Once they had fortified this, the rabble ruthlessly pillaged the surrounding countryside, unaware of how the Seljuks had now circled them.

In a flurry of fierce sorties, the Seljuks forced the People's Army back into the fort, then cut off their water supply, a well close by the gate and a nearby fountain. According to Beltran, the People's Army suffered hideous losses. They were now besieged, hunted, harassed and wounded, bereft of water and support and exposed to the late autumn heat. They grew so tormented by thirst they even drew blood from the veins of their horses and donkeys to drink. Some urinated into the hands of others, then supped it. Many dug into the moist ground and lay down, spreading the earth over them to allay the terrible heat. For eight days this agony continued. At last Rainald entered into a treasonable correspondence with the Turks and, in return for his life, agreed to hand over the others. The Turks placed some of their prisoners in a long line and used them for arrow practice; those they favoured were taken back to be sold in the slave markets.

Beltran now had his listeners spellbound. Meanwhile, he continued, back at Civetot, Walter Sans-Avoir and the other captains had heard about this disaster and hastened to help. The mob thronged along the road towards the deserted fortress without any order, although Walter and a handful of knights managed to keep a force of five hundred horsemen together. The Turks watched in astonishment, then trapped the entire army in a valley. Walter was killed in the first foray, seven arrows piercing his body. The Turks had won a great victory. The remnants of the People's Army fled back along the road. The Turks followed in pursuit and captured their camp, cutting down the Christian sick and enslaving the women. News of the disaster reached Constantinople, but all the Emperor could do was send troops to help those who had fled and hidden in rocky gulleys or caves . . .

The Poor Brethren received all this news with loud groans, cries and lamentations. Eleanor, warming her hands near a fire, heard similar sounds from other parts of the camp and realised that heralds were spreading the dismal news elsewhere. Beltran had not yet finished; his litany of woes continued. Other crusading armies had emerged under the likes of Gottschalk, a German priest so cruel and predatory that the Hungarian king had ordered the total destruction of both him and his army . . .

Eleanor listened carefully. She had read vague rumours about such hideous events in the letters,

35

memoranda and other missives dispatched to the chancery of Raymond of Toulouse. She and Hugh had been well educated by their widowed mother, a sharp martinet of a woman who'd mourned her husband at every waking moment; she had constantly reminded Eleanor and Hugh how God had taken her saintly man in the flower of his youth. She was also determined that both her children should rigorously study their horn books. They graduated on to Latin grammar and syntax, not to mention courtly French and even a few words of Greek. A harsh discipline! Eleanor often reflected on her bruised knuckles. She could still chant the Greek alphabet, as well as the more complex Latin tenses. Such a rigorous education had only drawn her and Hugh closer together, so that they had become like two peas in a pod. Even a drunken husband, the birth of a child who had died shortly afterwards, the upsetting of their world and the preaching of Urban could not shake that.

Once Beltran had finished, Eleanor accosted Hugh, demanding to know whether such terrible news could be true.

'There is worse,' he confessed, and took her to Raymond's chancery tent, where Eleanor, as she later wrote in her chronicle, quickly realised that God was not always with the cross-bearers. Raymond of Toulouse's clerks had also received dreadful news about Emicho, Count of Leiningen, who had used the call to Jerusalem to unleash a blizzard of hatred against the Rhineland Jews. Emicho truly believed he would be rewarded for his work with a diadem in Constantinople. He first tried his mischief at Speyer but then turned on

Mainz and the Jews who hid in the shadows of that great city, locked in their own world, garbed in their grey and purple robes, treasuring their traditions, studying the Torah and celebrating their calendar of feasts. Once at Mainz, Emicho, who believed a red cross had miraculously appeared on his flesh—probably a flea bite—together with William the Carpenter, Vicomte of Melun, viciously attacked the Jews there. The vicomte, a killer to the bone, had acquired his sinister nickname in Iberia because of his passion for hammering spikes and nails into the foreheads of his victims. These two assassins and their cohorts took the trampled corpse of one of their company, buried thirty days previously, and carried it through the city saying, 'Behold what the Jews have done to our comrade. They have taken a gentile and boiled him in water. They then poured the water into your wells to kill you.' Violence erupted. Many Jews fled for safety to the bishop's palace but were later betrayed. Emicho and William seized a leading Jew named Isaac. They put a rope around his neck and dragged him through the muddy streets to the place of execution, where they screamed at him to convert and be saved. Isaac signalled with his finger that he was unable to utter a word for his neck was choked off, yet when they released the rope, he said simply, 'Cut off my head.' They did so, then encouraged their followers to go on a bloody rampage. They killed about seven hundred Jews, who could not resist the attack of so many thousands. Various letters repeated the same horrors, a litany of hideous acts. Eventually Eleanor could read no more. She handed the documents back to the scribe and, followed by Hugh and Godefroi, left the chancery tent.

Later, Eleanor, Hugh, Godefroi, Alberic and Imogene gathered in a sombre mood for the evening meal of grilled rabbit meat and rastons. They met in the large shabby pavilion shared by Godefroi and Hugh; it reeked of scorched ox-hide, leather, sweat and charcoal. Father Alberic sang grace as Beltran pushed his way in and joined the circle just inside the pavilion's entrance. Behind him echoed the noises of the camp settling for the night. They all paused at the sound of a wolf howling mournfully at the full moon.

'A harsh day.' Godefroi bit into the half-baked bread, made a face and thrust the wine goblet to his mouth.

'Terrible news,' Alberic murmured. 'So many cross-bearers massacred. Peter the Hermit disgraced.'

'A rabble,' Hugh countered. 'They and others murdered Jews, massacring women and children! What has that to do with God's work?'

'We will pay for that,' said Alberic. 'Innocent blood never goes unanswered.'

'It's the fault of our leaders,' Hugh declared. 'The bishops, counts and nobles. They should impose order; there must be stricter discipline in God's Army.'

'But they are God's enemies,' Imogene retorted.

'Who are?'

'The Jews. They crucified the Lord. They said His blood should be upon them and upon their children.'

'But Christ's blood is meant to cleanse and sanctify,' declared Hugh.

38

'Or punish,' added Alberic, but his voice lacked any conviction. 'In truth,' he sighed, 'are they any different from us?'

'The Jews,' Eleanor asked, 'or the Turks?'

'Both!' Alberic muttered. 'The Jews? Who are they but God's children. Who are we? God's children. Who are the Turks? God's children, yet still we kill each other for the best possible reasons.' He glanced round. 'But *are* we God's children? Or is there no God and we are what we are, killers to the heart?'

His companions stared in puzzlement.

'Father,' Godefroi asked, 'do you regret coming?'

'No.' Alberic shrugged. 'I do not regret; just wonder.'

'But the Turks stole Christ's fief, His Holy City.' Beltran leaned forward, his unshaven, cold-pinched face bright in the firelight. 'His Holiness the Pope says it's our sacred duty to recover that fief, the Lord's domain, now in enemy hands, and restore it to its rightful owners. Surely, Father, if someone came to seize my house or your church it would be our duty to regain possession.'

'The devil rides a black steed,' intoned Peter Bartholomew, sweeping into the tent and sitting down uninvited. He stared around, eyes all fearful. 'I have heard the news,' he continued. 'The last days are upon us. Soon we shall see even more wondrous signs and listen to heaven-shaking news.'

'But what is that to us, brother?' Eleanor asked gently.

'The Lord Satan sows dissension here where there should be none,' Peter declared. 'We have sworn to do God's work. Is that not right, brothers

39

and sisters?' No one answered.

Eleanor watched Hugh closely. He had insisted that amongst the Poor Brethren, only the titles 'brother' and 'sister' should be used, and that each member must recite every day seven Paters, three Aves, two Glorias, the Dirige psalm and the Salve Regina. He had also compelled the Poor Brethren of the Temple to agree that money, plunder and the spoils of battle be shared equally. Discipline would be enforced, any violence against the innocent ruthlessly punished. Eleanor wondered about the Jews; those she herself had met seemed harmless enough, rather gentle, shy and frightened. True, she'd done them little good, but definitely no ill.

'You know our rules.' Hugh sipped at his wine. 'We stand by them. One more thing! Listening to what happened to Rainald. If we are captured,' he lowered his cup, 'let us not be cowards, but go to God with pure hearts, yes?'

A murmur of approval greeted his words. Hugh paused as Norbert joined their circle and squatted down.

'I heard you.' The monk pushed back his cowl. 'I was outside,' he coughed and rubbed his stomach, 'waiting for my belly to settle. I heard you mention the Jews, the Turks. Do you know what I think?' He gestured round. 'We are all killers. No . . .' He lifted a hand against their protests. 'Tell me, each of you, have you not lost your temper with a brother or sister and thought you could kill him or her? Have any of you said that?' The Benedictine's wrinkled face broke into a smile, lips parted to show blackening teeth. 'Remember,' he whispered, leaning forward, 'the thought is the father of the

40

word, which is the mother of the deed.'

'But your answer,' Hugh asked, 'is that it? That we are all killers?'

'It's not an answer.' Norbert chomped on his gums. 'Just something I have learned. Killing is about the will—that is what the great Augustine said. I mean . . .' Norbert's rheumy eyes stared at Eleanor, and his long fingers went out as if he wished to catch the tendrils of her black hair. 'If I planned to carry out an attack on your sister, to ravish her . . .' he playfully thrust his balding head forward; in return, Eleanor pulled an expression of mock-fear, 'then kill her, would you not have the right, Hugh, to defend her?'

'I would kill you!'

'No.' The monk laughed sharply. 'I said defend her. The two are quite different. Killing is about the will, what you intend to do.'

'You are a scholar of Augustine,' Alberic teased. 'You hold to his thesis of a just war.'

'Nonsense!' Norbert cackled. 'Oh, I've heard of Bonizo of Sutri's arguments about that, and how the Pope confers titles on warriors such as our glorious Count Raymond to justify their wars.'

Eleanor caught the sarcasm in Norbert's words.

'Titles such as *Fidelis Filius Sancti Petri*— Faithful Son of Saint Peter. Nonsense! The phrase "just war" is a contradiction in terms! How can a war ever be just?'

'So,' Godefroi asked, 'what is your reply? Why are you here?'

'Why not?' Norbert retorted. 'Oh brothers, I do not mock you. None of us knows why we really do anything. Why am I a monk? Is it because I have a vocation to follow the rule of St Benedict? To

41

serve Christ? Or was it to gain advancement and learning? Or because I sickened of listening to my mother couple with her lovers and wished to follow a more chaste life? Why have we come here? I tell you this.' Norbert's voice fell to a whisper. 'There are as many reasons for our pilgrimage as there are pilgrims. We may be *crucesignati*—signed by the cross—but we are all different. Ask yourselves but don't judge yourselves. Remember, our lives are taken up not by what we want to do but what we have to do!'

Eleanor pondered on Norbert's words as she, Hugh and Godefroi walked out across the camp, the silence broken by the neighing of horses, the barking of dogs and the cries of children. Lantern horns gleamed from the poles outside the great lords' tents. Camp fires flickered and crackled as they were banked down for the night. A cloud of smells greeted them: burnt oil, cooked food, wet straw and sweat, all mingling with the foul stenches drifting in from the latrines.

'Why are you here, Eleanor?' Godefroi abruptly asked as they stopped before her tent.

'Because of you,' she quipped, 'and you because of me?'

Godefroi laughed self-consciously and shuffled his mud-caked boots.

'Our life, as Brother Norbert said,' broke in Hugh, eager to save any embarrassment, 'is about what we have to do, or not do.' He stood, hands on hips, staring up at the sky. 'I know why I am not here,' he continued quietly. 'I am not here to kill innocent men, women and children. I am not here to plunder and pillage, ravage and rape.' He sighed deeply. 'I am here because I am here. True, I want to see the wonders on the other side of the world. I want to walk the streets of Jerusalem as Our Beloved Lord did, yet there's something else . . .' He shrugged, grasped Eleanor by the arms and kissed her gently on each cheek. Godefroi followed suit, though more awkwardly, then they were gone, their voices shouting farewells through the dark.

Eleanor undid the tent flaps. The lad guarding the tent was fast asleep beside the makeshift brazier. Eleanor roused him and gave him some slices of cheese in a linen rag. Once he was gone, she built up the brazier, tidied the tent and waited for Imogene to arrive. She'd glimpsed the widow woman deep in conversation with Norbert after the meeting had ended. Eleanor recalled Imogene's words about the Jews. She sat down on a coffer and watched a wisp of mist curl into the tent, thinking about Godefroi's question. Why *was* she here? To plead for pardon for the death of her drunken husband? To shake off the guilt of his death and that of her boy child, that glorious little spark of life, that flame that burnt so fiercely yet so briefly in her soul? For Hugh, the brother she adored, father and mother to her? Was it one of these or all of them? Was she part of something she would come to regret? The stories of Count Emicho, William the Carpenter and others revealed terrible savagery. She shuddered at the fate of those poor Jews, yet was she any different from the killers who had butchered them? Surely she was! Nevertheless, Hugh and Godefroi had assured her that once they crossed into the valleys of Sclavonia, fighting would break out, and they too would have to kill.

Eleanor stared at the tent flap. She felt deeply

43

uneasy about Hugh and Godefroi's reasons for taking the cross. True, they had been *crucesignati* in Iberia. They revelled in the legends of Roland. They sought absolution for past sins and were tired of the jousting and the tourneying between neighbours, but was there something else? The journey to Jerusalem could be understood, but since leaving the Auvergne, her suspicion had deepened that both knights nursed secrets. What date was it now? The middle of December in the Year of Our Lord 1096. Urban had delivered his sermon at Clermont over a year ago. Yes, that was right! She and Hugh had been in Compiègne when dusty messengers brought the news. She remembered one in particular, cowl thrust back, standing in their smoke-filled hall talking about an evil Turkish prince, Al-Hakim, who had razed the Holy Sepulchre church, inflicting indignities on his own people as well as Christians. Hugh had taken up the summons fervently, but when Norbert the monk had appeared, he began to change, becoming more sombre and reflective.

Eleanor chewed on her lip and quietly rebuked herself. She should have thought of this earlier. The seeds of her suspicions had been sown ten months ago, but she'd ignored them, taken up with the excitement, the frenetic preparations and the journey south to Auvergne. Godefroi's warm friendship had been most welcome, but again, events had been veiled by a mêlée of preparations. Yes, and something else. Alberic had been a constant visitor, often meeting Hugh and Godefroi by themselves. She recalled what she knew of the parish priest. He was undoubtedly a mysterious man, much better educated than the priests who

44

usually served the village churches. He and Norbert appeared to be old friends. The Benedictine seemed much travelled. Was he an excommunicate monk? Someone expelled by his monastery for making trouble? Jerusalem linked them all, but what bound Hugh, Godefroi, Norbert and Alberic so closely? She had been swept up in the preparations yet she had always sensed something amiss. Hugh had become more austere, praying more often, not so responsive to the laughing glances of the ladies and village girls. Moreover, since they had left the Auvergne, he had tightened the discipline of the Poor Brethren, publishing a divine office of hours, drawing up rules about meetings, dress and even diet. But why?

The march to the borders of Sclavonia had, despite the sheer glory of the mountains, been a tiresome trudge along muddy trackways. Eleanor had had plenty of time to reflect, to become more aware of the growing secrecy around her brother. In many ways Hugh reminded her of those knights from the great romances, who pursued some glorious, mystical vision. One thing she had discovered was Hugh and Godefroi's absorption with one particular chivalric poem: 'La Chanson de Voyage de Charlemagne à Jerusalem'. Hugh read this constantly. On several occasions Eleanor had asked to borrow his copy, and Hugh promised he would lend it to her, but he always found an excuse not to. This poem, together with a list of relics, seemed to absorb him whenever he was not busy with the Poor Brethren or conferring with Count Raymond. Eleanor had discovered the list of relics by sheer accident. A memorandum drawn up in

Count Raymond's hand was delivered by accident to her tent rather than Hugh's. She had asked her brother about its importance but he had dismissed it, declaring that it was simply a list of sacred items he would like to see. So much mystery!

Eleanor shivered against the cold and pulled her wrap closer about her shoulders. She was tired, eager for her narrow cot bed on the far side of the tent, yet she was determined to wait for the widow woman and resolve at least one mystery. She packed a few belongings for tomorrow's departure. She now regretted the few luxur-ies she had brought. She dressed the same every day: a linen shift under a brown serge gown with a leather strap around her waist; a deep cowl sheltering her head, whilst her legs and feet were warmed and protected by woollen stockings and ox-hide boots. She also carried a short stabbing sword in a sheath, Hugh had insisted on that. She was just finishing her preparations when Imogene, escorted by Beltran, reached the tent. They whispered their farewells and Imogene slipped in through the flap. As always she carried the battered leather bag containing her precious box. Eleanor smiled; Imogene nodded and crouched over the brazier. Eleanor shook off her tiredness.

'You were harsh against the Jews.'

Imogene simply shrugged.

'I mean,' Eleanor continued, 'you are, were, of the Jewish faith.'

Imogene's head came up; her mouth opened and shut.

'Oh, don't worry.' Eleanor smiled. 'I do not mean to threaten; you just talk in your sleep! Most of it is the jabbering of dreams, but I've heard you

46

pray the Shema. You mention the name Rachel, and sometimes you chatter in a patois I cannot understand.' She came and knelt beside Imogene. 'Please,' she begged, 'no pretence, not now. You are no longer with the rest; there is no need to chant the common hymn. I am not a threat to you. Does Norbert know?'

Imogene nodded, her dark eyes never leaving Eleanor's face.

'He knows so much, our wandering monk.'

'He has been to Constantinople,' Imogene replied. 'He and Alberic are more than what they seem; they search for something.'

'Yes, yes, I have realised that myself, but you . . .'

Imogene squatted on the floor and pushed back her hood, snatching off the coarse veil beneath. 'My birth name is Rachel. I am from Iberia on the borders of Andalus. The usual story,' she continued in a dry monotone. 'Portents and signs, a bad harvest, loans that could not be repaid. Of course the Jews were to blame, the usual scapegoats. My father was a merchant. He and my mother were trapped in their own house. They were burned to death along with my brothers and two sisters. I was six.' She smiled nervously. 'Small for my age. I escaped through a window. Night had fallen. I fled to a neighbour's house; they were kindly. My father had always told me to trust them. They took me in and sheltered me. I later found they were Jews who'd converted. I became one of them, given a new name and a new life. The couple were still Jewish and secretly continued to practise our religion. They kept the sacred vessels and their copy of the Torah hidden away. They secretly celebrated Yom Kippur, Passover, the Feast of the

47

Tabernacles and the other festivals. They also returned to my parents' house and gathered what they believed to be their ashes.'

'The wooden box contains these?'

'Yes. I hoped to bring them to Jerusalem, a righteous act for my parents. The Christian signs on the lid are part of the pretence.'

'And who are . . . what are you now?'

'Sister, I don't know.'

In the poor light, Imogene's face looked younger, paler.

'Truly I believe in nothing. Yes, that is correct.' She laughed sharply. 'How can I be Jewish when I believe in nothing?'

'And why have you decided to be honest now?'

'As Norbert says, why not?' Imogene pulled a face. 'After tonight's meeting of the Poor Brethren, I met Norbert and Alberic, and they assured me I'd be safe. We have so much in common. They are searching for something, something that is true in all this horror.'

'You know Alberic and Norbert from before?'

'Oh yes, they are constant travellers. They crossed into Andalus and visited my foster-parents' home. They are keen students of all things Jewish, be it the Kabbalah or the legends of the Temple Mount, the Dome of the Rock in Jerusalem.'

'What are they searching for?'

'God knows! Legends, relics, proof?' Imogene shook her head. 'They moved through the Jewish community asking questions, collecting information. I met them, and through them managed to meet my late husband Thomas, a wine merchant from St Nectaire.' She shrugged. 'The rest you know. I was a good wife, well respected. I settled in the area. My husband died. Urban preached his sermon at Clermont. By then, Alberic had taken the advowson of the local church. He'd been there for four years, exercising great influence over Lord Godefroi. Norbert seemed to have disappeared, then re-emerged as the Crusade was proclaimed. And then,' her voice faltered, 'came Anstritha, the wise woman, the one who was murdered by the mob.'

'What about her?'

'Nothing, mistress.' Imogene's voice turned weary. 'I have told you the truth about myself. It's wrong to tell you the truth about others.' She smiled thinly. 'I am not afraid of the truth. I suspect your brother and Godefroi already suspect who I am.' She got to her feet. 'Yet what threat do I pose, sister? Like you, I wish to journey to Jerusalem, but my reasons, like everyone else's, are a matter of the heart. Perhaps I will find comfort in bringing home the ashes of my parents; forgiveness for living after they died; absolution for my deception.' She undid her cloak. 'Get rid of my burdens and find some peace.'

Part 3

Radosto: The Feast of St Isidore, 4 April 1096

Dies quoque angustiae moeroris ac tristiae.
(A day also of bitter mourning and sadness.)

The *Dies Irae* of St Columba

'To the right!' Hugh de Payens' voice, dry and cracked, shrieked a warning.

Eleanor, standing between two high-wheeled carts, wiped the sweat and dirt from her face. She brought up the arbalest, then lowered it. The morning mist played tricks on her eyes and Eleanor, like the rest of her companions, was exhausted. She stared along the line of carts and makeshift barricades the Provençal captains had thrown up. The absence of their commander, Raymond of Toulouse, was deeply felt. Perhaps they should have taken up a better defensive position. The Provençal line, bending slightly like a bow, stretched between two copses of trees. Behind them open heathland ran down to a stream, where their horse lines had been fixed. Eleanor took a waterskin and drank greedily, splashing more on her face before handing it to Imogene, who squatted trying to organise the crossbow bolts on a tattered sheet. The widow woman, black hair bound with a piece of string, smiled back, then coughed, spluttering how she was full of the rheums, her throat sore, her ears

50

aching. She grumbled on as Eleanor patted her gently on the head. Over the last few weeks, during their nightmare journey from Istra down the Dalmatian coast, Imogene and Eleanor had become firm friends. They had, as Eleanor wrote in her chronicle, little choice but to unite against the dangers that confronted them. Imogene cursed as she cut her finger on the barbed edge of a bolt. She smeared some of the blood on her face.

'Just in case the Greeks,' she nodded towards the far haze of moving dust, 'overrun us. They won't rape the ugly ones!'

Eleanor stared despairingly up at the cloud-free sky. A buzzard came floating over and she wondered if the prospect of blood, her blood, had summoned it. The weather was turning balmy with the first hint of summer. They had travelled along the Via Egnetia to the Greek city of Dyrrachium and across northern Greece, arriving here outside Radosto only a few miles from Constantinople, yet their nightmare was not over. Alberic remarked how they were crossing Macedon, the wild, savage countryside that had once housed the great Alexander. Eleanor did not care for such history. The dark forests, rushing rivers, deep gorges and lonely meadowlands, from where the livestock had been driven away, were forbidding, rather haunting. Nevertheless, Macedonia for all its sombreness was a welcome relief from that nightmare road along the Dalmatian coast through Sclavonia. A dreadful dream of a journey, with the mist swirling as thick as fuller's cloth across a trackway slippery with ice and littered with boulders and fallen trees. On either side of this pathway rose thick, dense forests whilst the wind

51

cut along it like a razor. Nothing ahead, nothing behind but that mist curling like a host of ghosts.

Imogene said something. Eleanor was too tired to reply, and sat down with her back to the cart, staring across the heathland at the stream still bubbling from the spring rains.

Sclavonia! A barren land, Eleanor reflected, nothing but trees and mountains and that murk hanging like some vapour from hell cutting off sight and deadening sound. They rarely saw or heard any animal or bird. An eerie silence broken only by the sounds of their own straggling line of eighteen hundred souls on their horses and carts. The Poor Brethren of the Temple, their banner hanging limp from a pole, trudged along with the rest. Now and again the silent drudgery was shattered by swift, savage attacks. The Sclavs, who'd fled from their villages taking their livestock and precious food supplies with them, crept back to haunt the cross-bearers. They would follow the column, hanging on their flanks or rear, ready to attack any stragglers. They'd lop off heads, tie them to their standard poles and, if pursued, flee back into their mountain fastness. Eventually Count Raymond, tense and frenetic, moved mailed knights back to the rear of the column. He also asked Hugh, Godefroi and the Poor Brethren to sweep up the stragglers. A daunting task! A vigil that dominated the long, freezing days when the clouds seemed to descend so that when they did attack, the Sclavs were almost on them before anyone realised what was happening. Eleanor and the others fought back with crossbow, lance, spear and dagger. She recalled one attack. A Sclav, his bearded face all bloodied, climbed over the cart,

52

crawling towards her. She shattered his head with an axe and pushed his corpse, blood pumping out, off on to the trackway.

Day after day the same numbing routine, cold, silent and hungry, until those hideous figures came shrieking out of the mist. Eventually Count Raymond decided on more punitive measures. They could not pursue their tormentors, who fled back into their rocky hiding places, so the Count turned on any prisoners taken. Eyes were gouged out, noses slit, hands and feet hacked off. The captives were left blinded, disfigured, bleeding hunks of flesh as a stark warning to other tribesmen to leave them alone: Eleanor would never forget those screaming men and women left crawling blindly about on the ice-bound trackways.

Eventually they reached Scodra. Count Raymond tried to negotiate a truce with the King of the Sclavs, but the aggression continued until they crossed the imperial border and reached the territory of Alexius Comnenus around the town of Durazzo. They all breathed a sigh of relief, especially when the Emperor sent letters of peace and offered supplies as well as news about other Frankish leaders swiftly approaching Constantinople. Imperial scouts closed in around them: Cumans in their quilted armour, along with Turcopoles, Buglars, Patzinacks and other mercenary cohorts. The Poor Brethren of the Temple believed they were safe. Hugh and Godefroi were pleased to doff their chain mail and heavy helmets. Norbert and Alberic celebrated a Mass of thanksgiving on an altar set up on one of the great two-wheeled carts. Peter Bartholomew announced he had experienced a vision of the tears of St John, who, as in the Apocalypse, wept at the thought of how the Poor Brethren and others had suffered in Sclavonia. The respite proved illusory. The Emperor's mercenaries took to pillaging and harassing Count Raymond's army. Fierce sword quarrels took place in which two Provençal leaders along with knights, women and children were killed. Even Bishop Adhémar of Le Puy received a knock to the head, and had to be sent under safe conduct to the city of Thessalonica.

By the time Count Raymond's army reached the town of Roussa, its patience was exhausted; the townspeople there were unable, or unwilling, to trade, and fighting broke out during which shops and warehouses were pillaged. Running fights took place between townspeople and Count Raymond's followers. Greek troops appeared, mounted men-at-arms with their oval shields supported by mercenaries, mounted archers and, more dangerously, Catephracti, the heavy-mailed cavalry of whom, Hugh assured Eleanor, Count Raymond was very wary. A truce was eventually arranged. Greek envoys entered the camp to beseech Count Raymond to accompany them to Constantinople to meet the Emperor, who was already negotiating with other Frankish leaders. The Count accepted the invitation and travelled on in haste, leaving his eighteen-thousand-strong host under the joint command of the Vicomte of Béarn and the Count of Orange; two young men who, in Godefroi's opinion, hardly knew the difference between north and south, let alone how to command an army.

Three days had passed since the Count had left. The army had slowly moved on, close to the town of Radosto, still shadowed by imperial troops.

There had been further clashes, and pillaging by the cross-bearers, for despite all the proclamations and ordinances, not all companies followed the same strict discipline as the Poor Brethren. The worst of these was a gang of ribalds from Montpellier called the Beggars' Company, led by Jehan the Wolf. A notorious character, Jehan had been hired by the city fathers to drain Montpellier's moat and ditches. He did so, but also developed a skill second to none of poaching geese and ducks from the same moats and ditches, birds that belonged to local farmers or the city guilds. He then set himself up as a successful fowler, selling fresh bird meat to all and sundry. When the call from Clermont came, Jehan realised rich pickings were to be had elsewhere. He immediately used his wealth and notoriety to organise his own company, most of whom were denizens of the city slums. The Beggars' Company swarmed with codgers, counterfeiters, jesters and japers, moon people and tumblers. Such men and women thought Jerusalem was only down the road or just beyond the far horizon. The harsh journey down the Via Egnetia had shocked and embittered them. As Father Alberic commented, the Beggars' Company had no knowledge of scripture except for one verse: 'Live for today, do not worry about tomorrow or about what you will eat, drink or clothe yourselves in.' Jehan and his legion of imps truly believed the Lord would provide, and if not, they would gladly give heaven a helping hand.

Jehan was assisted by two lieutenants, ugly bruisers who rejoiced in the names of Gargoyle and Babewyn. These organised his horde of rogues, and as they approached Radosto, the Beggars' Company simply disappeared. After an absence of four days, they returned bringing back cattle, sheep, chickens and fresh meat for the pot, as well as valuable tapestries, cloths and precious goods, gifts they claimed from grateful local inhabitants. No one questioned them, though Hugh whispered hoarsely that they'd pay soon enough for the feast Jehan had prepared. None of the captains of the companies or the great lords had the authority or status to bring Jehan to account. More importantly, none of them could resist the smell of freshly cooked meats, spiced and garnished with herbs, that wafted through the camp.

Like some King of Misrule, Jehan entertained all the leaders to a great banquet. Eleanor, Hugh and Godefroi attended, their bellies sick for food, their throats craving the lush wines and fresh fruits on offer. The banquet was a clever move. Count Raymond was absent. Jehan played on the hunger and bitterness of the cross-bearers, turning them into his accomplices. Platters of fresh meat, duck, swan, pork and beef, were served in the light of roaring fires and flaring pitch torches. Jehan entertained them with tumblers and mummers as well as recounting a tale of how he had once swindled a fat wine merchant and a pompous canon of Montpellier.

'I ordered some wine,' he roared from his throne-like chair. 'I told the merchant's apprentice I would pay for it once it was delivered. He followed me to the cathedral. I told him to wait outside while I went in and accosted the canon. I told him I'd brought my nephew to be shriven as

56

he had an insatiable hunger for money, a deep avarice, so would the canon talk to him and, in return, accept as a gift the barrels of wine I'd brought on the cart? Of course the canon agreed. He followed me outside and glimpsed the apprentice guarding the wine. I told him to wait, approached the apprentice and said that the fat, wealthy priest beckoning at him would settle the bill.' Jehan's story ended in roars of laughter at the mutual bewilderment of both confessor and penitent: the latter demanding money whilst the priest reproached him for his avarice. Truth eventually came with time, but by then, both Jehan and the wine had disappeared.

Eleanor regarded Jehan as a lying boaster, though she marvelled at his cunning. Hugh and Godefroi, however, as they surveyed what was being served and the plunder Jehan had gathered on his so-called foraging, tried to reassure themselves that what he had brought was legitimate. After all, if the Emperor wouldn't supply them, what choice did the cross-bearers have but to take it for themselves? As Hugh and Godefroi watched Gargoyle, Babewyn and others display the glorious raiment and precious jewels they'd brought back to the camp, their anxiety deepened. They were confirmed in this by Theodore, a wandering Greek mercenary who had joined Count Raymond's army and become closely attached to the Poor Brethren. Theodore claimed to have been born near Smyrna, of Greek and Norman parentage. He was certainly an expert swordsman, who owned his own destrier and pack horse. He was of medium height, his dark face bearded. In character he was courteous and kind,

57

and he soon impressed Hugh and Godefroi with his knowledge of the Turks, the Greek army and the countryside they were travelling through. He also proved himself to be an able fighter, allowing Hugh and Godefroi to examine the special armour he wore: a mail-lined jerkin over a leather corselet made out of lamellar with a gorget of similar material and a ridged steel helmet. He was also skilled with the bow and couching a lance. A born soldier, Theodore had fought against Bulgar, Alan and Turk. He fascinated the Franks with his description of the Turks whose territory they were about to invade, describing them as swift fighters, deadly and ferocious, and skilled in mounted archery, which always confused their enemies. He also described the rigid discipline of the Emperor's armies, its heavy and light cavalry and its well-organised infantry led by the Imperial Guard. He explained how Alexius organised his army into *turma* of about three thousand men, which in turn were subdivided into eight *numeri* each of about three hundred and fifty, delineating the various officers and standard-bearers as well as their military code. The Byzantine army was also well supplied in the field, being supported by siege trains, engineers and physicians. Hugh was deeply impressed by such organisation and began to impose similar discipline on the hundred or so Poor Brethren. He organised them into units of ten which he called a conroy, dividing the knights from the serjeants and allocating duties such as cooking and physic to various individuals, including even women and children.

Theodore arrived late for the Beggars' banquet but immediately engaged Hugh in hushed conversation, talking quickly in the lingua franca of the Middle Sea. Hugh listened intently, then turned and whispered to Eleanor how Theodore believed Jehan's men had not just collected supplies but had attacked and pillaged the villa and estates of a high-ranking local notable, a crime the Greeks would not ignore. The following morning, Theodore's prediction was proved correct. The sun had hardly risen when scouts galloped into the camp, shouting how an imperial army was emerging out of the mist in column of march and deploying for battle. At first, the Frankish commanders thought this was simply a manoeuvre and moved to the outskirts of Radosto only to find their way blocked by imperial troops. Hugh and Godefroi were summoned by the Vicomte de Béarn for a hasty meeting near a clump of trees. Envoys were dispatched but imperial troops drove them off with a hail of arrows. Apparently the Greeks were intent on battle and all the Franks could do was sit and wait. Eleanor closed her eyes and dozed. After last night's feast, she was no longer hungry but felt thirsty, tired and slightly sick, her joints aching. For a brief while she wondered if the whispers circulating the camp spoke the truth. Had they made a mistake? Should they have come? Was this truly God's work?

'Eleanor! Eleanor!' She startled awake as her name was shouted. A group of horsemen—Hugh, Godefroi, Beltran and Theodore—came galloping up. Hugh threw himself from the saddle. 'What is it?' Eleanor pulled herself up; she had been so lost in her thoughts she'd ignored the growing noise from the camp. She turned and glanced out between the carts. In the far distance, the glint of armour and the flutter of coloured banners threatened whilst the dust-laden breeze carried the ominous sound of trumpet and drum.

'Theodore believes the Greeks are massing for an attack. It will come soon.' Hugh grasped Eleanor's shoulders, his fingers squeezing hard. She glimpsed the fear in his eyes. 'Eleanor,' he whispered, 'I love you, but in the name of God, is it to end here? For the love of heaven, Count Raymond has gone to meet the Emperor, so why are the Greeks attacking?'

'Revenge!' Eleanor stared out at the distant dust cloud.

'I agree.' Beltran had also dismounted and came swaggering across with Theodore, their dark faces sweat-soaked and anxious.

'Negotiate!' Eleanor rasped, pointing at the dust cloud.

'Too late,' Theodore declared. 'Lord Hugh, we need to prepare.'

All along the Frankish line, the captains were trying to impose order. The Vicomte de Béarn and other commanders, garbed in full chain mail, conical helmets over their coifs, long oval shields fastened to their saddle horns, galloped up. They were desperate to close any gaps between the carts and deploy a mass of archers behind them. The vicomte reined in before Hugh.

'What more,' he yelled, 'can we do?'

'Close the line further.' Hugh shouted back. 'Close it fast. Place your horses here,' he indicated each end of the line, 'and here.' He pointed to the centre. 'Hold them in reserve. The same with some of the foot. Whatever happens, our line must not break. My lord,' Hugh grasped the vicomte's reins, 'we must, if we can, treat with the Greeks.'

'About what?' the vicomte screamed back above the rising din.

'Why do they attack?' Hugh shouted.

'Because they are Greek schismatics!' one of the vicomte's companions yelled. 'Worthy of hell fire, jealous of our work!'

'Nonsense, my lord.' Hugh placed his hand on the vicomte's mailed knee. 'My lord, if we can, we must negotiate.'

The vicomte nodded. 'There'll be bloody bustle first,' he murmured. 'God wish the count was here. Hugh,' the vicomte gathered his reins, 'you remain in the centre.' Then he was off.

Hugh began massing his own company before moving on to the Beggars further down the line. Banners and pennants were unfurled, crucifixes latched to poles raised and fixed on carts. Children, the aged and the infirm were sent back to the horse lines down near the stream under the protection of a group of women armed with spears, heavy arbalests and pouches of bolts. Rusty armour was hauled out of baskets and sacks. Short-sleeved mail shirts were quickly donned; body armour, buckram stuffed with wool, fastened securely. Pot-helmets, *chapeaux de fer* or kettle-hats, were hastily strapped on. Long shields were slung on soldiers' backs or placed across gaps between the carts. Horns and trumpets shrieked. Eleanor was given a bow and a quiver. She peered between the carts and groaned. The Greeks were now moving slowly but ominously towards them. A long line of foot, shields locked, spears jutting out, a moving wall of barbed iron. Here and there the Greek ranks broke to allow squadrons of heavy horse to come through, their riders desperate to restrain their destriers and keep to the line of the march. Standards were raised to shimmer through the dust. The air throbbed with the clash of cymbals, the shrill of trumpets and the deep lowing of battle horns. Godefroi came riding up. Eleanor hurried across and grasped the bridle of his horse. He leaned down, his face and head almost hidden by the chain mail coif, and released the strap across his mouth.

'Eleanor, I swear, if we survive today I will do some great service for God, assume the cowl, become the Lord's monk.' Then he was gone in a flurry of hooves.

Eleanor laughed, coughing on the dust as she walked back to the cart.

'A lovers' farewell?' Imogene teased.

'A true troubadour,' Eleanor replied drily. 'High romance. If he survives, Lord Godefroi will become a monk!'

Imogene's sardonic reply that she would enter a nunnery was drowned by the raucous blast of trumpets. The Greek line of march was quickening. The earth shook with the stamp of feet, the clatter of steel, the shrieks and yells of men and the loud neighing of horses. All along the Frankish line men and women were notching arrows or pushing bolts into the grooves of crossbows. Hugh reappeared beside Eleanor, coif back, and clambered on to the cart. Eleanor peered between the slats as the Greek line stopped abruptly. The shield wall opened. Bare-headed men dressed in jerkins and breeches streamed out. They raced towards the Franks, leather straps whirling above their heads.

'Slingers!' Hugh shouted. 'Hide! Heads down, shields up!'

Eleanor and Imogene hid beneath the cart. The air sang with the jarring hum of angry hornets. Polished pebbles smashed against the cart, followed by chilling screams from either side. Hugh, shield over his head, stood up.

'Archers,' he yelled, 'ready—loose!'

The clatter of stones was answered with the twang of bows, the click of catches, followed by a sound like that of a giant bird's wings snapping furiously. Eleanor stared round the end of a cart at the figures dancing in the dust clouds. She notched her arrow, pulling back the bowstring even as Imogene released the catch on her crossbow; both arrow and quarrel disappeared into the haze. Shouts of 'Toulouse, Toulouse!' rang out. Eleanor glanced down the Frankish line; corpses, bloodied and torn, were already being dragged out. On the cart above her, Hugh was roaring at them to ready and loose again. Eleanor did so, hands and fingers sweat-soaked, Imogene breathing curses beside her. Were they going to die? It was muscle-aching work. They notched and loosed, speeding arrow and bolt at that moving line of figures dancing like demons. All the clamour of hell surrounded them. Brief memories of Eleanor's childhood sparked: her father, a distant figure riding into a courtyard, cloak billowing about him; her mother hastening out to greet him . . . Hugh, standing on the cart above her, shook her from the reverie. She heard him yell.

'Axemen!'

The Greek shield wall had opened again. Long-haired, bearded mercenaries clad in leather hauberks were racing towards them, shield in one hand, two-headed axe in the other, a horde of shrieking men. Some collapsed in the dirt as arrows pierced them in the face and chest. Others reached the carts, climbing up to be met by whirling sword, mace, club and spear thrust. One of them broke through the gap between the carts. Eleanor tripped him up with a lance whilst Imogene, screaming hysterically, clubbed the back of his head to a bloody pulp. On the cart, Hugh and other mailed knights held off the attackers whilst those who did break through were caught by the waiting infantry. A nightmare vision of hissing steel, spurting blood, angry faces, hideous cries and the soul-wrenching sounds of metal and wood smashing out life. A brief respite, then a fresh ferocious assault. Eleanor felt delirious. Bodies were piled either side of her, then she heard a roar, and the attack began to falter, the axemen withdraw. Hugh, all blood-splashed clambered down from the cart. His chain mail had caught pieces of human flesh, his face was splattered with gore. Eleanor turned away and vomited, aware of Imogene's arm around her shoulder.

'Eleanor?' Hugh pulled her hands apart. 'Godefroi and the other knights attacked the Greeks in the flanks; they are withdrawing.'

Eleanor nodded. She did not care. She just crouched by the wheel; she had descended into hell. Children were crying, sobbing furiously, footmen were moving amongst the wounded. The enemy were given short shrift, a mercy cut across the throat, the same for those Franks the leeches could do nothing for. Dust devils billowed across. Waterbearers with buckets and ladles moved along

64

the line of men baking under the sun. The Beggars' Company were already pulling the dead of both sides away from their carts. The Vicomte de Béarn and his officers came galloping up. Eleanor leaned against the cart; Imogene pushed a ladle of water into her hand. She slurped at it, staring out over the battlefield. The dead lay mostly in contorted positions, but occasionally so peacefully, heads resting on arms, they seemed asleep. The summer heat, hot and clammy, intensified the agony. The cries of the wounded drove away the marauding buzzards but not the flies hanging in black clouds around gruesome wounds. A child was weeping uncontrollably. A woman wailed. Voices shouted for leeches or a priest. Rahomer, one of the Poor Brethren, had taken an axe cut to his shoulder and was sobbing with the pain. A leech tried to dress the hideous wound. Eleanor glanced away. Hugh was talking to the vicomte. Eleanor rose and walked over even as the vicomte nodded in agreement.

Hugh shouted for Theodore, Beltran and Alberic to join him.

'We'll seek a truce,' he informed them breathlessly. 'This is madness. We must discover why the Greeks have attacked so fiercely.'

A short while later, carrying a leafy bough hewn from a tree and flanked by Theodore and Alberic, the priest bearing a cross lashed to a pole, Hugh galloped into the dusty haze, Beltran following behind. The Franks dragged the dead, now stripped naked, ghastly bodies with their shiny purplish wounds, to the funeral pyres hastily erected near the stream. The mound of corpses was sprinkled with oil. A priest intoned the

Requiem. A torch was thrown to engulf that monument of the dead in sheets of flame followed by plumes of black smoke. The acrid stench of burning flesh curled along the battle line. Godefroi came riding up, his face still full of battle fury. He looked absent-mindedly at Eleanor and cantered off to where the vicomte and other commanders had created a gap between the carts to ride out and stare across the battlefield at the gathering mass of Greeks. Envoys from the enemy camp came galloping through the murk carrying peace boughs. The Franks accepted these, allowing the Greeks to scour the field for their own dead and wounded. Eleanor slumped down. Imogene squatted next to her. They shared a cob of hard bread, some bitter wine and a few dried figs.

'We are supposedly marching to Jerusalem, the Heavenly City,' Eleanor murmured. 'Yet here we are in the meadows of hell!'

'Sister?'

Eleanor glanced up. Norbert stood over her. The Benedictine's gaunt face, skin peeling, was spotted with blood.

'It's Fulcher the Smith.' Norbert indicated with his head. 'He is dying of his wounds. He says he must speak to you before he is shriven.'

Eleanor rose to her feet. She felt so dazed, Norbert had to steady her by the arm as he led her down the line of carts. They passed groups clustered around screaming, moaning men and women. Others were repairing weapons. A few knelt and prayed around some small statue of the Virgin or their patron saint. Smoke floated across, thick and rank. It broke to reveal Fulcher propped against some baggage; he lay shivering, the dirty

66

bandage around his neck and chest blood-soaked.

'I cannot stop the bleeding,' the leech murmured. 'Wounds everywhere.'

Eleanor knelt down. Fulcher's eyes fluttered. He tried to grasp her hand but he was too weak. Eleanor, hiding her own weariness and fighting to control her stomach, ignored the fetid stench around them.

'Arrowhead and sling shot,' Fulcher gasped, 'struck almost immediately.' He blinked. 'A wound to the back. Anyway, God wills it. Listen.' The smith turned and Norbert withdrew. 'Listen closer.' Eleanor did so. 'I've watched you,' the blacksmith gasped. 'I trust you, Lady Eleanor. I must speak to you. I was in the coven that killed Anstritha. No, hear me! You are not from the Auvergne, sister—where we live in a world of witches and warlocks. Anstritha had been a wandering woman, skilled in herbs, who came and settled in our village. She was a stranger. We had suspicions about her. She kept to herself, though God knows she was friendly enough. She was young and comely. Some of the women envied her, whilst the menfolk lusted after her. She had money and, to all intents and purposes, led a goodly life. It didn't save her. Stories were rife, tragedies and misfortunes were laid at her door. A week after Michaelmas last, I and other sinners who drank at the Vine of the Lord . . .' Fulcher gasped, a pink froth bubbling between his lips, and his eyelids fluttered. He took a deep breath. 'We were given a secret message. No one knew its source. On a certain day we were to meet out along the heathland just as Father Alberic tolled the Vespers bell. We did so, gathering one by one in a grassy hollow; its sides rose high to hide the glow of the fire burning there. We thought it was a joke, but the message had mentioned Anstritha so, full of ale and mischief, we agreed. We were to come hooded and masked, and so we did, though I recognised them, Robert the Reeve and other sinners.' He paused, gasping for breath.

'Who?' Eleanor asked.

'I cannot say, sister, I am bound for God's judgement seat. I do not wish to lie or condemn another. My soul is black and heavy enough already.' He paused in a fit of coughing.

Eleanor grasped a battered waterskin and held it to his lips. Fulcher's face had taken on a deathly pallor. Eleanor glanced quickly around. The blacksmith's story had made her less aware of the bloody mayhem around her. She abruptly thought of Hugh galloping off towards the Greeks and quietly prayed he would be safe.

'Sister, for God's sake I'll be brief.' Fulcher's fingers fluttered against her wrist. 'A horseman appeared, cowled and visored. He told us a hideous story of how Anstritha was truly a witch who deserved to die. How she dug her fingers deep into the sockets of dead men's eyes and bit off the long yellow nails from withered hands as she harvested the bodies of hanged men. How she made the black sacrifice in the dead of night and sacrificed bowls of blood to the demons of the air. Nonsense,' Fulcher whispered, 'but we believed him. He insisted we should cleanse such filth from our village. He left a wineskin and a piece of silver for each of us. We were bought,' he coughed, 'body and soul. We were told to wait for a sign, and when it came to act. On the night she died, we assembled hooded and visored in the tap room of the Vine of God. The taverner was with us. You, Lord Hugh and Godefroi were absent. Robert the Reeve, I am sure it was he, led us to Anstritha's house. Sister, it was a blasphemy! Anstritha was in her small buttery, brewing ale. We burst in and seized her, but even then I knew something was very wrong. Anstritha fled to the church. I was already regretting my part. I returned to her house, not to plunder but to search for evidence. I found nothing that would be out of place in a nun's cell, but more importantly . . .' he struggled to pull himself up, 'the horseman was there. Again his head and face were covered. He had already searched the house. I carried my hammer but he was armed with sword and dagger. He told me to be about my business. I realised we'd been used. I fled; I was frightened. By the time I rejoined the rest, Anstritha was captured. She was strapped and bound like some outlaw caught red-handed. I tried to speak to her, to console her. She asked if I could hear her confession. I told her I was no priest, but she insisted. Sister, my guilt deepened. Anstritha had a pure heart. Others came to taunt her. She whispered the Contrition and said I was to take her left sandal and give what I found to someone I trusted, "a new Veronica"'

'I am sorry?' Eleanor interrupted.

'Sister, I tell you what I know. Go amongst my belongings.' He banged his head against the baskets and panniers piled behind him. 'Take the small one, now.' He pushed himself forward, allowing Eleanor to free the saddlebags, two pouches held together by a strap. 'Keep them,' he gasped, 'and all that is in them. God knows there is no one else. Now, sister, I must confess . . .'

'Who was this horseman, this stranger?'

'I don't know. Anstritha did claim she had travelled to Outremer. She told me that she had secrets of her own. Just before I left, she admitted how her present troubles were the fault of a half-brother who'd plagued her life.' Fulcher coughed on his own blood. 'Sister, it was dark, she was terrified, as was I. She would say no more. The fire roared and they hanged her above it. Anstritha's blood is now on my hands and those of others. We have to pay, I know that.'

Eleanor, more to humour him than anything else, kissed him on the brow, muttered the Jesu Miserere, took the bag and left Fulcher to Brother Norbert's ministrations. She'd hardly returned to where Imogene lay sleeping beneath the cart when shouts and cries sent her running to a gap. Hugh and his companions came thundering back. A cart was pulled aside and the riders galloped through, accompanied by a high-ranking Greek officer in court dress, a long, ornate gown that hung midway down his boots, bright and richly embroidered with gold thread. Behind him was a young servant boy dressed in green. Immediately they were surrounded by the vicomte and his commanders and a heated discussion ensued. Eleanor hurried to join the fast-gathering crowd. Jehan, leader of the Beggars' Company, was summoned and the debate continued. From the people around her Eleanor learned that the Greeks had attacked because a nobleman's villa had been plundered: the owner's wife, together with his two daughters, had been brutally raped, then hanged from the beams of their own house. The servant boy had

70

escaped but would recognise the attackers, and the finger of suspicion was already pointed at Jehan's company. The Greeks had issued an ultimatum: the perpetrators must be identified and summarily punished, otherwise a fresh attack would be launched. Jehan tried to defend his company, but the vicomte ordered him to co-operate or be expelled.

The entire Beggars' Company was summoned and lined up along the carts. Shouts of defiance— 'Toulouse, Toulouse!'—were swiftly quieted by the vicomte's commanders, drawing their swords, whilst Hugh, now their envoy, stood up in his stirrups and proclaimed that rape and murder had nothing to do with their quest. 'Moreover,' he continued, 'if justice is done, the Greeks will offer provisions and escort us safely to the great city.' Shouts of abuse echoed, followed by more cries of 'Toulouse, Toulouse!' Nevertheless, the mood shifted as more people joined the throng. The servant boy dismounted and, accompanied by Hugh and Beltran, walked along the line of Beggars. Four men were identified. They shrieked their innocence as Hugh ordered them to be dragged out. The servant boy, grasping the crucifix Alberic thrust into his hand, shouted his oath that he'd spoken the truth. The men's fate was sealed. Another quarrel took place between the vicomte and the Greek. The vicomte pointed to Hugh. The official nodded in agreement, bowed and, turning his horse, galloped off, followed by the servant.

The four prisoners were hustled out from behind the line of carts and forced to kneel on the ground, still littered with corpses and broken weapons. Alberic moved along, crouching before each one, hand lifted in absolution. He had just reached the third when Greek horsemen emerged, riding slowly up to watch what was happening. Alberic finished. Hugh, carrying a basket, stepped forward. He drew his sword and, like a harvester collecting grain, neatly severed each of the condemned men's heads, a slicing cut that sent the head rolling like a ball. Blood spurted up as the corpses toppled over. Eleanor looked away. Once Hugh was finished, he collected the heads, put them in the basket and, walking towards the line of horsemen, placed it on the ground before them. He returned, cleaned his sword on the clothing of one of the corpses, resheathed it and strolled back to the watching wall of Franks.

Bread, meat, wine and ripe fruit began to reach the camp just before nightfall. Carts piled high with produce were escorted into the camp by Turcopole mercenaries in flowing sky-blue robes, white turbans on their heads, black horn bows thrust into side pouches on their saddles. The arrivals were greeted with dark looks but Hugh, unperturbed by the brutal executions, went out to talk to the Turkish officer, who smilingly agreed to his request to stage a display of mounted archery out on the open meadowland. Hugh, holding Eleanor's hand, watched the rider circle round a tree stump, horse and officer acting as one. The nimble mount turned and twisted even as the Turcopole, low in the saddle, loosed shaft after shaft into the stump.

'This is what we will face, Eleanor,' Hugh murmured, raising a hand in thanks to the officer. 'These are the enemy, not Greek women and girls. Do you know they were mere children, raped, tortured and hanged before their mother, who was forced to witness it. If I had my way, I would enforce strict discipline on this rabble. Anyone who raises a hand against an innocent should be executed; it is the only way. The Greeks do not wish to fight us. They see us as defence against the Turks. Yet there is more bad news.' He pulled a face. 'Our leaders are arguing in Constantinople; they cannot decide on who will lead the army.'

'Hugh, look at me.'

He did so.

'Tell me,' Eleanor stepped closer, 'why are you here? To impose order, to create a brotherhood, or something else?'

He slowly wiped the sweat from his dirty face.

'I asked you a question, brother, a direct question that deserves an honest answer. We are travelling across the world to Jerusalem, yet there is more to it, isn't there, than the freeing of Christ's Sepulchre, the liberation of the Holy Places. You, Godefroi, Alberic and Norbert, there is something else, some secret.'

He opened his mouth to reply.

'Hugh, I know you like no one else does. You don't lie. Sometimes you simply don't tell the truth! I have asked you to lend me that poem, "La Chanson de Voyage de Charlemagne". What is in that, Hugh?'

He scraped his boots on the ground and, leaning down, took off his spurs, jingling them in his hand.

'I promise you this, sister,' he smiled, 'I will tell you everything, but not now. We face problems enough. My execution of those men is not popular.'

'Nor was their crime,' Eleanor retorted. She

stared at her brother. His unshaven face looked harder, more resolute. She felt tempted to tell him about Fulcher, but decided to wait. They were bound for Jerusalem, but Hugh and, to a certain extent Godefroi, Alberic and Norbert too, apparently had their own private crusade. She was sure it was not her own imagination, but decided to accept Hugh's reticence for the time being.

They returned to the camp now all a-bustle, bitterness at the Greek attack and the subsequent executions swiftly receding as the food and wine were distributed. After Vespers, Eleanor, Hugh, Godefroi, Alberic and Norbert joined the leaders of other companies in a tented enclosure lit by cresset torches lashed to poles. The vicomte and his colleagues stood on a dais and openly debated what was to be done next. Shouted argument and counterargument ensued, wine and full bellies quickening tempers. Many claimed Count Raymond should not have abandoned them. A few voiced the wish to return home. Eleanor felt tired and sick. She excused herself and returned to the cart where Imogene, helped by a nearby family, had set up tent. Beyond the ring of carts, the torches of scavengers and other searchers moved around the battlefield. Guards on foot also patrolled in the jingle of armour and the creak of leather. Eleanor was about to settle down when she remembered Fulcher. She found the pannier where she'd hidden it and shook out the paltry contents: a dagger, some nails, a medal, pieces of silver and a thick-soled sandal, its leather upper prised loose from the stitching. Eleanor put her fingers inside and drew out a neatly folded piece of smooth vellum. She unfolded this; it was larger than she'd thought. The vellum was slightly oiled, the best to be found in any chancery or scriptorium. In the poor light she could make out a drawing like a map and the clearly written letters above it.

'Under the Rock,' she translated, 'look on the treasures of God and the face of the Lord.' She moved the lantern horn closer. The diagram meant nothing to her, nor did the words. She sat down, refolded the piece of vellum and tucked it into the hem of her cuff. Fulcher had evidently thought this was important; so had Anstritha. Was this the manuscript the mysterious horseman had been searching for? Anstritha had been out to Outremer; so had Norbert and Alberic. Had they discovered something precious there? Eleanor closed her eyes. She recalled that list of relics held by her brother, and yes, something else: Hugh and Godefroi chanting that poem they so zealously read. Those words on Anstritha's manuscript sparked a memory of verses in the 'Chanson' about the face of Christ. Was there more to the Poor Brethren of the Temple? Anstritha and Fulcher had both died violently, as had Robert the Reeve. Was the latter's death an accident? And was the horseman now one of their company? They had never really discussed Robert's death. The reeve was undoubtedly a toper, but how had he drowned in that stream? Did he know something? Had he been inveigled outside and murdered?

Eleanor heard sounds, her name being called. She crawled to the mouth of the tent and pulled back the flap. Hugh crouched there.

'Sister,' he smiled, 'a decision has been made. We, the leaders of the Poor Brethren, will

75

leave immediately tomorrow morning for Constantinople to take urgent council with the Lord Raymond.'

Part 4

Constantinople: The Morrow of the Feast of St Athanasius, 3 May 1096

In quo cessabit mulierum amor et desiderium.
(A day on which the love and desire of women will cease.)

The *Dies Irae* of St Columba

Eleanor de Payens of Compiègne in the county of Champagne, *crucesignati*, cross-bearer, sister of Hugh, widow of Odo de Furneval, always swore that the city of Constantinople, old Byzantium, was the nearest thing to her image of the heavenly Jerusalem, despite the treachery, murder and intrigue brewing in that great city by its inland sea. Eleanor and her companions reached Constantinople around the Feast of St Mark the Evangelist. Theodore, their guide, described the city as a rough triangle bounded on two sides by the sea and enclosed within massive twin walls. They entered through the Golden Gate, three sets of soaring bronze doors enclosed by a white-brick, red-tiled wall, which, in turn, was surmounted by two massive golden statues of Victory and four huge elephants carved from the same precious

76

metal.

The Poor Brethren joined Count Raymond at the luxurious villa the Emperor, Alexius Comnenus, had provided for the Provençal leader just off the great highway leading up to the Golden Gate. The count received them well. He grew furious at the news about the Greek attack, though he was full of praise for Hugh's actions. He was restless, still in deep negotiation with both the other leaders as well as the Emperor's court. He insisted that they relax whilst they waited. They bathed, dressed in fresh flowing robes, ate soft fruit-bread and fresh lamb roasted in mint and spices, and drank wines that had once, Theodore assured them, drenched the mouths of Alexander the Great and his generals.

In the days following, Theodore proved to be a knowledgeable, courteous and highly intelligent guide. He showed them the glories of the city. They were ushered up marble steps into the great palaces where Varangians, warriors from the north, stood on guard in their gold-edged scarlet cloaks. On their heads were plumed silver helmets, in their hands the two-headed axes that distinguished them as the Immortals, Alexius' imperial body guard. Past these pattered servants in their silver-slippered feet, hurrying to do the will of the Basileus, the Elect of God, their Christ-Adoring Emperor. Eleanor and her companions also walked the great city walls, thirty feet high and seventeen miles long, and from the summit of the Golden Gate watched the caravans of carts, camels, donkeys and horses bringing in the produce of the empire.

They visited the harbours and quaysides of the

Golden Horn where triangular-sailed fishing smacks cut the light-blue, sun-dazzled waters, past imperial galleys with their banks of oars and the huge dragon's heads arching out over carved prows which, Theodore confided, spat out streams of mysterious Greek fire. In the cool of the evening they wandered the streets, escorted at all times by mercenaries who ensured that these Franks were kept safe and did not wander where they shouldn't. After the dusty open roads, rocky meadowland and thick forests of their recent march, Eleanor found the contrast dazzling. In the teeming city bazaars, bearded, hawk-eyed men shouted at them in a variety of bewildering languages as they offered camphor oil, sesame, silk from Cathay, spices such as sandalwood and rolls of heavy embroidery. From open-fronted cookshops traders served platters of honey cake, walnuts, chilled cherries and goblets of Chian wine. Afterwards they walked in the imperial gardens, where the Judas trees blossomed and the wild vines grew heavy and lush. Along the waterways cutting through these paradises sailed gilt-edged pleasure barges and imperial galleys resplendent in their pennants. Eleanor would remember such luxury and opulence during the storm of war, disease and famine that would later engulf them. She also kept to her promise that she would discover what secret desires prompted the hearts of those in her company. She began to hint at this whenever she was alone with Hugh, though this was a rare event. Count Raymond depended on Hugh, especially in his discussions with the other lords about the setting up of a council of leaders, establishing a common fund and sharing provisions.

All the great lords were now arriving in Constantinople, bringing with them men of every nationality and tongue. Eleanor had glimpsed these leaders as they visited the luxurious villa to confer with Count Raymond. Hugh of Paris, brother to the King of France, was the first Frank to arrive in Constantinople. The French prince's small fleet had been shipwrecked, many of his troops drowned, their sea-drenched corpses washed up in inlets and on islands. Nevertheless all these corpses, so it was rumoured, bore red crosses, a miracle, a sure sign that they had fulfilled their vow and would receive God's reward. Godfrey of Bouillon arrived, iron-haired and harsh-faced, with his ambitious wily brother Baldwin, whilst Adhémar of Le Puy, the scheming, warlike bishop, still nursing his sore head after the attack on him in Sclavonia, led in the rest of Count Raymond's troops to be comfortably quartered in the fields and meadows beyond the city. Robert 'Short-breeches', Duke of Normandy, red-haired and even more red-faced, jovial and laughing, lazy and feckless but a superb horseman and a skilled warrior, came swaggering in. Finally Bohemond, the Norman Prince of Taranto, yellow-haired with the face of a hunting eagle, who stood over six feet, with the powerful arms of a swordsman. A Norman who took to fighting like a bird to flying, Bohemond was no friend of the Greeks. He had fought to carve himself an empire in southern Italy and Greece, only to be repulsed. He now brought five hundred knights under his scarlet banner, eager for Jerusalem but with an equally sharp eye for any territories and fiefs along the way that he could claim as his own. Bohemond was joined by his nephew Tancred de Hauteville, the finest swordsman amongst the Normans, a bird of similar feather to Bohemond though one more concerned about his soul and the blood on his hands than seizing some rich fief.

All these seigneurs gathered like a host of hawks in Constantinople. The Emperor, cunning as a serpent, received them with exquisite gifts: gold and silver, precious cloths, jewelled saddles and harness, fresh robes, baskets of sugared fruits and wines cooled by snow from Olympus, caskets and coffers of gleaming sapphires, small ingots of ivory, damascened covers and finely wrought weapons. Alexius feted and entertained the leaders whilst their followers, seventy thousand strong, stayed outside the city, fed and watered but closely watched by squadrons of Turcopoles in their pointed helmets of grey damascened steel, turbans of white cloth wrapped around their brows. The Turcopoles sported leather body armour over loose jerkins with breeches pushed into high-heeled riding boots. All were well armed with lance, bow and sword. Hugh took careful note of these and ruefully wished the great lords would do likewise: their future enemy, the Seljuk Turks, were similarly armed and adopted the same hit-and-run tactics in battle, to devastating effect.

Alexius, for all his generosity and advice, viewed the Franks as a farmer would savage dogs whom he'd brought on to his land to drive off wolves: they had to be carefully controlled. The Franks might be dedicated to God's work, but Alexius was determined they would also do his. He demanded oaths of fealty from the lords and, with various degrees of chicanery, they gave these, promising to hand over any cities taken in return for supplies and military assistance. Alexius swore to put twenty thousand men at their disposal under his chief Turcopole Tacticius, a wily veteran commander of Greek and Turkish parents who'd had his nose bitten off in a fight and replaced it with a false one of gleaming steel. Tacticius also entertained the lords to series of splendid banquets. The Franks, accustomed to draughty, smoke-filled halls adorned with dirty tapestries and warmed by filthy rushes on the floor, were suborned by gleaming hangings, marble walls, luxurious cloths and bathhouses that smelt fragrantly of sandalwood and attar of roses. The Franks mingled with sloe-eyed women garbed in saffron silk, rose and blue linen, with purple cords, tasselled with gold, around their slim waists. Alexius opened his treasuries, distributing gold bezants amongst the captains and copper tartarons amongst their followers. Nevertheless, he walked a dangerous path. When the lords assembled to take their oaths, one of them unceremoniously sat down on the Emperor's vacated throne and had to be roughly pulled off by his colleagues. Further altercations occurred as some of the leaders openly voiced their suspicions of Alexius. Eventually, however, an agreement was reached, the die was cast; an advance guard would cross the Arm of St George into Anatolia, where Sultan Kilij Arslan hoped to destroy them as he had the hordes of Peter the Hermit. That charismatic former leader of the People's Army was now a discontented, broken man who had merged the pitiful remnants of his erstwhile horde into what everyone was now calling the Army of God. All Peter could do was mourn that the Holy Spirit had deserted him and that he and his followers had been justly punished for the sins they'd committed.

On her part, Eleanor was determined to have words with Hugh and Godefroi. Once in Anatolia, they would face dangers as great as any in Sclavonia. Accordingly, whenever possible, she questioned Hugh, who remained taciturn until the eve of the Feast of St Athanasius. A banquet had been arranged for the following evening where Hugh hoped to host the leading men of his brotherhood and, once again, enforce the rule, which he had made even more rigorous. On the afternoon beforehand he and Godefroi, accompanied by Theodore, took Eleanor into the city along narrow lanes and alleyways, past the markets and bazaars, the rancid-smelling runnels and busy jetties into the great Augusteon Square: a spacious expanse ablaze with sunlight that struck off the ivory-white marble porticoes and walls all emblazoned with gold, silver and bronze. The square was dominated by a huge statue of Constantine as well as the cavernous entrance into the golden-domed Cathedral of Hagia Sophia, Holy Wisdom, where long-haired priests prayed and chanted amidst clouds of incense.

Inside the cathedral, Theodore first showed them the image of the Virgin, whose tears dropped without ceasing, then the tablets of stone Moses had taken from Mount Sinai, the bronze trumpets of Joshua that had brought down Jericho, and the Staff of Aaron. All these relics were revealed to the constant chanting of '*Kyrie Eleison, Christe Eleison*'. Finally, Eleanor was shown various images of the face of the Saviour; she was taken from one side altar to another to study paintings and icons framed in silver, gold and precious stones.

'Look, Eleanor,' Hugh murmured, 'see how each is the same, or almost so.'

The different renderings gave individual interpretations of the Divine face, yet there was a marked similarity between them all. A long face, with very expressive eyes, a slim nose and full lips above a firm chin. He was moustached and bearded, and the long hair, reddish-brown, hung braided on each side in a fashion similar to how some Jewish men still wore it. Afterwards they left the hallowed precincts and crossed the Augusteon Square, where they stopped to admire the twelve bronze figures that moved to show the direction of the wind. Theodore then led them down a maze of alleyways to the quayside, a veritable Tower of Babel with different tongues shouting in shrill voices. The Greek mercenary hired a shabby chamber above stairs in a tavern, ordering wine, bread and a highly spiced fish dish, which he carefully shared out into bowls.

Hugh and Godefroi had apparently taken Theodore completely into their confidence. Eleanor was pleased with that. Theodore was of similar mind to them and her admiration for this good-humoured, resolute and patient man had deepened over the last few weeks. He smiled and winked at her as Godefroi intoned the grace. For a while they ate in silence, then Hugh cleaned his dish with a piece of bread, popped it into his mouth and sat staring at his sister.

'You would have told me your great secret?' she teased. 'I mean, eventually?'

'We had to be sure. Theodore here, like Brother Norbert and Alberic, has journeyed to Jerusalem; he too has learnt about the rumours.'

'Hugh, what rumours?'

'We are journeying to Jerusalem,' Godefroi began, 'to liberate Christ's fief from the Turks who occupy the Holy Places . . .'

'Godefroi,' Eleanor smiled, 'I know where we are going and why.'

'Do you?' Hugh asked. 'Eleanor, there are as many reasons for being on Crusade as there are cross-bearers. Bohemond of Taranto wants to carve out a principality. He failed to do so in Italy, Sicily or Greece. The same is true of our other leaders. Robert of Normandy held a duchy but he became bored, preferring the excitement of travel and the roar of battle to governing lands. The same applies to us. Did you want to stay in Compiègne till some knight offered for your hand, whilst we whiled away our days at tournaments, launched *chevauchées* against our neighbours and waited to be summoned by Count Raymond for another sortie into Iberia, or by King Philip because of a border dispute with Flanders?'

'Eleanor,' Theodore added, 'you of all people must realise this: the liberation of Jerusalem and the recapture of the Holy Sepulchre is a vision as sacred as that of any man or woman wishing to leave this life to serve God as a monk or a nun. To fight your way into heaven,' he smiled, 'is an ideal worthy of any knight.'

'Yet there is more?'

'There always is, sister.'

'You have taken the oath?' Eleanor asked.

'I am one of you,' Theodore replied, 'for the

same reason as you, but yes, there is more. I am a son of a Norman knight and a Greek mother who died shortly after giving birth to me. My father married again. He made it very clear in letters and proclamations that the offspring of his Norman wife would inherit.' He pulled a face. 'So I began to travel. Believe me, *adelpha'*—he used the Greek term for sister—'it was wonderful to wander, to be free, to see the marvels of Constantinople, to visit the ruins of Athens and stand in the nave of St Mark's in Venice or the great cathedrals of Rome. Yet there was something else.' Theodore spread his hands. 'You and I have a great deal in common. I, too, started to search for something substantial to my faith, something real—'

'As did Anstritha,' Eleanor interrupted. 'She also had her secrets.' She quickly described her conversation with Fulcher. 'Did you know anything about this?' She turned on her brother.

'Yes, yes.' Hugh refused to meet her eye. 'Let me explain, Eleanor, why we took you to Hagia Sophia. Holy Wisdom.' He laughed sharply. 'That is what this is all about. Either Holy Wisdom or Holy Money! Every cross-bearer in our company has his or her own reason for this journey. Some of these we know.' Hugh paused as if listening to the sounds drifting from the tavern below or the smelly alleyway outside. He circled his hands. 'One reason perhaps could unite us all: relics.'

'Relics?' Eleanor queried.

'They are in great demand,' Theodore explained, 'by both the angels and the demons, which is,' he drummed his thickset fingers against his wine goblet, 'why I am here, along with your brother, Godefroi, Alberic and Norbert.'

Eleanor stared at the lancet window. The piece of stretched linen had been removed to let in the light. She quickly recalled the stories about various churches and their hunger for relics.

'Pieces of bone,' she murmured. 'Shards of cloth, dried flesh, flakes of skin.'

'True,' Hugh replied, 'but listen, Eleanor! Norbert has travelled to Outremer. He has been to Constantinople and visited Jerusalem.'

'As did Anstritha.'

'So I understand, but let me explain. Norbert was expelled from his monastery because of his mockery of certain relics held by his community. He was not stripped of his orders, just given licence to leave. At first he considered preaching against the veneration of what you call pieces of bone and shards of cloth; then he met Alberic and they both came to Constantinople.'

'What!' Eleanor exclaimed.

'Alberic left his parish church for this Crusade. He claims he is in the thirtieth year of penance for the betrayal of his master. He was born of noble Saxon family and became a member of the housecarls, the personal bodyguard of Harold Godwinson the Saxon king defeated by William the Norman at the battle of Senlac thirty years ago. Alberic has described, how, in the final moments of the battle, as the sun set that October day, the Saxon line finally buckled. He believes he should have stayed and died beside his master. Instead he fled. For a while he sheltered in the wild wastes and the great forest that border the southern coast of England. He became a hermit, torn by guilt, a desire to make reparation, to seek forgiveness for what he still regards as a betrayal. For a while he called himself Judas. Eventually he found that even living in his own country, however reclusive he remained, only deepened the wound. So he took ship to France and wandered the roads. He eventually met Norbert, who recognised him as an educated man. After a prolonged stay at Soissons, Norbert arranged for Alberic to be ordained . . .'

'Do Alberic and Norbert know you are telling me this?'

'Of course,' Hugh smiled. 'Norbert asked you to speak to Fulcher; he later heard that man's confession.'

'And would you ever have spoken?' Eleanor accused.

'Yes,' Hugh insisted, 'but as I shall explain, there is also great danger in all of this. Anyway, Alberic and Norbert took to wandering. They witnessed all forms of cruelty and began to doubt the truth of religion, any idea of a loving God or the Incarnation of the Christ.' Hugh sipped at his wine. 'Little wonder,' he added. 'I have been down the same path myself. At last they visited Jerusalem, where they sheltered for two years next to the Holy Sepulchre.'

'They were not persecuted?'

'Contrary to belief,' Theodore spoke up, 'the Turks regard Christ as a great prophet. The real persecution took place under the mad caliph Al-Hakim, who treated his own subjects as barbarously as he did others before going completely mad and declaring himself God. No, Alberic and Norbert were left alone. During their stay they heard rumours about great treasures in Jerusalem, relics of the Passion that would prove not only that Christ died but that he rose from the dead. I, too, have heard similar stories.'

'According to Alberic and Norbert,' Hugh continued, 'who have studied manuscripts such as the Life of St Nino, beneath the Dome of the Rock where Solomon's Temple once stood are sealed chambers that used to house the stables of the great Jewish king. In there lie marvellous relics closely associated with the Passion and Resurrection of the Lord. The two of them faithfully collected these stories, and it rekindled their faith. As Norbert remarked, what use debating about logic or philosophy? Instead they recalled the words of St Paul: "If Christ has not risen, then all that we do is in vain." They concentrated on this: whatever cruelty ravished the earth, whatever terror stalked, if the Lord Christ came out from His tomb glorified and resurrected, then there were hidden, greater truths. Think, Eleanor! If someone arrived here now and could prove that Jesus of Nazareth remained a corpse, what use is there in us being here? What use the Mass, the Eucharist, the Sacraments, the Gospels? We'd all go home. However, if Christ did rise from the dead, leaving all other questions aside, that is our faith. If such relics exist, the Holy Sepulchre must be liberated. It must become the centre of the Church, and if beneath the Dome of the Rock lie true relics, evidence for Christ's Passion and Resurrection, then . . .' Hugh held his hands up, 'why shouldn't we go to Jerusalem?'

'And who is party to this?'

'Everyone here, as well as Alberic and Norbert, whom we trust.'

'And Anstritha?' Eleanor opened the wallet on her belt and brought out the piece of parchment

Fulcher had entrusted to her. She opened this up and pushed it across to Hugh: he seized it, studied it and passed it round the others.

'Further proof,' he murmured. 'I do not know what Anstritha found. Norbert and Alberic only told me after she was killed how she too had searched for certain relics. Alberic hid when she came to seek sanctuary in his church; he was terrified she might name him as an accomplice.' Hugh drew a deep breath. 'Anstritha was the widow of a physician. She journeyed to Jerusalem where she met Alberic and Norbert. They became members of the Temple Brotherhood, a secret community dedicated to discovering relics of the Lord's Passion. Anstritha never mentioned any half-brother, hidden menaces or secret enemies, but she did collect information about the Dome of the Rock, hence this map. Alberic later persuaded her to return to France, where she settled at St Nectaire. When the Crusade was preached, Norbert, recalling my family's links with the Benedictine order, journeyed to ask for my help.' Hugh leaned forward, face excited. 'When Jerusalem falls, we shall seek out these treasures of God. Look upon the face of Christ, reveal them to the rest of Christendom! Proof that Our Lord lived, died and was resurrected, leaving sacred marks on certain cloths.'

'And Veronica?' Eleanor asked. 'Fulcher gave me that name.'

'The woman who cleansed Christ's face as he was being led out to crucifixion. According to some legends, Veronica also provided the mandylion, which covered the divine face in the sepulchre, as well as the shroud in which His body was wrapped.

Legend has it that a woman should keep these sacred cloths and be given the title "Veronica". Those icons you viewed in Hagia Sophia? You noticed the similarity in different paintings from different eras? My belief, as well as that of the Poor Brethren, is that they are all based on the real image of Our Saviour, which has now disappeared, though we shall find it.' Hugh paused as Eleanor raised a hand.

'You mentioned the Resurrection? This is more than a holy relic? The relics we studied in Hagia Sophia, they are all based on the real likeness of Christ?'

'A miraculous likeness,' Hugh replied. 'Transferred to cloth by divine means. Proof that Christ did suffer but rose again. These relics are not just ordinary ones, but living proof of our belief.'

'And Norbert and Alberic have discovered evidence for this?'

'Norbert was allowed into many monasteries to study in their scriptoria and libraries and trace the history of these holy Images. About a hundred years ago a group of refugee Greek monks set up a cult in Rome near the abandoned church of St Boniface. They worshipped an icon that one manuscript describes as an image of Our Lord Jesus, not fashioned by human hand, imprinted on a shroud. According to another document, the Acts of Thaddeus, Jesus wiped his face on a cloth folded in four yet left his image on it. More importantly, Pope Stephen II delivered a sermon, oh, some three hundred years ago, in which he described a famous cloth.' Hugh closed his eyes as he recalled the lines. ' "Wonderful it is to see or

90

hear such a thing, the glorious face of Jesus, and the majestic form of his whole body has been miraculously transferred. For those who never had the opportunity to see his earthly appearance, they can do so as it has been imprinted on the linen."'

He opened his eyes. 'Don't you see, Eleanor—an image of Christ as he really was?'

Eleanor turned to Theodore. 'And you believe this?'

'Passionately, sister. I too wish to secure my faith on something.'

'You mentioned danger?'

'And their name is Legion,' Godefroi replied, leaning across the table. 'Eleanor, we have seen what is happening within our own small communities. Churches, monasteries and abbeys are founded and each hungers for its own relics. Can you imagine what would happen if the relics we've described were brought into the marketplace to be sold to the highest bidder? A veritable fortune could be made. A king's ransom demanded. We know little about Anstritha. She was frightened to tell Alberic and Norbert the full truth, but her half-brother may have been a man called the Magus, named after Simon Magus, the magician who tried to buy the spiritual powers of St Peter and was punished for his sins. This Magus lurks deep in the shadows. He peddles sacred relics as a butcher would hunks of meat. He has been hired by city communes and councils to secure relics by fair means or foul, usually the latter. We believe, though we have little proof, that this Magus is probably the masked horseman who stirred up the villagers against Anstritha, silenced her mouth once and for all and ransacked her possessions, possibly searching for the map you have given us. The Magus tried to steal the corpse of St Modaldus from the Church of St Symphronius in Trier but failed when her body began to bleed. He was more successful in other ventures: the body of St Sanctus from a church in Meaux and that of St Nicholas from Myra which he sold to the city of Bari.'

'Who is he? Where is he?'

'We don't know. He may be one of us, but,' Hugh pointed at the square of parchment, 'he would be deeply interested in that. Perhaps,' he shrugged, 'he is a member of the Beggars' Company. If so, there will be further trouble with that coven.'

'They have already invoked the blood feud against us,' Theodore added quickly, 'for the death of their comrades.'

'Rapists and murderers,' Eleanor retorted. 'Count Raymond fully approved of what Hugh did.'

'I hope God does.' Hugh replied wearily. 'The Beggars will have to be watched, but in the end, the relics of the Lord's Passion are what we seek. Eleanor, we waited until now to tell you the full truth, for to do so earlier may have been dangerous. The Magus will strike at anyone who has knowledge of this, and that now includes you. The dangers, as Godefroi said, are many. Alberic and Norbert are devoted servants of the Poor Brethren but they have brought a legion of other troubles with them.' Hugh walked to the window, then crossed to the door. He opened this, closed it and returned to the table. 'We all know about the Holy Father's sermon at Clermont, but that is not the full truth of our situation. Alberic and Norbert are our teachers in this. They also spent years with the teachers of Islam, who have a faith as certain and firm as ours. They too have their own codes and laws. They too regard Jerusalem as sacred. They call the Dome of the Rock "a Noble Sanctuary, the Haram", a revered site. According to their faith, the great Prophet Muhammad, having fallen asleep while praying in his home town of Mecca, was woken by the Angel Gabriel. He mounted a winged horse called Al-Buraq and was taken "to the most furthest place", the Dome of the Rock. Once there, the great Prophet ascended into heaven to pray with Abraham, Moses, Jesus and the other leading prophets, as well as receive final instruction for his teaching.'

'The Dome of the Rock is a Holy Place for all faiths,' Theodore took up the story, 'and, therefore, a powerful attraction for fanatics, be they Frankish, Muslim or Jewish. One Muslim group, a heretical sect called the Fedawi—the Devoted Ones—are committed to guarding the Dome of the Rock and all its secrets. They are assassins garbed in white with blood-red girdle and slippers. Each carries two long curved daggers. They answer only to their leader, Sheik Al Jehal. They are feared and hated by other followers of Islam, who regard them as heretics because, full of wine mixed with opium, they will strike at those who oppose them or whomever they regard as an enemy.'

Hugh fumbled at his wallet and drew out a roll of parchment.

'Alberic and Norbert had to flee Jerusalem. Their search for the secret chambers provoked suspicions amongst the Fedawi. One morning they woke to find a dagger thrust into the bolster of a bed with a scroll bearing a warning.' Hugh unrolled the parchment and read its contents:

What you possess shall escape you in the end and return to us.
Know that we hold you and will keep you until the account is settled.
Know you that we go forth and return as we wish.
Know you that by no means can you hinder us or escape.

Hugh threw the parchment down on the table. Eleanor picked it up and studied the writing. The Norman French letters were perfectly formed.

'This was delivered to them?' she asked. 'They were marked down for death?'

'Something similar,' Theodore replied, 'but that,' he pointed to the parchment, 'was delivered to us.' He leaned underneath the table, undid the straps to the panniers he usually carried over his shoulder and drew out two long curved daggers bound together by a blood-red cord.

'We are,' intoned Hugh as if reciting a prayer, 'the Poor Brethren of the Temple; we will, God willing, take Jerusalem and the treasures it holds. We will be a community zealous in our service to the Lord, dedicated to preserving His name and the glory of His Passion. We do not seek the blood of Jew or Muslim but we will follow our vision, for as the Book of Proverbs says: "Where there is no vision on the earth, the people perish."'

'And the warning?' Eleanor asked, curbing her

94

fear.

'The same as that given to Brother Norbert and Father Alberic,' Hugh replied softly. 'Pinned to a bolster two nights ago. The Fedawi know what we intend, and they are waiting!'

Part 5

Dorylaeum: The Feast of St James the Apostle, 25 July 1097

Hominumque contentio mundi hujus et cupido.
(A day when strife amongst men and the lusts of this world are over.)

The *Dies Irae* of St Columba

Deus Vult! God wills it! The hoarse battle cry rang through the valley, echoing up to the pine-edged hilltops, scattering the birds from the cypress trees. Yes, *Deus vult*, Eleanor reflected, as she sat on a pile of cushions in the looted tent close to the battlefield of Dorylaeum. Dust devils swirled through the flaps of the gorgeous but fire-singed pavilion of expensive cloth with its ornate gold fringes. To the right of the flap stretched a great splash of dried blood; Eleanor tried to ignore this as she dictated to Simeon the Scribe, the man of a thousand faiths, as he described himself. A Copt, a prisoner whom Eleanor had rescued from the blood-spattered mace of Babewyn, Simeon sat waiting patiently for his 'mistress-sister' to collect her thoughts. He had everything ready: the writing

95

tray, the sharpened quills, ink horns, pumice stone, a little sand, as well as rolls of looted parchment. Simeon, whose Coptic name Eleanor found difficult to pronounce, stared adoringly at his saviour whilst quietly congratulating himself on his innate skill at surviving. A trained scribe, know ledgeable in Greek and Frankish, not to mention Latin and the lingua franca of the ports, he had served Fatimid, Seljuk, Greek and Frank as well as Armenian, Syrian and Jewish masters. He was a skilled scholar, and could prepare manuscripts, write in cipher, and worship God in any way his masters wanted him to. On the morning of 19 July 1097, Simeon awoke a devout Muslim; by the time he succumbed to a fitful, nightmare-ridden sleep that same day, he was, according to the subtle tale he told Eleanor, a devout Christian captured by the Sultan of Rhum outside Nicomedea. Nevertheless, Simeon, as he now called himself— after Simeon Stylites, the hermit who lived for years on top of a pillar—truly liked Eleanor. He admired her solemn pale face, framed by its veil of black hair, and those lively smiling eyes. If she wanted to recall the stupendous events, as she described them, that accompanied the Franks and their foolish journey to Jerusalem, then he was her man, though he fully intended not to share her fate. If the Turks attacked and were victorious, Simeon quietly promised himself that he would hide as he had done last time, survive the axe, sword or lance and declare himself the most devout of Muslims.

In her turn, Eleanor studied Simeon out of the corner of her eye: his dark face, the neatly clipped and oiled beard and moustache, his bony body, long arms and slender fingers. Quite an elegant man, with his bracelets, the earring in the left earlobe and the loose dark green robes he wore with a white cord around the waist. Simeon was a born story-teller, Eleanor reflected, and that was what she needed. Others were writing chronicles, accounts and letters about what was happening, so why shouldn't she continue hers with a little skilled help?

'Write it down as I describe it,' she said to Simeon.

He brought both hands together and bowed.

'As you say, mistress-sister, so shall it be done!' His liquid dark eyes were full of amusement, his face composed in a mask of mock servitude.

Ah well, *Deus vult*, and so it was, Eleanor reflected. They had left Constantinople, ferried across the Arm of St George in barges to begin their journey through Anatolia, the Sultanate of Rhum. From the start they had been shadowed by Turkish scouts. The Army of God were following the same path as Peter the Hermit's horde, and the Turks had deliberately left the remains of the thousands they had slaughtered at Civetot and elsewhere as a grisly warning. Bits of rotting skeletons, decapitated heads, skulls on a row of poles, in spiked bushes, on rocky outcrops or around wells and waterholes glared ominously at them. The signs of such a great massacre dampened the ardour of some, though others grew fervent for revenge. The Army of God moved slowly in phalanxes, long lines of carts, horses, donkeys and camels. Alongside these trudged columns of men, women and children, baking under the strengthening sun. Their destination was the Turkish-held city of Nicea with its forbidding towers, huge gates and flaking yellow walls. An impregnable fortress, Nicea was defended on three sides by impressive fortifications and on the fourth by the Askanian lake. The Army of God, however, were in good spirits. They were well supplied with corn, wine, wheat and barley, whilst the route to Nicea was clearly marked along the rutted, tangled path by scouts who nailed up wooden or metal crosses.

In the main it was a pleasant journey. Eleanor had ridden in one of the carts, reflecting more on what she had learnt in Constantinople than what awaited them at Nicea. Norbert and Alberic had become friendlier, welcoming her as a true sister as if some invisible barrier had been miraculously removed; even Imogene, who tended to keep to herself, commented on that. For the rest, Eleanor wondered about the Fedawi and their threats. How could they be so close to Constantinople? Had they disguised themselves, blending in with the merchants or Turcopole mercenaries who swarmed everywhere? Theodore, in recognition of what they had told her, rather shyly gave Eleanor a small icon painted on wood, very similar to those images she had seen in Hagia Sophia, a reminder of the bond between them.

Eleanor could now understand Hugh's enthusiasm, as well as the strict discipline imposed on the Poor Brethren of the Temple. They were marching to Jerusalem not just to recover the Holy Sepulchre but to discover proof of Christ's Passion and Resurrection. According to Hugh, they must be victorious and purify themselves, in order to be worthy to receive such holy relics. Little wonder too about the secrecy. Relic-hunters like the Magus, whoever he might be, would murder for such religious objects, whilst the Fedawi would never allow entry to a place they had chosen as their own.

Eleanor, seated on the cart jolting along the trackway, wondered if the Beggars' Company, marching a little ahead of them, could be a refuge for such outlaws. Beltran distrusted Jehan deeply and had warned her to be wary of that rogue and his coven. Indeed, since leaving Constantinople, Beltran had attached himself to Eleanor and Imogene, paying particular attention to the pretty widow. Like Theodore, he proved to be a genial companion who, by his own confession, had hardly left Provence, being steeped, as he put it, in all its wonders, particularly the poetry and songs of the south. He was not a knight but a serjeant, a *nuncius* or envoy, well placed to learn all the gossip of the camp and the bickering between its leaders.

After the long march they eventually reached Nicea. The Turks had withdrawn into the city to await any attack. Hugh took Eleanor to view the massive fortifications, the lofty yellow brick walls with more than a hundred towers all protected by a double ditch. Eleanor had scarcely returned to her tent when the cry *'Au secours! Au secours!'* was raised. Warning horns and trumpets blared. She and Imogene hurried down the narrow gulleys between the pavilions leading to the centre of the camp. Here stood a huge cart, poles on each corner displaying the battle standards, containing a great wooden altar surmounted by a stark black cross. Two men, dressed like monks in long grey robes, stood with their backs to the cart wheels, swords and daggers drawn. They faced a threatening line of Frankish foot armed with lowered spears and pikes.

'Spies! spies!' a voice accused. 'We caught them trying to leave camp with drawings and numbers.' One of the trapped men raced forward, whirling sword and dagger, only to be stopped by a surge of pike thrusts that almost lifted him off the ground. He struggled like a landed fish, legs kicking, gargling on the blood spilling out of his mouth. The other immediately threw down his weapons and knelt, hands extended in a sign of surrender. He was swiftly seized, bound and dragged away. A short while later Hugh came hurrying back, even as the alarm was raised again: a blare of horns and trumpets, men shouting battle cries, war horses being quickly led out. He grasped Eleanor and pushed her inside the tent.

'They were spies,' he announced breathlessly, pausing as Beltran, Theodore and Godefroi thrust into the tent behind him. 'The captured one has confessed. Kilij Arslan, Sultan of Rhum, is marching straight towards us with thousands of horsemen!'

'Where, when will they attack?'

'Bohemond besieges the northern side of Nicea, Godfrey of Bouillon the east and we the south, the same direction as Arslan. We will bear the brunt of the first attack.'

He had hardly finished when there was a surge of noise from outside, a renewed blowing of trumpets followed by screams and cries. They hastened out to see people pointing. Eleanor stared in horror at the hills behind the camp where the pine trees clustered close together like a green-black wall. Everyone was staring at them: boys and women collecting water in jars; a cluster of monks, Ave beads wrapped round their hands, gathering for the midday prayer; a cook, all bloodied to his elbows, a dead chicken dangling from his left hand; a young boy with a mongrel puppy in his hands; knights in linen undergarments, all gazing at the horror coming from the hills. Eleanor's throat felt dry and narrow. She blinked and stared again. Hundreds if not thousands of horsemen, in flowing white robes, sunlight dancing off their helmets, were moving out of the trees like a flood of ants towards them. Already a dust haze was rising. The distant thunder of hooves shook the earth; coloured banners snapped in the breeze. Some children playing amongst the decaying stones of a cemetery laughed and shrieked, pointing their fingers.

'They say they've brought ropes,' Beltran murmured. 'To bind us and lead us into captivity.'

The crowd could only stare. A monk began to chant a psalm: *'Domine libera nos*—Lord deliver us.'

'You pray,' Hugh shouted. 'The rest to arms, to arms!' The menacing spell was broken. Jars were dropped, cloaks doffed, baskets placed on the ground, camp equipment pushed aside. Knights, serjeants, monks and priests, every able-bodied man, hurried to arm against that river of horsemen sweeping down to engulf them. For a short while the enemy disappeared into the tree-covered slopes, only to surge out again. The Turkish battle cries, a piercing, ululating screech, echoed shrilly above the drumming of hooves. The enemy's coloured banners could now be clearly seen. The

101

Turks reached the foot of the slope just as the Frankish line, knights in half-armour, on clumsily strapped saddles, burst out of the camp. The Frankish mounts were fresh, much heavier and moving at full charge. The Turks, bloodied on the pathetically armed mob of Peter the Hermit, were taken completely by surprise at the sheer fury of the Frankish attack. This only deepened as the phalanx of armour and heavy horse crashed into them like a fast-moving river hurtling up against some makeshift bridge. The Turks, on smaller, lighter mounts, were simply engulfed, then cut up into small groups, which had to face further Frankish attacks. The air rang with the horrid crash of battle, screams and yells. Banners floated down. The ground became strewn with white-garbed corpses. The Turks, not used to such violent hand-to-hand combat, simply broke, retreating up the slopes pursued by the exultant Franks. By now the news of this first skirmish was spreading through the Army of God. Normans, Rhinelanders, Flemings, French and Greeks flooded into Count Raymond's camp. Eleanor watched them prepare, donning body armour, strapping on helmets. The mounted knights gathered, masked by a screen of dust and smoke deliberately created to blind the Turks already massing again on the tree-lined heights.

Hugh, Godefroi, Beltran and Theodore, now properly armoured, collected their oval shields and maces. Norbert and Alberic, faces flushed, joined the foot gathering behind the horse. Fresh fires, deliberately started, poured out more black smoke, concealing what was happening in the Army of God. The Turkish cavalry gathered again for the charge. Their stratagem was simple: to attack, pin the Franks against the walls of Nicea, destroy them and relieve the city. As Eleanor wrote later in her chronicle, the Turks made two mistakes. They believed that Count Raymond's host was the entire Frankish army, and that its fighting qualities would be no better than those of Peter the Hermit's ragged followers. They were soon proved wrong. In the early afternoon, the white-robed horsemen again poured like a waterfall down the slopes. The Franks, behind their screen of black smoke, watched, waited, then charged. The swift, heavy iron wall of mounted knights shattered the enemy and the Turkish line crumbled. The Franks swept through, cutting and slicing, drenching the ground in so much blood it poured in rivulets down the slopes, then turned and charged again. The Turks broke and fled. For a while the Franks hotly pursued them before returning in triumph to the camp, spears and lances displaying grisly trophies, herding lines of prisoners, the decapitated heads of their comrades tied around their necks.

The captives were paraded, taunted and humiliated. One of the catapults Alexius had provided was pushed down to the edge of the great moat around Nicea. As the sun set, the severed heads, gathered in fishing nets, were catapulted into the city. Some smashed in a gruesome pulp against the parapets. Others cleared the battlements, and even from where she stood, Eleanor could hear the groans of the population imprisoned behind the walls. Kilij Arslan had failed! The Army of God now turned on the prisoners. They were herded into the centre of the camp and forced to kneel so they could be decapitated. Simeon the scribe was amongst those captured in the baggage train. Desperately he pleaded for his life. The executioners ignored him. Eventually he broke free and fled through the camp, pursued by Gargoyle and Babewyn, the lieutenants of Jehan the Wolf. He ran screaming down the narrow lanes mocked and pushed by drunken spectators. Eleanor, who had retreated to her tent, heard the uproar and went outside. Simeon almost ran into her and collapsed at her feet. Babewyn and Gargoyle grasped him.

'I did not beg, mistress.' Simeon paused in his writing.

'No, Simeon, you did not. You simply said you didn't want to die. You claimed you were a Catholic captured by the Turks. If I remember correctly,' Eleanor added drily, 'you even quoted canon law, though that made little difference to those two grotesques.'

'Camel turds,' Simeon whispered. 'But thanks to you, mistress-sister . . .' He leaned forward. 'Oh, by the way, can I take the oath as a Poor Brother of the Temple? I know things.'

'Do you, Simeon?' Eleanor narrowed her eyes.

'I know secrets about the hidden things. I have heard the whispers.'

Eleanor glanced quickly at Imogene stretched out sleeping on a pile of cushions.

'Simeon, I am always amazed at your skill for listening.' She smiled. 'But let us return to our chronicle.'

'Of course, mistress-sister, though I must add my thanks to you and your noble brother for saving my life. I am so grateful . . .'

'The chronicle, Simeon . . .'

'Yes, mistress-sister . . .'

Babewyn had seized Simeon by the throat, struggling to keep him in position so that Gargoyle could swing his mace. Eleanor had screamed at them to stop, but only the arrival of Hugh and Godefroi, their swords drawn, forced the two killers to retreat. Drunk and mouthing filthy curses, they staggered away. Eleanor took Simeon into her entourage as the Army of God turned from celebrating its victory to the grim business of besieging Nicea. The city baffled them. No such fortifications had faced a Frankish army in the west. They also had no boats, so attack from the lake was impossible. The moat in front of the walls stretched over two yards wide and the same deep. The first defensive wall beyond was at least six feet thick and nine yards high, with towers jutting out to defend the approaches. Even if this was breached, the towering curtain wall behind it, eighteen feet thick, was protected by a fresh range of towers from where archers and slingers, not to mention engines of war, could rake attackers with a blizzard of missiles. Frustration mounted amongst the Army of God. The jubilation over Arslan's defeat soon evaporated as they tried desperately to take the city. The moat was filled in at a certain point and makeshift catapults and mangonels pushed across. They and the soldiers who manned them were swiftly engulfed in a flood of arrows, stones, javelins and sheets of roaring flame. Mantlets, screens of aspen and willow woven together, were built to protect the archers, but these too were ravaged by oily fire poured from the battlements.

One morning Count Raymond, escorted by

Hugh, Godefroi, Eleanor and others from the Poor Brethren, rode out along the moat to search for any weakness. From the fortifications rose jeering insults and a rain of arrows, which fell short. It was a clear, warm day, the breeze sweet with the fragrance of pine, cypress and the fruits ripening in the nearby orchards. The count reined in.

'We have plenty of wood,' Raymond's one good eye glared at Hugh and Godefroi as he gestured at the trees, 'but what can we do with it?'

Hugh grasped the reins of the count's horse. 'Come, my lord, there is something.' They galloped further along the evil-smelling moat.

Eleanor found the palfrey she had been given sluggish, reluctant to move, so Theodore reined in, moving between her and the Turks lining the battlements. He grasped the palfrey's reins and winked at Eleanor.

'Just in case,' he murmured, 'the Turks might glimpse your beauty and sally out.'

Eleanor blushed, and Theodore began to sing a troubadour song about a maid locked in a tower. Eventually Hugh led them to the most eastern part of the wall.

'Look, my lord.'

Eleanor followed her brother's direction.

'Theodore told me about this,' continued Hugh. 'Stare hard at the base of the tower: the brickwork is crumbling, the legacy of a previous siege.'

Count Raymond stared, then clapped his hands in glee. Two days later a testudo, fashioned out of cypress, willow and aspen under a roof of holm oak, its leather covering saturated with wet sand, crossed the makeshift bridge to pound at what Eleanor had christened 'the Leaning Tower'.

Archers sheltered beneath the eaves of the testudo's broad sloping roof and loosed at the enemy along the battlements. The engineers soon broke through the wall, shoring up the breach with beams as they picked feverishly at the crumbling masonry behind. Eleanor stood watching, safe behind a line of shielded carts. The tower collapsed just as darkness fell, but the following morning the camp was roused by trumpet cries. Eleanor, bleary-eyed, rushed out of her tent and joined the throng streaming down through the shifting mist to the eastern side of the moat. They stopped and stared in disbelief of the Leaning Tower. During the night, the defenders, working feverishly, had repaired the breach. Count Raymond's anger knew no bounds, and like Achilles, he retreated to sulk in his tent while other leaders pressed on with the siege. Yet despite Kilij Arslan's defeat, the Niceans were ferocious in the defence of their city. The enemy had desecrated their dead so they retaliated by lowering hooks on ropes to seize the corpses of Franks; these were pulled up, stripped and hung over the walls to rot. If the Army of God attacked, stone and arrow shattered head and neck; if the Franks broke through, they were swiftly deluged by flaming missiles.

For a week the siege became a desultory affair of two enemies watching each other like circling dogs, then, abruptly, the atmosphere changed. Count Raymond bustled about accompanied by Tacticius the Greek commander. Ballistae and mangonels from the arsenals of Constantinople appeared in the camp. These were wheeled down to the Leaning Tower to launch a scathing attack of missiles and rocks that drove the defenders from the walls. A new breach was opened, and when darkness fell, the night was illuminated by roaring fires and the light of flaming missiles hurled at the tower. This time the Turks had no opportunity to repair the damage. The star-lit sky was streaked with orange tongues, the silence shattered by the whoosh of missiles, the crash of wood and stones and the cries of both defenders and attackers. As soon as daylight broke, the Poor Brethren of the Temple, to shouts of *'Deus vult!'* and 'Toulouse!', prepared to lead Count Raymond's force across the makeshift bridge over the moat. Hugh and Godefroi kissed Eleanor before tightening the chain-mail bands across their faces, which left only their eyes exposed. Helmets were strapped on, shields fastened to arms and swords drawn.

Hugh and Godefroi led their company down to the bridge whilst archers, crossbowmen and engineers loosed volley after volley at the walls. The catapults edged even closer to intensify the barrage. Eleanor watched, heart in mouth, as Hugh and Godefroi crossed the rickety bridge. Smoke billowed about, screams and shouts echoed. The knights of Toulouse thronged all about her. Standards were unfurled, men-at-arms in full battle gear waited to reinforce the first assault on those formidable defences. The horror and din of battle whipped Eleanor's senses as if some wandering demon had seized her soul, her mind, her imagination. She looked up at the empty blue sky bending over those soaring yellow-brick fortifications. Arrows, sling shots and other missiles scored the blue. Oaken bundles, smoking evilly, swept through the air, spouts of flame erupted from the battlements. Eleanor glanced again. Hugh and Godefroi, shields up, were halfway across the bridge when an ear-splitting roar cut through the noise of war. Men were pointing at the battlements where scarlet and gold banners displaying the gorgeous eagle of Alexius Comnenus were being draped and hoisted. The city had fallen! Greek forces were inside. The Turks had surrendered! Trumpets called the retreat. Hugh and his company fell back even as more imperial banners fluttered from the ramparts above them. A loud screech cut the air. The great gates of Nicea swung open and Catephracti, blue-silver insignia fluttering from their spear points, came thundering out. Imogene cursed and immediately left, searching for Beltran. Eleanor, feeling weak, eager to escape the confusing storm of war, returned to her tent. She went to lie down on the ready-made palliasse but startled in horror at the two curved daggers, white bone-handles gleaming, pushed deep into the bolster, their blades tied together by a ribbon of blood-red cord . . .

'Know ye,' a voice whispered behind her, 'what you possess shall escape you and, in the end, return to us.'

Eleanor turned slowly. At first she could see nothing, then she made out a shadow outlined by the slit in the tent through which the mysterious intruder must have entered. He sat cross-legged on the ground, garbed in a white robe, head and face swathed in a black turban exposing only the eyes.

'The witch woman's chart.' The voice stumbled over the Norman French. 'I know Fulcher gave it to you.' He extended a gloved hand; the other tapped the hilt of the dagger in the red waistband.

Eleanor tried to speak but couldn't.

'The chart!' the man insisted.

'My brother,' Eleanor stammered. The sounds from outside grew stronger, followed by shouts of someone approaching the tent. Eleanor glanced at the main flap then back, but her mysterious visitor had vanished.

Simeon the scribe, talking as ever—God had given him a tongue as nimble as his pen—burst into the tent gabbling the news. How the Emperor had brought ships in ox-drawn carts to the Askanian lake and sent them up against Nicea. How these ships had even captured the wife and family of the Governor of Nicea as they tried to escape. The Turks soon realised that if the Army of God manned those ships, their city would certainly fall and be devastated by fire and sword. They had immediately entered into secret negotiations with Alexius, promising to surrender to him if they and their possessions were spared from the Army of God. Alexius had agreed, sending a high-ranking envoy named Boutoumites into the city to accept the surrender. The leaders of the Army of God had had some inkling of this, but when the news became public, the Franks immediately accused Alexius of duplicity and treachery.

Rumours were rife that Boutoumites had encouraged Tacticius to persuade Count Raymond to attack, writing a note: 'We have the game in our hand, assault the walls. Do not let the Franks know the true situation but, after sunrise, let them attack the city.' The leaders of the Army of God knew about the ships and the pressure these would place

110

on the Turks, but they never expected such a swift surrender. The Emperor had kept them in the dark and by nightfall his deceit was common talk around the camp. Tempers rose, especially amongst the Normans from southern Italy led by Bohemond and Tancred, so Alexius moved quickly to mollify them. Cartloads of fresh provisions and wine, baskets, coffers and chests full of precious stones, gold and silver, stacks of weapons, piles of embroidered cloths and lines of sleek, plump horses were dispatched into the camp. The Poor Brethren of the Temple drew their share, ten gold bezants, which went into the common coffer under Godefroi's care. Later that same night, Eleanor, Hugh, Godefroi, Alberic, Norbert, Theodore and Simeon gathered to meet. The scribe had been taken on to their council because of his clerical skills as well as his knowledge of the shrines of Jerusalem, particularly the Dome of the Rock. Theodore hosted the meeting, welcoming their new recruit, and pointing out that Simeon's only protection against the rancour of the camp was Hugh and Eleanor, so it was little wonder the scribe had enthusiastically taken their secret oath. On that night, as all the gates of Nicea were opened and the heralds proclaimed how the Army of God would soon march for Antioch, Eleanor told them about her own mysterious visitor.

'But who could it be?' Alberic asked. 'Every one of the Poor Brethren was mustering before the Leaning Tower.'

'It must be someone in the Army of God,' Eleanor insisted. 'The same thing happened in Constantinople.'

'The Fedawi,' Theodore explained. 'Perhaps

111

their assassins lurk hidden amongst us? It is foolish to speculate, but at least we know the importance of Anstritha's map. Lord Hugh, you have it safe, yes?'

'Yes,' Hugh replied absent-mindedly. 'You have all seen it, but come . . .'

They turned to fresh news. Bohemond's phalanx was to leave immediately the following morning. Count Raymond wanted the Poor Brethren of the Temple to join these and act as a link with the rest of the army. No one disagreed, eager for what Hugh called the 'proper pilgrimage' to begin in earnest.

Eleanor would never forget their departure. They left Nicea just before the sun rose swiftly in sheets of red-gold flame against the light blue sky. A fitting start for what proved to be a time of wrath, of anger, the beginning of the horrors. Yet, as Eleanor wrote in her chronicle, it started ordinarily enough. She sat perched on one of the carts, Imogene squatting next to her as Bohemond's column trudged down the old Roman road stretching to the valleys and dusty plateaus leading down to Antioch. They crossed stone bridges built by the ancients over streams and rivulets, and passed the occasional decaying Byzantine guard tower. On either side rolled wild meadows sprinkled with hardy summer flowers; now and again, long strips of ochre-tinted ploughland; here and there a solitary farmstead usually built around the shell of a ruined villa. Clumps of sycamore, holm oak, grey ash, willow and cypress broke the undulating landscape. They passed lonely villages with their dusty trackways, wandering goats, domed wells, silent vineyards and wine presses. The morning air rang with the clatter and rumble of carts, the jingle of harness, the clink of weapons, shouts and cries from the trudging men-at-arms. Dust clouds swirled, staining the black robes of the monks. Spear and lance tips caught the sunlight and flashed it brilliantly back. Faces, white, red and brown, became laced with sweaty dust. Children played or fought with each other. Hymns were chanted. A group of nobles in gorgeously coloured robes left the column escorted by their grooms clad in green and brown; hawks fluttered on their wrists, or strained against the perches, making the jesse-bells tinkle. Young men, leggings pulled up, stood in the streams, busy with string or net to catch fresh fish. Eleanor considered it was more like a day out in the country, visiting friends or enjoying the good weather, than marching to war. Scouts came galloping back: they had glimpsed Turkish patrols but nothing happened that day.

By evening they reached a crossroads near the yawning mouths of two lonely valleys, apparently empty except for the boulders, rocks, shrubs and trees dotting their sides. In between the valley mouths stretched a large, reed-ringed marsh. Bohemond, alarmed by increased sightings of Turkish patrols as well as rumours that the valleys on either side might house more, used the marsh to protect the rear of his camp. Nothing happened that night; it passed quiet and peaceful under the stars. At sunrise the priests gathered the people around the altar carts. Candles glowed in lantern horns and incense circled up into the heavy morning mist as Tancred led a *comitatus* of knights to scour the valley to the east.

As Mass finished, Tancred came hastening back with alarming news: Turkish horsemen were emerging out of the mist further down the valley. The Franks, still jubilant over what they considered their victory at Nicea and lulled by the calm morning, became excited and curious. Horsemen galloped off to catch sight of the enemy. Women and children mingled with the leaders at the front of the column; eventually these were forced back, becoming an unruly mob. Eleanor glimpsed Bohemond in full chain mail, a towering figure on his powerful black war charger. Riders, casting up clouds of dust, came galloping towards him, turning in the saddle and gesturing back. Eleanor recognised Hugh, Godefroi and Theodore. What they announced must have been truly alarming. Bohemond turned to face the people, ordering them to move back. Hugh, Godefroi and the rest forced their way through, jumping from their saddles, screaming for their harness and weapons.

'Eleanor, Eleanor!' Theodore pushed her back towards the tent. He snatched up a wet rag from just inside and wiped the dust from his face. 'Arm yourselves,' he gasped. 'They aren't Turkish patrols. Kilij Arslan's entire army is coming out of that valley, thousands and thousands of horsemen. They'll sweep us away!' He gestured at Imogene, who stood horror-struck. 'Arm!' he yelled, then he snatched at the reins of his horse and clambered into the saddle. 'Lord Bohemond is sending me back to hasten on the rest. Eleanor . . .' He meant to say more, but shrugged, turned his horse and galloped off.

Terror and panic swept the camp as more scouts

rode in. The Turkish battle lines were fast approaching. Bohemond forced his way through the gathering troops, imposing order. Carts were pulled into position. Oxen and donkeys were swiftly unhitched, their pack saddles and baggage used to defend gaps. Bohemond ordered all horsemen to the front. The rear of the camp would be protected by the marsh whilst a semicircle of foot and archers would guard its flanks. Battle instructions were shouted, armour and harness quickly donned and clasped, swords and daggers loosened in their sheaths. The anxiety spread, apprehension deepened. Men knelt praying, sobbing for help.

'Here they come!' shouted a voice.

Eleanor, standing on a cart, watched the haze swirl out of the mouth of the valley. It ebbed and flowed to reveal flashes of colour and the glitter of armour. A rumbling thunder shook the earth. The cloud of dust billowed then broke. Eleanor caught her breath at the power of the enemy. Hordes of horsemen armed with round shields, their bows already strung, arrows notched. They came on in a thunder of hooves, a pounding of drums and a clash of cymbals. They broke into a trot, a dense throng hurling itself towards the now silent Frankish lines. Screams pierced the air. Green banners flowed and rippled in the morning breeze. The Franks, standards now unfurled, answered with their own battle cries then, like lurchers in a hunt, burst into a furious, galloping charge. They should have smashed into the enemy like a battering ram, but the Turks divided abruptly to the left and right. As they did so, their mounted archers loosed shaft after shaft at the Frankish

115

lines before closing in on the flanks with axe and scimitar, grappling hooks being thrown to drag the mailed knights from the saddle. Steel, flint and rock bit into head and stomach, smashing blows that severed hands, arms and legs. A second phalanx of Frankish knights prepared to charge but the Turkish horse, light and swift, came round the embattled first line and raced past the waiting ranks, loosing a deadly hail of arrows. Horses collapsed; others were panicked into galloping, only to be surrounded by Turks who closed to bring both horse and rider crashing to the ground. Bohemond could take no further provocation. The battle standards of Normandy unfurled, the air ringing with his war cry, his knights broke into a full charge against their tormentors.

Eleanor, drenched in a sweaty dust, the strengthening sun beating down on her, could see the Turkish tactics of attack and faked withdrawal. More enemy forces appeared. Eleanor glanced around. The camp was in chaos. Men, women and children now realised that if Bohemond's men broke, the Turks would sweep through and massacre them. The air became a hellish din of horns, drums, cymbals and trumpets, all mingling with the shrieks, yells and crash of battle. Vultures appeared in the blue skies, forbidding black shadows hovering over that place of blood. The wounded were being dragged back to receive the attention of leeches or shaven-pated priests. One knight, bruised and battered, came clutching his side and collapsed by the cart. Eleanor, startled out of her shock, jumped down and ripped off his mail hauberk and jerkin. Beneath these, his shirt was sticky with blood. She went to staunch the

116

wound, blackish red with the flies already hovering close.

'No, leave me to a leech,' the man gasped. He grasped Eleanor's arm and gestured to the front. 'They need water.'

Eleanor called to a leech kneeling beside another man, his limbs jerking, the death rattle noisy in his throat. The leech shrugged, pushed a wine-soaked rag into the dying soldier's mouth and hurried across. Eleanor rose, calling Imogene and a cluster of women and children to bring waterskins, jugs, anything that would hold water. Some of the priests were already organising this as well as putting on white vestments and hurrying to the battle line to offer absolution and the Eucharist. Eleanor reached the rear rank of horsemen, a host of stinking, wounded knights, blood seeping through their chain mail, faces masked red. They sheltered and rested against the corpses of their horses, the bellies of which were already swelling. Some knights seemed to have swam in blood, swords red to the hilt, maces and axes smeared with gore. Angry eyes, glazed with the fury of battle, glared at her. She offered water, which was snatched and drunk greedily. Flies buzzed in dark clouds. Ahead of her echoed the raucous noise of battle. Bohemond had changed his tactics. The army was losing too many horses, so the Franks now stood in a curving arc of steel against the Turks, who attacked them then swiftly sheered off as they delivered shower after shower of barbed arrows. Men cursed and prayed as they rose to rejoin the battle. A few joked how, when they seized the Turkish camp, they'd bathe in water gushing from crystals, wear garlands of flowery spiken mixed with roses and sprinkle cinnamon in their hair. Others stayed nursing hideous wounds, cuts, slashes and bruises.

Eleanor glimpsed Hugh sitting exhausted on his horse, Godefroi beside him. She called their names but the ground shook with the thunder of a fresh charge and the ear-piercing whistle of the Turkish war cry. Arrows whipped through the air; a horse whinnied in agony. Men screamed for respite. Eleanor wanted to reach Hugh, but a heart-chilling shout sent her racing back to the camp. She stopped by a cart and stared in disbelief. A troop of Turkish horse had found its way across the marsh and was racing into the far side of the camp. Here and there men-at-arms and archers tried to hold them back, but the Turks spread out like angry hornets, shooting arrows before drawing their curved swords to cut to the left and the right. Women, children and priests were slashed and hacked. The Turks were dismounting in groups of twos and threes, seizing fleeing women, stripping them and throwing them down on to the ground. Eleanor felt as if she was carved from stone, with no life in her legs. She felt imprisoned by what she saw, as if asleep, suffering a nightmare that had to be endured. A line of foot was forming to protect the rest of the camp, but beyond these sprouted scenes from hell. A priest, still in his vestments, was fleeing for his life only to have his head sliced open with one swift cut. A monk was staggering backwards, facing the pursuing horseman, who paused, then leaned slightly to one side so his sword neatly severed the monk's head. A soldier stood trying to free a shaft embedded deep in his chest. A Turk was getting up from raping a woman even as the knife in his right hand gashed her from groin to neck. Others were pillaging a tent, running out with jugs and basins and what looked like severed heads.

The line of Frankish foot between Eleanor and the Turks moved forward. From behind, archers loosed arrows that hit friend as well as foe. A further shout. The Frankish line surged more swiftly as a conroy of horse dispatched by Bohemond charged into the camp, attacking the Turks now trapped amongst the tents and carts. Eleanor felt the tension ebb, though her stomach clenched and spasms of pain coursed up her legs and across her back. She couldn't open her mouth. Frankish knights now hacked at white-robed horsemen whilst on the breeze shouts of 'Toulouse, Toulouse! *Deus vult! Deus vult!*' grew stronger. Theodore had been successful! The rest of the Frankish army had debouched on to the battlefield, flinging themselves at the Turkish flanks, whilst Adhémar's company, armed with maces to shatter bone rather than swords to slice flesh, assaulted the Turks from the rear. Hoarse voices shouted further news, Bohemond was leading his line forward; the battle had turned.

Eleanor joined Imogene beneath the cart to drink watered wine and chew on dry bread before crawling out to help the wounded, console the survivors and assist with laying out the dead. Late in the afternoon Frankish horse appeared, the riders sporting the ghastly trophies of their great victory on the end of their lances or tied by the hair to their saddle horns. They brought splendid news: the near defeat had turned into a great victory! Angels in gleaming armour had been seen fighting

119

on the side of the Army of God. The Turks had been completely routed, their camp taken and ransacked. The riders brought orders: the rest of the army must move down to occupy the Turkish camp. Jubilant, singing hymns, the entire army swept up the valley to seize, as Peter Bartholomew proclaimed, 'the tents and possessions of their enemies'.

On that night a great banquet was held, the darkness lit by hundreds of camp fires and pitch torches. Freshly slaughtered meat was roasted on makeshift grills and spits. Songs, hymns and drunken shouts resounded up to the surrounding hills. *Deus vult! Deus vult!* The cry was repeated. The Army of God rejoiced beneath the dark blue velvet sky, the stars brilliant as if an angelic host was also watching. The revelry, however, was broken by the faint sounds of keening and mourning. Eleanor had seen the dead laid out in rows. Men, women and children, mothers and priests as well as warriors like Tancred's brother: a long line of blood-splattered corpses. The stories were rife about the rape and killing perpetrated in the camp by the Turks. The Poor Brethren of the Temple had certainly lost several of their number: Richer the Fuller, Osbert and Anna, Matilda of Aix with four of her children, William the Brewer, his wife and three children, all wrapped in shabby shrouds. Graves had been hacked from the ground. The corpses, each with a small wooden cross, were assigned to the earth, their souls to God in joyful expectation of the rapture, the final resurrection. The kin of the dead were given special rewards in the distribution of the spoils. Heaps of treasure, lines of horses and stacks of weapons had been put on show. Chests and coffers brimming with jewelled plate, cups of ivory, onyx and jasper, golden goblets, gilded armour, bejewelled sheets, embroidered cloths, elaborate harness fashioned out of blood-red leather, cloaks, gowns, shoes and girdles, medallions and coins, the likes of which had never been seen before.

Now, as the darkness deepened and the celebrations echoed to the heavens, the leaders of the Poor Brethren camped around their fire. All were exhilarated and jubilant. Alberic and Norbert had received light wounds before escaping from the massacre, Hugh and Godefroi likewise, though both had their horses killed under them. The main topic of conversation was the ferocity of the Turks.

'Count Raymond,' declared Hugh, biting into a piece of blackened beef, 'says the war is changing. *Bellum in extremis*—war to the end.'

'That is the only war there is,' Norbert replied. 'As I said, no war can be just, no war can be holy.'

Eleanor, half asleep over a cracked goblet of wine, tried to clear her soul of the gruesome images of the day. Beltran was agreeing with Hugh how little mercy could be shown or expected. Theodore, exhausted after his furious ride for help, was smiling at Eleanor over the flickering glow of the fire.

'Our cause is just!'

Eleanor startled at Peter Bartholomew's trumpet-like voice.

'Satan walks,' the prophet continued, 'Satan rides like a great lord. We must arm ourselves against him, take up the weapons of salvation.'

Hugh caught Eleanor's gaze and indicated with his head that they should withdraw. Peter

Bartholomew continued his prophesying as they both retreated into darkness. Hugh grasped her hands.

'Eleanor, Count Raymond really asked us to join Bohemond so I could watch for something.'

'What, Bohemond himself?'

'No.' Hugh drew closer. 'Godefroi knows this as well. Do you remember at Radosto how the Greeks attacked as soon as Count Raymond left? How they seemed to know our movements? How they deployed so swiftly?'

Eleanor nodded.

'Well,' Hugh shrugged, 'this morning Kilij Arsan learned very quickly that Bohemond had become separated from the rest of the army.' He took a deep breath. 'Eleanor, we might have a traitor in our midst. Count Raymond now sees a bear behind every bush; perhaps the Poor Brethren of the Temple shelter one.'

'Why us?' Eleanor replied hotly. 'Why not the Beggars' Company? They provoked the Greeks at Radosto.'

'Ah, yes,' he replied, 'but only amongst the Poor Brethren was it first known that Raymond had left for Constantinople. The rest learned much later whilst the Greeks were ready, just looking for a cause . . .'

'And?'

'We know the Turks have spies in our camp,' Hugh continued, 'as we have in theirs. Count Raymond received an anonymous message that if he was looking for traitors then he should search for them amongst the Poor Brethren of the Temple.'

'A lie!' Eleanor countered. 'Someone trying to

122

create trouble.'

'Count Raymond trusts us,' Hugh replied, 'me, you, Godefroi and the others, but as he pointed out, Alberic, Norbert and Theodore have wandered the face of God's earth, so whom do they truly work for? Do we house a traitor, sister?'

Eleanor reflected on Hugh's question as she sat in that plundered pavilion and watched the flies dance in the shaft of sunlight piercing a tear in its cloth.

'Mistress-sister?' Simeon the Scribe stared around. The pavilion was now empty. Imogene had left saying she wished to share a cup of wine with the brethren. 'Sister, a spy?'

'You know, Simeon . . .' Eleanor smiled. 'I trust you whilst you can only trust me.' She touched the tip of Simeon's nose. 'Moreover, you were not at Radosto.' She gazed round. She'd welcome her own tent, poor and shabby though it was. This one reminded her of blood, the terrible massacre she'd witnessed. The army planned to march to Antioch within three days. She'd be pleased to leave here. There were too many demons, blood-splattered and wicked, clustered about.

Part 6

Antioch: The Feast of St Godric, 21 May 1098

Vexilla Regis prodeunt.
(The standards of the King advance.)

Venantius Fortunatus, 'Hymn In Honour of the Cross'

'O Key of David! O Rod of Jesse! O Morning Star!'

Eleanor de Payens shivered as Norbert and Alberic intoned the Advent 'O' antiphons. Outside Hugh's tent it was black and cold. Inside a meagre fire and two evil-smelling candles shed a little light and warmth against the stink and the freezing cold. 1097, the year of iron and blood, was drawing to a close. When they left Dorylaeum the Army of God thought they would celebrate the great feast in the real stable at Bethlehem whilst their battle standards fluttered above the ramparts of Jerusalem. Instead they had marched on to the plains of hell and encountered Antioch, a city of iron and steel, a huge, dangerous boulder blocking their path. Antioch! The Army of God dared not go round it because the city controlled northern Syria. It could cut off their lines and sever any help from the Emperor and the west. Yet what help? Eleanor wondered as she stared down at her bitten fingernails.

She tried to curb the wave of self-pity and stared

124

round the tent. They had left Constantinople seventy thousand strong; now they were fewer than fifty thousand. A long trail of funeral crosses and burial mounds stretched back across Asia. An army of ghosts must now march with them. She closed her eyes briefly and gave thanks that at least those dear to her had survived. Hugh and Godefroi, Alberic and Norbert, Theodore, Beltran and Imogene, but, she stared swiftly around, they were all now grey people: grey-haired, grey-faced, grey-souled, ekeing out a grey existence in that sinister half-light of the year before the brooding mass of Antioch. Again Eleanor tried to check herself. There were those other grey shapes left along the dusty highways and roads. Little wonder wolves had come down boldly to the gruesome feast provided. Lions, scenting the rotten smell of decaying flesh, had slunk close. Bears abandoned their lairs for the feast and dogs the hovels they lived in, filthy beasts, soon joined by every creature that could smell carrion-tainted corruption from afar. Vultures, shadowy flocks of them darkening the sky, became their constant companions. These foul birds of the air so filled their bellies they grew too fat for flight, so trees, bushes and gorse became sprinkled with gore from their feathers whilst bits of putrid flesh and drops of blood fell on the trudging column. Were they cursed? Eleanor recalled passing a crumbling graveyard. She forgot which village in which province, they all seemed the same now, but she certainly remembered that one! A hag, a crone crawled out from between the rotting masonry of a cemetery; she was scrawny and squalid, her hair all matted and tangled. She danced round on the top of a table tomb screaming

125

curses in a screeching voice until some unknown archer loosed an arrow straight through her throat. They left her sprawled in a pool of blood. No one cared, but had they killed a witch?

'Eleanor? Eleanor?'

She glanced up. Hugh, eyes all red-rimmed, stared down at her. She shook her head and got to her feet. Her brother grasped her hands.

'Eleanor, you are looking well!'

'Brother,' she joked, 'no better than you.'

'This siege must be broken!'

'How?' she retorted. 'Shall we sprout wings and fly?'

Hugh released her hands, murmured something about Bohemond and walked away. Eleanor closed her eyes and whispered a quick prayer. She'd been too harsh. They were all hungry, cold and wearied. For a few moments she thought of other Christmases in their manor house at Compiègne: the crackling logs, the sweet smell of fresh meat, of goblets brimming with wine.

'I must stop it!'

'Stop what, mistress-sister?'

Eleanor opened her eyes. Simeon the Scribe was staring at her.

'I must have some meat,' she retorted.

'Not human flesh?' he joked. 'Mistress, we should retire.'

She followed Simeon out of the tent and through the silent, cold camp. Here and there cooking fires flickered. Men, women and children grouped around seeking warmth and food. Standards, dirty and tattered, fluttered on poles. Eleanor glanced away. The very sight of her companions deepened her depression, the darkness in her own soul. When she reached her own tent, she asked where Imogene was.

Simeon shrugged. 'The same place! Beltran knows where food is. So, where food and Beltran are, Imogene always follows.'

Eleanor sat down on the soaked cushions. Simeon cut their freshly cooked meat into small pieces, placed some on a scrap of parchment and handed them to her.

'Eat, mistress, and look.' He opened his leather jerkin, taken from a dead soldier, and pulled out a small wineskin. For a while, they sat sharing this between them. Simeon busied himself lighting a small fire, gathering twigs, pieces of rubbish to burn. The smoke smelt foul, but the weak flames provided some warmth.

'Mistress, why not return to the chronicle? It is better than sitting here staring into the flames. I tell you, more souls have been lost looking into fires . . .'

Eleanor, feeling better after the meat and wine, even though her stomach now hurt, nodded in agreement.

'It's best,' she whispered. 'Yes, it's best . . .'

They made themselves as comfortable as possible. Simeon, Eleanor reflected, had become very useful. Again she cursed her bitterness. Simeon was a friend. He'd told her a little about his life. How he'd lost one wife full of fever whilst his second wife and young son had been captured by Turkish bandits.

'God knows where they are, mistress,' he'd remarked. 'Perhaps one day . . .'

She realised that Simeon too carried his own book of sorrows, his own bag of pain. The scribe

127

had become an expert at filching food, even the odd little luxury. He had responded to her protection with deep loyalty. He had also persuaded her to talk, describe what they had been through, insisting that she continue to write her memories down.

'Others are doing it,' he pointed out. 'Stephen of Blois writes copious, detailed letters to his wife.'

The depredations of the march and this long, dreadful siege had certainly curbed Eleanor's enthusiasm for reflection, for memories. Simeon tried to prompt her with news, scandal, rumours and gossip. She recalled Hugh's warning about a traitor, a spy, but as Simeon had pointed out, the Turks had a legion of spies throughout the camp. They would certainly be busy collecting news about the condition of the Franks, which would make the hearts of those in Antioch rejoice. Ugly rumours were also being spread. How an army was gathering in Egypt to march, pin the Army of God against the walls of Antioch and utterly destroy it. More importantly, Simeon's sharp observations about religion had begun to influence Eleanor's own attitude, though not her faith. She still believed in the power of the Mass, the Eucharist, prayer and the need to be shriven of one's sins. Nevertheless, during the journey she had begun to question the truth about the Army of God and Urban's great vision. *Deus vult!* Did God really want this? she wondered. Death, cruelty, rape and rapine? The barbarous greed of their leaders, lords constantly fighting amongst themselves over which cities and towns they should hold?

'Mistress,' Simeon intervened. 'Dorylaeum, we left Dorylaeum, remember? It was the height of

128

summer . . .'

They'd left chanting the Veni Creator Spiritus, which was just as well, Eleanor reflected, for they needed all the help God could give them. The leaders had decided to keep the Army of God together even though this meant foraging for food and water became more intense. The taste of victory soon turned sour as they trudged in the wake of the Turkish army, which had already devastated the bleak countryside with fire and sword. The only comfort was that they met no opposition. The Franks had replenished their armouries with lances, axes, swords and maces; these, together with their great oval shields, were slung on the carts from where women and children, silent now, stared sorrowfully around at the burnt villages and the blackened crops of wheat, barley and millet they passed. Hunger and thirst soon stalked the Army of God. The vultures became busy again, their great white-haired heads constantly blood-stained. They shadowed the army like a host of demons. Beneath them floated the hawks, kites, buzzards and fantail crows that also gathered eager for the feast of flesh. Wells and cisterns had been deliberately polluted. Eleanor approached one, leaned over its crumbling wall and stared in horror at the severed head of the camel floating there, its dirty grey hair all fly-infested, yellow teeth bared, bloodshot eyes glaring, the murky slime from its severed neck fouling the water. Other horrors affected them. Hordes of flies and reptiles that swarmed out of the undulating yellow hills and deep dusty hollows on either side of their route. Black-red dragonflies, yellow-black hornets and strange lizards, that kept changing colour from a dusty grey to a muddy red as if some mysterious angry fire burnt inside. Such creatures were their constant companions. All these frightened them whilst myriads of pot-bellied black flies wriggled into mouths, noses and ears or crawled under collars or cuffs to torture their sweat-soaked bodies. Around them the landscape stretched bare. The peasants and farmers had fled. Only occasional scouts were glimpsed, bearded men in evil-smelling goatskins riding shaggy hill ponies and armed with long tufted lances. No one could tell whether they were Turks or simply local inhabitants, for they scattered like quail under the shadow of a hawk when the knights rode out to meet them.

The army crossed arid scrubland, dotted with tamarisk and acacia bushes that sprouted from rugged masses of rock, their surfaces smoothed by wind and rain. A nightmare of winding chasms and dark brooding valleys, so hot and unwelcoming Simeon claimed they were crossing the lip of hell. Eleanor heartily agreed. Sometimes they would shelter from the noonday heat in caves, but even there, danger lurked: blue and green lizards darted in and out of crevices, and were just as dangerous as the vicious-looking snakes, horned and decorated in macabre colours, which struck fast and furious at the unwary. Armour-plated black scorpions and scuttling spiders as big as a man's hand only heightened their terrors.

Eleanor reflected on Simeon's description: if daytime was one lip of hell, night-time was certainly the other. They pitched their tents, if they could, and gathered around weak fires of dried dung, wormwood and whatever bracken they could find. Darkness was truly a time of terror! Eleanor never understood how such a deserted place could conceal so many creatures. Wolf jackals howled at the sweet fleshy smell of their restless horses and braying donkeys. Fire beetles flared eerily out of the dark. White moths flew in over the camp fires whilst the exhausted pilgrims screamed as bats, with their half-cat, half-monkey faces, chattering and swishing, swarmed in to feed on the myriad of insects. Eagle owls, fierce and fiery-eyed, joined other predators: jackals, snakes, huge rats, as well as the occasional lynx that slunk into the camp to seize dogs, birds, pets and, on one occasion, a sleeping girl. Eleanor herself soon experienced the dangers of leaving the camp. One night, alarmed by strange sounds, she went beyond the line of carts. She heard a soft growl and, turning to her left, glimpsed what looked like balls of green fire staring at her. A dark shape emerged from the darkness, a squat head with grinning mouth displaying sharp fangs and flecks of bubbling froth on a curling upper lip. Eleanor screamed, lashed out and the striped hyena swiftly disappeared into the darkness.

The effect of such hardships on the Army of God soon became apparent as they journeyed through the stifling heat. Hunger was commonplace. Leaves, bark, flowers and berries were eagerly seized and eaten. Some were poisonous, and more corpses and graves trailed their route. Horses, donkeys and dogs died. Pack animals became a rarity, so goats, sheep, cows and even dogs were used to carry the baggage until their skins became scuffed and worn. Knights rode oxen or trudged wearily in the wake of the carts.

Water became equally precious; those wells, streams and waterholes the Turks had missed were soon turned into nothing better than muddy messes. People left the column to dig at roots, searching for any moistness. They prayed for rain, yet the sudden violent storms only brought fresh hardship. Simeon taught them how to build screens of poles, interwoven with palm fronds, prickle pear and acacia twigs, to protect their tents; these became ragged and torn but could be quickly repaired with goatskin. The abrupt, tempestuous sand storms, however, became the bane of their lives, especially at night, when the heavy clouds rolled in, hiding the stars and plunging everything into an inky blackness. Blinding flashes of yellow forked lightning silenced the growls, howls and deep coughs of the night prowlers. The air became heavy, and hot, thick flying sand pelted them so all they could do was shelter and pray for it to pass. Jagged holes would appear in the clouds, then close again, whilst the rain would fall, streams of icy water turning the ground into a sticky yellow mud that coated everything. The night would pass. The storm would break and the sun rise to blister rock and burn the ground, then by noon the dust returned to redden eyes, clog the mouth and block the nose.

Some pilgrims just disappeared; others turned back. Even their leaders began to falter. Tancred of Hauteville and Baldwin of Boulogne decided to take a different route through the Cilician mountains. They reached Tarsus, drove out the Turkish garrison, then fought each other for control of the city. Tancred, furious, had to withdraw and return to the main army. Baldwin

132

followed because his wife was dying, but when she was gone so was he, with a conroy of knights, to Edessa in the land of the Armenians. Here he became the adopted son of Tholos, the ruler of the city. Treacherous as ever, however, Baldwin conspired with certain leading men in the city and Tholos was literally thrown to the dogs.

Peter Bartholomew, their self-proclaimed prophet, now came into his own. For most of the journey he had kept quiet, apart from the occasional outburst. As they suffered the horrors of their march from Dorylaeum, he seemed to survive only on brackish water, and began to preach and proclaim his visions. How in the dead of night he had dreams in which the trumpets of the Apocalypse summoned him to watch what was about to happen. How fire would fall from heaven to destroy the impious, yet this fire was only the harbinger of even greater calamities. Thunder and lightning delivered further visions. Plagues would be released to the clash of cymbals. Earth, air, water and fire would become polluted by the horrors God intended to unleash on the world. The Angel of Wrath would fly over ruined cities, whilst a devil named Wormwood lurked in the shadows, ready to strike. Very few understood him; even fewer cared. Nevertheless, after the morning Mass, or in the afternoon when the Ave Maria was recited, Peter would often climb on to some cart and preach about the pale horse, mounted by Death, which rode on their right flank, whilst black horses carrying Famine and Hunger galloped to their left. Of course the curious asked if God was punishing them rather than the Turks. Peter would blink, stare into the middle distance and immediately launch into another vision he'd received.

Eleanor wondered if Peter really had become witless. Beltran and Imogene insisted that he be banned from preaching and kept close, but Hugh thought differently. Now and again he would take Peter off into the dark, and they would sit away from the camp fire and talk quietly together. Once Eleanor asked Hugh what the topic of conversation was. Hugh merely gave that lopsided smile, his eyes not meeting hers. Indeed, brother and sister rarely talked during the march. Hugh was constantly employed by Count Raymond for this task or that, whilst Eleanor's companions were either Beltran or, more usually, Theodore. On that occasion, when questioned about Peter, Hugh gnawed his lip and was about to walk away, but Eleanor caught him by the sleeve.

'Hugh, we face horrors enough without Peter's trumpeting. Why do you allow it?'

'Very simple, sister.' Hugh stepped closer, his face coated with a fine sheen of dust. 'Peter reminds us that this is God's journey. True, we call ourselves the Army of God, but in fact, Eleanor, we're not. We have blood on our hands. We are as vicious and as cruel as our enemies. Nevertheless, God uses us for his own secret purposes. We will reach Jerusalem. We will discover the treasures there. Peter is important in this. If his voice echoes like a trumpet, then I say it is God's trumpet reminding us why we are here.'

Theodore thought otherwise and approached Eleanor with a plea to talk quietly to Peter to try and calm him. Eleanor repeated Hugh's words. Theodore shook his head.

'Sister,' he replied, 'the pilgrims thought they would march through Asia into Syria and take Jerusalem. We have lost some twenty thousand souls through hunger, thirst, desertion, war and weakness. If we are not careful, the Army of God may think itself cursed, and then what?'

Eleanor realised that both Hugh and Theodore were correct: they were walking a narrow bridge. The Army of God must be virtuous, but if it lost hope, then what future was there? What vision existed? Hugh also sensed this and did his best for his own company. He would gather the Poor Brethren of the Temple and lead them in Compline or Vespers, or simply stand on a cart, a solitary stark figure, reciting his Ave beads and inviting others to join him.

The Army of God continued its march, beginning its climb through the mountains leading down to the plains of Syria and the city of Antioch. As Peter Bartholomew so eloquently proclaimed: their ascent was, in fact, more of a descent into a cruel hell of tortuous shale-strewn trackways lined with dark, sombre forests, along ledges that turned treacherous underfoot, especially when the autumn rains set. Little wonder Hugh and Godefroi called them 'the Mountains of the Devil' or 'the Mountains of Hell'. Now and again they found some respite in one of the scattered stone-walled villages with their brown-domed churches and flat-topped, mud-brick cottages with cow and goat pens hidden behind. At least the inhabitants did not flee. Squat, sallow-faced men, garbed in old armour and reeking of cattle, dried milk and dung, came out to greet them. They carried crosses and offered wine and stale bread, explaining how they were Armenian Christians, hostile to the Turks. When Eleanor, Hugh and other leaders of the Poor Brethren met them in the dusty porchways of their round churches, they found the Armenians equally wary of the Franks. In truth, they offered little help and stole whatever they could. They also relayed false information, telling them that Antioch was an open city where the Turks were preparing to flee. Count Raymond, recovering from a near-fatal illness, believed them and immediately dispatched a conroy of five hundred knights, but the news proved false. On one subject the Armenians were adamant: the way ahead was bleak and treacherous. And so it proved.

The Army of God climbed across a landscape of plunging gorges, narrow winding tracks, twisting paths, icy air, biting winds and mist as thick as vapour from a steaming pot. Men, horses and pack ponies missed their footing or were too weary to be wary and slipped into the yawning darkness below. Knights found armour and harness a great burden and offered to sell them for a few coins; when they found no buyers, they cast their heavy loads into the chasm. Nights were long and cold. Sometimes it was impossible to kindle fires as they perched on ledges and trackways under brooding cliffs. Bishop Adhémar kept their spirits up by insisting that they intone the Ave Maria, whilst Hugh continued to lead the Poor Brethren in their own devotional hours. Eleanor found it difficult to reflect. She could only concentrate on each day as it came, plodding through that grim, horrid place listening to Simeon the Scribe whisper how they would soon be out of the Mountains of Hell. Eventually they

136

were. Early one morning they breasted the peaks and began their descent into green-carpeted valleys, down through soft meadowland and fields where barley, wheat and millet had been freshly harvested. Simeon pointed out the various trees: sycamore and oak, laurel, terebinth and palm. They feasted on the soft, plump fruit of olive trees with their knotted trunks, shiny green bark and lance-like leaves. They collected the fruit of fig, almond, apple, apricot and pear. They wondered at the purple pomegranate and plucked at carob trees for their medicinal use while gazing hungrily at the fat-tailed sheep browsing in the grasslands and the occasional black-nosed gazelle that sped hastily across their path.

Eleanor felt as if she had been reborn as Simeon described the great variety of birds: shrikes, goldfinches with rose-coloured breasts, cranes and white storks. They slaked their thirst at pools where river warblers sang, and in the grassy fringes, crickets and grasshoppers chanted their monotonous hymn to the sun. Food and other supplies became plentiful through barter or foraging. No Turkish forces appeared; news of the defeat at Dorylaeum had spread on the wind. The only threats were the scattered garrisons locked up in their hilltop fortresses. According to scouts, the way to Antioch lay open. The Poor Brethren, like the rest of the Army of God, relaxed. They camped in the meadowlands enjoying the sun, filling their bellies and, as Peter Bartholomew declared, shaking off the dust from the devil's mountains. A census was taken. The wounded were moved to be tended by leeches and priests. Animals were let out to graze. Clothes were stitched, darned, washed and stretched out to dry. Armour was cleaned with sand, weapons were sharpened, harness, carts, baskets and panniers repaired. Eleanor bathed, washed and mended what she could and seized any hour for rest and sleep. The journey from Constantinople had changed her. She was now less certain about everything; more concerned about those around her than reaching Jerusalem. She put this down to exhaustion, yet there was something else. It was as if all her old certainties had been shaken. Such quiet reflection soon ended. Eleanor became alarmed at disquieting rumours about Antioch. How the city was heavily fortified, so impregnable its inhabitants openly boasted that it could only be taken by treachery, surprise or starvation.

'The latter is out of the question,' Hugh announced at one of their meetings. They sat under the spreading branches of an old oak tree sharing a wineskin and a dish of fruit. They revelled in the warmth of the autumn sun, their nostrils tickled by the sweet scent from the nearby orchards mingling with the fragrance of wild flowers.

'Why?' Peter Bartholomew asked.

'We have no siege weapons,' Hugh replied, 'and it would take weeks to hew wood, fashion planks and construct engines of war. We have lost engineers and masons. The Emperor Alexius is a hundred miles away, unable to help us. Antioch is our real challenge. Let me explain.' He snapped his fingers. Simeon produced a scroll of parchment and unrolled it. They gathered closer to study this finely drawn chart of Antioch.

'The first line of defence,' Hugh explained, 'is

the river Orontes, which cuts across the plain of Antioch. Beyond that, the great wall of the city rises at least thirty-two feet high. This wall is so thick, one of our great carts could be rolled along its ramparts with horsemen riding on either side.' He stilled the rising clamour. 'It runs two miles along the Orontes, then on either side it climbs to encircle the city as well as contain three great hills. On the highest of these stands a towering citadel that dominates everything. When we march there we will leave the foothills and occupy the northern plain. Looking across it, we will see the river, a stretch of land, the great ditch and then the might of Antioch. We will have to camp in front of the city. The flanks and rear of Antioch are protected not only by that wall but also by the sheer height of the three hills. On the flanks and rear stand no gates; only small postern doors served by narrow trackways. It would be impossible to camp there. The ascent itself would be very, very dangerous and easily detected by guards on the wall or the citadel.' Hugh paused. 'Think of climbing the cliffs we have recently crossed, then having to scale a wall, whilst we can only camp on a ledge so narrow, only a few men at a time could assemble there.'

'So our attack,' Imogene asked fearfully, 'must come from the front?'

'Yes, and again there are great difficulties.' Theodore pointed to the chart Simeon still held between his fingers. 'The curtain wall is very thick. The city has many gardens and fruit orchards, whilst a stream runs down from those three hills through a watergate on to the plain.' He wagged a finger. 'Remember that! Antioch is furnished with enough water and produce to withstand a siege for

139

a while. Moreover, that wall is so long and so massive, we simply do not have the siege equipment to break, shatter or undermine it.'

'What about gates?' Beltran asked.

'Five in all,' Theodore declared, 'along the great wall facing the plain. All of these are flanked and protected by massive square towers rising sixty feet into the sky. From these towers the gates, as well as all approaches to them, can easily be protected.' Theodore paused at the groans of his companions.

'We have given the gates names,' Hugh declared. 'The furthest east, leading to Aleppo, will be called St Paul's. The second, moving from east to west, is the Dog Gate, which opens on to the river. The third, where the Orontes skirts the city wall, is the Gate of the Duke. No,' Hugh fended off a question, 'this is not as vulnerable as you think, as it is protected by a tangle of marsh. Further along there is a bridge spanning the Orontes; at the end of this stands Bridge Gate. The most western gate leading down to the port of St Simeon and the sea is the St George Gate. What you must realise is that to attack any of these gates we have to cross the Orontes. However, because we don't have enough men to attack all five at the same time, the Turks can sortie from any other gate left free and trap us against the walls.'

'Hugh speaks the truth,' Theodore confirmed. 'We cannot lay siege to all five gates.'

'So the Turks can come and go as they please,' Imogene declared. 'Either through one of those main gates or through the postern doors up in the hills that we cannot guard.'

'Could we cross the Orontes?' Eleanor asked.

'No,' Theodore replied. 'The Turks would hurl

140

missiles at us, launch sorties and trap us against the river or the wall. Moreover, that stream as well as the Orontes turns the ground very marshy, ill-suited for a camp especially as winter approaches, when the rains and snow will soon swell the waters.'

'Think!' Hugh plucked the chart from Simeon's fingers. 'Antioch is like a sprawling garden that can only be entered from the north whilst those inside may leave by a number of routes.'

'Then why besiege it?' Beltran asked. 'Why not just go home?'

'God will help,' Peter Bartholomew declared.

'With what?' Beltran jibed.

'His help!' Peter Bartholomew's shout sent the birds fluttering above them. 'He will help! He will send his angels.'

'I sincerely hope so,' Beltran whispered, though loud enough for the rest to hear.

Eleanor realised the coming siege would be a crisis. She had a deep sense of oppression and found herself going more often to Alberic or Norbert to be shriven. These men of God, however, were resolute in their belief that the army would eventually be victorious. Both encouraged Peter Bartholomew's increasing urgency to describe the visions of the night.

The Army of God prepared itself and moved down towards Antioch. A brief but brutal foray was launched to capture the so-called Iron Bridge, which forded the Orontes to the north-east of the city and controlled the road to Aleppo and Damascus. A savage mêlée ensued, with the Franks forming testudos to take the fortress commanding the bridge. Eventually it fell, and the

141

Army of God moved into the foothills leading down on to the plain of Antioch. They deployed before the city during the last week of October, just before the Feasts of All Saints. Camp was pitched and Eleanor rode out with commanders of the Poor Brethren to view the city's defences. These seemed absolutely formidable: a range of turrets and towers above which the green sheen of orchards shimmered. Hugh and Theodore's description was perfectly accurate. The Orontes twinkled in the sun; on the other side of it lay a stretch of marshy land, then that wall with its massive towers, one either side of all five gates. Above these frontal defences rose the peak of the highest hill which, Eleanor learnt, was called Silpius; from that soared an impregnable citadel with a commanding view of the countryside on all sides.

The Army of God immediately moved to besiege some of the gates. Bohemond, supported by Robert of Flanders, set up camp before St Paul's Gate on the far east of the city. Raymond of Toulouse encamped in front of the Dog Gate, Godfrey of Bouillon before the Gate of the Duke. Bridge Gate and the St George Gate, however, not to mention the Iron Gate, the heavily fortified postern door at the rear of the city, were left unguarded; the Franks simply lacked the men to besiege these as well. The Army of God glared at the obstacle before them whilst the Turks beyond the walls stared back. Debate raged fast and furious. What was to be done? A great council was convened. A large pavilion plundered from the enemy was erected, the ground beneath it covered with looted prayer carpets. Godfrey of Bouillon

142

was given the chair of state, beside him Adhémar of Le Puy in full episcopal robes. Special stools were arranged for the rest: Hugh of Paris; the yellow-haired giant Bohemond; Robert of Flanders, constantly stroking his own face; Robert 'Short-breeches', Duke of Normandy, flushed as ever, one hand on the buckle of his war belt, the other grasping a goblet of wine. Next to these sat their Greek adviser Tacticius, his false metal nose gleaming in the sunlight. Count Raymond, grey-faced and sweat-soaked, after recovering from his malignant contagion, opened the debate. Behind him Hugh and Eleanor were given places of prominence to witness what happened. In the end, nothing did. Count Raymond advised a swift, brutal assault on the city but the rest declared they would wait. The council meeting broke up and everyone drifted away to pursue their own gains.

A strange period, as Eleanor wrote in her chronicle, as if it was a holy day during a festive season. The Turks were locked up in Antioch so the Army of God was free to go on a foraging spree of plunder and rapine, scouring the surrounding countryside for food, wine, women and livestock. For two weeks they gobbled the rich fat of the land. The entire camp was given over to revelry and drinking. They almost forgot Antioch until the Turks struck, sallying out in swift, savage raids. They left by the Iron Gate at the rear of the city, seized the heights above Bohemond's camp near St Paul's Gate and poured down a heavy hail of arrows and other missiles. To bring the battle to the enemy, Bohemond retailiated by building a tower he named Malregard, or Evil Look, to protect his position, whilst Duke Godfrey constructed a bridge of boats across the Orontes to reach the Gate of the Duke. Meanwhile, Tancred took the heights above the St George Gate and bided his time.

The siege now began in earnest. The days of revelry were over. The Army of God had plundered vineyards, pits of grains and orchards, their trees bending heavy with fruit. Now, as the winter rains lashed in, the countryside was stripped bare of produce. The Turks released Armenians into the camp to act as spies but kept their wives and children as hostages to fortune as well as to war. If any of these spies were caught, Bohemond had them paraded before the walls and summarily decapitated. The Turks responded just as cruelly. The Armenian patriarch who sheltered in the city was taken up on to the ramparts and hung upside down over the battlements, where the soles of his feet were beaten with rods. Frankish prisoners were also exhibited on the walls before being decapitated, their heads flung by catapults into the camp. Eleanor was one of those deputed to collect such grisly objects and wrap them in linen for decent burial. She did so carefully even as she wondered about the cry of *'Deus vult!'* and the will of God. One burial particularly haunted her, that of Adelbaro, Archdeacon of Metz. He had gone into the woods near Bridge Gate to play dice with a young woman from the camp. They regarded it as a festival day, taking wine, fruit and bread. A Turkish troop burst out of the city and invaded the orchard, driving out all who sheltered there, including Adelbaro and his sweet maid. Both were captured and taken back into the city. Just before darkness fell, Adelbaro was dragged up on to the battlements and decapitated, whilst the young woman was publicly stripped and repeatedly raped, her cries ringing out through the darkness. At dawn she was stabbed and her head was cut off. Just as Father Alberic was finishing Mass, the whoosh of a catapult cut across his blessing and the severed heads of the pair were hurled into the camp. They bounced along the ground, then stopped, objects of horror with their gaping mouths and startled eyes. Theodore, Eleanor and Simeon collected them in linen sacks and buried both together in a hole beneath a pile of rocks, whilst Alberic sprinkled holy water with his asperges rod. Afterwards Eleanor sat and sobbed in her tent as Simeon the Scribe, anxious about his mistress-sister busied himself over this task or that. From outside came the sound of more catapults delivering their gruesome burdens. Shouts and cries echoed. Somewhere a monk began to chant the hymn 'In Cruce Christus Dominus Vincit Mundum'—'On the cross Christ the Lord Conquered the World'.

Eleanor listened to the words and began to laugh. What conquest? she reflected. What world? She lay down on the cot bed, crossed her arms and stared at the light pouring through the tent flap. She recalled the prophecies of Peter Bartholomew about the Apocalypse. Were they all part of that Apocalypse? Was she really dead and living in hell? What had all this cruelty to do with the cross of Christ? She, Hugh, Godefroi and the rest were no better than babbling babes; they'd had little inclination of the bloody cost of this undertaking. As if mocking her, Eleanor heard the whoosh of catapults, the cries of the besiegers, followed by shouts from the archers closer to the walls; above all this rose a Turkish voice chanting a prayer. Eleanor knew what was happening. In revenge for the execution of the archdeacon and his mistress, more prisoners were being herded down to the river bank to be executed. Eleanor began to shiver, then burst out crying. Imogene came in and crouched before her. Eleanor just stared back. She was not ill, she assured herself; in fact she felt as if she could perceive everything most clearly. She gazed at the Jewess so determined to bury her parents' ashes within the precincts of the Holy City. Eleanor could understand that. Yet even Imogene had changed. Jerusalem did not concern her now; only Beltran. He had become Imogene's life; her second, or even first reason for being here. Over the last few months Imogene had distanced herself. Sometimes Eleanor would catch the woman staring curiously at her, but she very rarely talked about Beltran, though she often tried to draw Eleanor about what might happen once Jerusalem was taken. Eleanor had ignored her questions, being more concerned with the present than any future plans.

Eleanor continued to lie there, staring into the middle distance. Imogene offered her some wine. Eleanor refused, so Imogene left. Simeon the Scribe, crouching in the corner, crept out to fetch Hugh, who came and sat beside his sister. He coaxed her to drink the wine Imogene had poured. Eleanor did so and felt her body being warmed. She drew a deep sigh, sat up and then attempted to stand. Hugh told her to stay.

'It's nothing,' Eleanor murmured. She put her head into her hands, staring down at her battered ox-hide boots caked in yellow mud.

'It must be something,' Hugh insisted.

'It is.' Eleanor forced a smile. She gestured at the tent flap. 'Brother, the killing, the blood, the revenge, the agony, the pain. Is this really God's work? Are we here so that Bohemond can carve out a kingdom? You've heard the rumours. Bohemond wants Antioch for himself.'

'It is necessary.' Hugh's voice was fierce and resolute. 'Sister, what we do now is truly filthy. I know that. Godefroi and I have been talking. We have taken a great oath. If the Lord delivers Jerusalem into our hands, if our lives are spared to achieve that, if we can look upon the Holy Face, then we will found a holy order of poor knights who will take the vows of monks and dedicate themselves to protect God's people.'

Eleanor hid her smile. The fire in Hugh's heart only burned stronger; he was no longer talking to her but preaching his own private Crusade.

'What you see here, Eleanor, is the truth,' he continued. 'This so-called Army of God does include men and women of vision, though many are here to indulge their filthiest passions.' He blinked, pausing for breath. 'I speak not only of the likes of Jehan the Wolf and his lieutenants, Gargoyle and Babewyn, but also of our leaders. Nevertheless, here before the city of Antioch, God will purge them all.' Still absorbed in his own dream, Hugh patted her hand and left the tent.

Eleanor laughed quietly to herself.

'As the child,' she murmured, 'so the man; as the tree, so the branches.'

'Pardon, mistress-sister?' Simeon the Scribe scrambled to his feet, face all concerned.

147

'Hugh.' Eleanor spoke over her shoulder. 'Ever since I can remember, he has been the preacher and I have been his congregation.' She walked to the entrance of the tent, pulling her cloak closer about her. As she lifted the flap, she almost walked into Theodore, who grinned and stepped back.

'I heard you were ailing.' He smiled and extended a hand. 'You wish to walk?'

Eleanor agreed, and they went out into the frenetic bustle of the camp. Under iron-grey skies, tents and bothies were being erected. Carts were being pulled across the narrow thoroughfare to block any attack by enemy horsemen. Camp fires spluttered, cauldrons bubbled. People stumbled about dressed in the now common colours of brown and grey. A blacksmith was trying to fire his forge. A group of Saxon mercenaries were sharpening their swords on a whetstone. A knight in rusty chain mail led his thin-ribbed horse carefully through the camp, picking his way around ropes, pegs and mounds of refuse. Smoke billowed and swirled. The cold breeze blew the various smells: the stench of the latrines and horse lines mixing with the odours of sweat, leather, burning wood and roasting meat. The Beggars' Company had gathered around a cart, eager to share the plunder it brought.

Eleanor and Theodore walked in silence down to the edge of the camp where the standards and pennants fluttered. Eleanor stared at the slight ridge of land that rose before falling down to the Orontes. On the near bank lay a heap of corpses, blood spilling out from their severed necks. On the ridge above it stretched a long row of poles; each bore the severed head of a Turk, positioned where

148

it could be seen easily by the defenders of the city. Eleanor shivered. Theodore put his arm about her shoulder. She did not resist.

'It's only beginning,' he whispered. 'We have gorged ourselves after our hunger upon sweet bread, figs, fruit and wine. People think this is the Promised Land, flowing with milk and honey. Eleanor, fresh horrors are about to emerge. We've plundered the countryside bare. Constantinople is an eternity away. We've bathed in pools, occupied plundered houses, but now what?'

'*Deus vult!*' she whispered. She turned, freeing herself from his grasp, and stared full at him. 'Do you really believe that, Theodore? That God willed this, the sickness, the savagery, the fighting, the blood, the severed heads, the catapults? Look at poor Adelbaro and his mistress playing dice in an orchard. Was that what God intended?'

'I don't know.' The Greek's usually merry eyes were now black and hard. 'Eleanor, I believe in the truths of our faith, that Christ the Lord is God incarnate, but also that real religion is a matter of the individual soul, the mind,' he tapped his head, 'nothing else. In here, in our minds, our souls, we have Jerusalem, the Holy Sepulchre and Calvary. Here we have the Sacred Face. If we cannot worship Him in our own inner sanctuary first, then what is the use of searching for something else?' He shrugged. 'I've just learnt that!'

Eleanor remembered his words as the siege tightened and the Army of God bayed like a pack of ravenous wolves before the walls of Antioch. November came in a flurry of sleet and rain. The ground turned soggy underfoot. A creeping fear seized the camp. Count Raymond had spoken the truth: the city should have been assaulted immediately. Now everything had changed. Yaghi Siyan, the protuberant-eared, white-headed Governor of Antioch, had perceived the weakness of the besiegers and sent hasty messages to Aleppo and Damascus pleading for help. He also dispatched his horsemen in brutal forays through the various gates to plunder and ravage the Army of God. The Turkish archers, in gleaming breastplates and colourful robes, rode swift-footed ponies, bows pulled back, arrows notched ready to drop a deadly hail into the enemy camp. At night the misery continued, the Turkish catapults hurling fiery missiles into the tents. The pain turned into agony. Heavy rains swelled the Orontes. Icy sleet pounded the sodden, thinning tents, rotting bowstrings, spoiling rugs and carpets, polluting food stocks. Eleanor did what she could to assist. She filched, begged and scoured the camp, then she cooked and broiled the morsels into the most savoury messes.

Eleanor now regretted what she called her miasma of fear. She drew strength especially from Theodore. Instead of talking about the siege, he chattered constantly about his own dreams of a whitewashed villa set in vineyards with orchards full of pears, apples and almonds alongside fields burgeoning with millet and wheat. The Greek won Eleanor over with his vision of life, of ordinary things, peace and stillness. Eleanor reflected and vowed that she would come through this nightmare to find her own salvation. What could misery and despair achieve? Tomorrow always brought new hope. So she struggled along with the rest, even boiling leather straps to fashion a weak soup. She

150

foraged with the other women, grubbing for shoots and roots, anything that could be cooked in boiling water.

Advent came. Bohemond planned a great foraging expedition to bring in supplies. It ended in disaster. His company was ambushed even as the rest of the army were attacked by Turkish horsemen; they streamed into the camp, slicing and cutting, casting firebrands and loosing flame-edged arrows into the tents. Eleanor, now resolute, grasped a pike and fought alongside the other women. What did she care if Christmas had come and gone? Here was her life, squelching in mud, pike out, jabbing at horsemen in billowing robes who thundered past her. Nevertheless, when the attack ended, wise-thinking heads brought important issues to the fore. Bohemond had left to forage and been ambushed. At the same time Yaghi Siyan had quickly learnt that Bohemond was absent and dispatched his raiders to wreak hideous damage in the camp.

'Strange,' people murmured, 'how the infidels were so closely informed about what was happening.'

The new year of 1098, as Eleanor reflected in her chronicle, brought little cheer. The portents for the future looked dismal. The threat of total and absolute failure swept the camp. Eleanor realised it might all be coming to an end but took comfort in the belief that she had done her best. She could do no more, so she and Simeon spent their time chronicling the past and ignoring the future. She wished Hugh and Godefroi would visit her, but they had become virtual strangers, until one January night when Hugh swept into her

151

stinking goatskin tent, and asked her and Simeon to join a secret council convened by Count Bohemond.

At first Eleanor objected, but Hugh grasped her by the shoulders.

'Eleanor,' he hissed, 'times have changed. No more sword! More wit, more wisdom! Come with us.'

He led her and Simeon across the bleak, foul-smelling camp to Bohemond's tent. Inside, the Norman, dressed in a furred robe, his long yellow hair falling down either side of his face, sprawled on cushions talking quietly to Theodore and Godefroi. He paused as Eleanor entered, remembered his manners, scrambled to his feet and gave the most elaborate bow before gesturing at the heap of cushions and bolsters prepared for them. Eleanor sat down. She stared at the great Norman; those piercing blue eyes in the ruddy, weatherbeaten face glared back. Bohemond could never stay still; now he turned and fidgeted. Occasionally he would glance at her lecherously, look away, then stare piteously as if beseeching her help. Wine was poured, precious sweetmeats served. Bohemond waited until the tent emptied of servants before getting to his feet. He went outside, breathing noisily as he stared around, ensuring no eavesdropper lurked. When he returned, he flopped down on to the cushions and jabbed a stubby finger at Eleanor.

'You are our Trojan horse.'

She stared steadily back.

'The Trojan horse: you know the story?' he asked.

Eleanor nodded.

'We cannot take Antioch.' Bohemond shook his head. 'Not by storm or by stealth. Remember the Antiochene boast, that their city can only be captured by starvation, surprise or treachery. We have decided upon treachery.' His powerful face creased into a smile, then he tapped his chest as if confessing his sins. 'Well, not all of us, just me.'

'My lord,' Eleanor spoke up, 'what need of me? You talk of stealth and treachery. How can I assist you in that?'

'Oh, very easily.' Bohemond pulled himself up and stretched, and Eleanor realised why he was such a fearsome figure amongst the Franks. He was square-shouldered, slim-waisted, a powerful, deep-chested man, his long square face framed by that yellow hair, those eyes, icy blue, constantly moving, constantly searching. She stared round the tent at the various scraps of armour and harness, weapons piled in a tangle, manuscripts tossed in a heap. Here, Eleanor reflected, was a man eager to grasp something, anything. At first Bohemond acted the blustering soldier, revelling in his own achievements, pretending to be drunk, cursing the other leaders, describing how he would have arranged matters. As Eleanor sat and watched, she realised that Bohemond was a very dangerous man. He acted as if he was tipsy, yet he was cold-stone sober. He clasped Godefroi and Hugh as if they were comrades-in-arms, then he would move on to a story about his father or his brothers, his wars in Sicily and his hatred for the Greeks, before returning to the siege. Eleanor realised he was trying to prepare her as a man would seduce a woman, offering signs of his bluntness and honesty, his desire to do what was right. What also emerged

153

was his deep hunger for Antioch. He had seen the city and wanted it for himself. He'd realised he couldn't take it by force so he would try other means. He stopped abruptly halfway through a tirade against Godfrey of Bouillon and glared at her.

'Eleanor, you want to save your soul?'

'It is already saved, my lord,' she answered. 'Christ's blood has bought it.'

That confused him. He blinked, slurped from his goblet and slammed it down. He glanced at Hugh and Godefroi then at Theodore, Simeon and Eleanor. At last, as if tired of the pretence, he moved his hand across his face, stroking his brow, eyes closed tight.

'If we don't take Antioch,' he said slowly, 'we might as well go home.'

Eleanor, tired, exasperated at this meeting, which seemed to be leading nowhere, lost her temper.

'My lord, why are we here?'

Bohemond's head went down, that glorious mane of hair shrouding his face, then glanced up. 'I am asking you to sacrifice yourself,' he said. 'All right.' He pushed his hands forward, palms towards her, fingers extended in the sign of peace. 'I've blustered, I've bragged, I've threatened, I've promised, but at the end of the day, Eleanor de Payens, I need you. Now I can sit here and give you sweet verses from the troubadours, lines from the poets—'

'My lord, why are we here?' Eleanor insisted, 'What do you want from me?' She glared at Hugh, who looked away. Godefroi, embarrassed, simply stared down at the floor and shuffled his cup.

154

Simeon plucked nervously at his jerkin. Theodore sat, one hand over the lower part of his face, as if he sensed what was coming.

'Very well.' Bohemond took a deep breath. 'We will never take Antioch by force. We can build towers, we can launch forays, this, that and the other. The Turks know exactly what we are doing. They have spies amongst us. If I discovered who they were, I would take them out myself, drag them down to the river bank and pluck their heads as a farmer would a flower, but what is the use of that?' He smiled at Eleanor. 'Terror without a reason is diabolic; terror with a reason is understandable, it's logical. Now, Eleanor, this is what I plot. I want spies to go into Antioch, and this is how it can be done. Theodore is a Greek mercenary. He will enter the city with his wife, namely you. He will claim he has had enough of the Frankish army and wants to sell his sword to the victorious party. If he brings the sister of a high-ranking Frankish knight, together with her scribe and maidservant, people might accept that he is speaking the truth. In a word, Eleanor, you, Theodore, Simeon and Imogene will enter Antioch as our spies. Once there you will seek out someone, anyone, who will betray part of that wall to us.'

Eleanor stared across the table at Theodore. She was putting her life into this man's hands. She trusted him, yet she didn't really know him. She glanced at Hugh, who stared resolutely back.

'It is a sacrifice,' Bohemond said softly, 'that you and your companions will make on behalf of us all. We must have someone behind the walls of Antioch. Someone quick-witted who will seize any opportunity and use it for the Army of God.' He pushed himself closer so Eleanor could view his face in the light of the needle-thin candle: strong and brutal, the golden moustache and beard streaked with grey, the skin all peeling but his eyes blazing with passion. She recognised that look; she'd seen the same in her brother's eyes. She looked at Godefroi, who was still staring into his cup. Simeon stirred restlessly.

'There is no need for you to come,' Eleanor whispered.

'No, mistress-sister, I will be safe with you.'

Bohemond's lip curled in a smile. 'Well said, Simeon,' he declared. 'Eleanor de Payens is your sure defence. If she left you here, those in this camp who resent your presence might act. Moreover, we need you in Antioch. You know the ways and customs of the enemy, their tongue. You could be of great assistance.'

'And what if,' Eleanor asked, 'we go through the gates of Antioch and are arrested, taken up on to the battlements. Theodore and Simeon are executed. I am raped, stabbed and decapitated and our heads are flung back into the camp. There is that risk.'

'Of course,' Bohemond agreed, 'as there is every risk that Turkish light horse might attack the camp tonight and you could suffer a similar fate.' He drummed his thick, muscular fingers on the top of the small table before him. 'Think, Eleanor! The Turks will do you no harm. Why should they? If deserters from this army are brutally executed, that would discourage others. Already men are leaving, mercenaries selling their swords to the highest bidder. Why should they execute you and

156

Theodore? No! No! They will boast of your presence. Who knows,' he joked, 'fortune might smile on you. You could be treated as guests of honour, given furnished quarters, good food and drink, a chance to bathe, to be clean and warm, well away from this stinking, freezing camp.' He paused. The tent flap shifted; a draught of cold air seeped through.

'There is something else.' Hugh spoke up.

'My lord, wait.' Eleanor held up a hand. 'We are in the retinue of Raymond of Toulouse. Does he know?'

'Yes, and he agrees,' declared Hugh. He leaned across the table and grasped his sister's hand. 'If you don't want to go, you need not, we shall think no worse of you. Count Raymond also believes the only way Antioch will fall is through treachery. For that we need someone we can trust.'

'You said there was something else?'

Hugh let go of her hands and turned, staring at the tent flap. 'Listen, Eleanor!'

She did so. Faint sounds: a woman screaming, a man shouting curses.

'Bishop Adhémar believes,' Hugh said softly, 'that one of the reasons we face such obstacles is because the Army of God needs to do reparation, to purge itself, to express sorrow for its sins. He has persuaded our leaders that all women must leave the camp. People like yourself and Imogene will be escorted to the port of St Simeon to await events. The whores, prostitutes and camp followers are to be summarily driven out.'

Eleanor gasped in surprise.

'It is harsh,' Bohemond spoke up, 'but necessary. For God's sake, woman, we are

157

supposed to be the Army of God, yet we house a crowd of tinkers, moon people, troubadours, whores and catamites. Bishop Adhémar is right! Our camp should be purged, the army must cleanse itself, express its sorrow and receive absolution. We are not talking about women like you, but others. They bring nothing, they offer nothing, yet they eat and drink and impede our progress. Within the week they will be driven from the camp.'

'And Imogene?' Eleanor asked. 'You called her my maidservant.'

Hugh looked at Bohemond, who nodded slightly. 'Imogene must go with you.'

'Does she know?'

'No. You will simply say that she must follow you. She will be given no opportunity to discuss this or talk to anyone about what is happening.' Hugh paused. 'It is logical for you to take a servant. Moreover, Imogene cannot stay here to chatter her surprise and, perhaps, her disbelief at your desertion.'

'Such an observation,' Godefroi spoke up, 'might endanger you.'

'And Beltran?'

'He does not know, nor will he. Only Count Raymond and the people in this tent know the truth. It's best that way.'

'You see,' Bohemond took up the thread, 'we want you not only to enter Antioch and discover ways of betraying it, but, if possible, discover who the Turkish spies in our army are. Now of course we know there are Armenian traders,' he lifted a hand in a weak apology to Simeon, 'but is there someone else who has an ear at our council door

158

and informs Yaghi Siyan about what we plan? I ride out to forage and I am ambushed. At the same time, because I have left the camp, the enemy attack. Coincidence or a plot? Is there a traitor?'

'And what happens,' Simeon spoke up, 'if we fail, if we are captured or betrayed?'

Bohemond chewed the corner of his lip, refusing to meet Eleanor's eye. 'If that happens, and we discover it, we will bargain for your lives. If we fail, I will have Masses sung for your souls.'

'And what happens if *you* fail?' Eleanor asked. 'What if the army moves down to the coast to take ship?'

Bohemond pointed at Theodore. 'He has gold, silver and letters hidden away in a certain place in our camp. If the Army of God retreats, Theodore will seize the opportunity to leave as swiftly as possible. After all, what is the point of staying in Antioch if it will never be ours?'

Eleanor caught the change in his voice. Bohemond had nearly said 'mine'. He smiled to himself as if realising the mistake he'd narrowly missed. 'Antioch must be taken,' he continued. 'Once we have that, we shall march on Jerusalem.'

'And when do we leave?'

'Now!' Hugh spoke up. 'Tonight, sister. The moon is only a quarter, the sky filling with clouds; there will be more rain. You will be led down to Bridge Gate and left to your own devices. The real danger is being recognised by our own soldiers and attacked as traitors, or by Turkish guards thinking you plan mischief. If you do enter Antioch safely and are accepted, Theodore knows what sign to give. Until then, sister, I shall pray, as will everybody in this tent, that you remain safe. Will

159

you go?'

Eleanor glanced at Theodore. She wanted to refuse, yet she understood the logic of Bohemond's plan. If things didn't change, the army would simply rot away. The great cause would collapse and what could she do but wait with the rest? Yet in the end, her life would depend on that dark-faced soldier sitting opposite, so calm and poised. Despite the ravages of the weather, the deprivations of the siege, Theodore always kept himself clean and washed, his black moustache and beard neatly clipped, even oiled. A wild thought occurred to her. What if Theodore was a traitor? What happened if she was taken into Antioch and betrayed? The Greek glanced directly at her, liquid dark eyes full of amusement. Eleanor trusted few men: Hugh and Godefroi, but Theodore was a third. The die was cast. She was committed. She pushed back the cushions and rose.

'I will go, and as you say, it's best if we are gone within the hour. After all,' she laughed sharply, 'what possessions can I take? What do I have?'

Bohemond rose and embraced her, followed by Hugh and Godefroi. Hugh came back and held her again, pressing her close.

'Little sister,' he said, 'take care. So much depends, so much.' He squeezed her again, kissed her on each cheek and, spinning on his heel, left the tent.

Theodore escorted her through the camp. The Greek was well armed and carried a bundle ready to leave. Behind them Simeon was praying quietly under his breath in a tongue she could hardly understand. They reached their tent. Eleanor

160

pulled back the flap and went in. Thankfully Imogene was by herself.

'We have to go,' Eleanor declared. 'Imogene, we have to go now. You must follow me; you must trust me. Take what you can. We are not going far.'

Imogene went to protest but Eleanor pressed her finger hard against the woman's lips. 'If you do not go, you will not be allowed to stay in the camp. You must trust me and follow me. Have I ever betrayed you?'

Imogene, face startled, eyes full of fear, shook her head.

'Then come!'

Imogene, of course, grasped her carved wooden box and a few meagre possessions. Eleanor did the same. Simeon packed his writing tray and leather pannier, then they rejoined Theodore. As they walked through the camp, Eleanor kept her eyes to the ground to hide her own nervousness. They reached the picket lines and slipped through. Apparently the guards had been withdrawn and they made their way across the muddy, slippery ground down towards Bridge Gate. The night was dark, the wind chilling and cutting. From the shadowy battlements pricks of light glowed. Theodore stopped abruptly, putting down his small roll of baggage and bringing up the arbalest he carried. He opened the pouch on his belt and, taking out a bolt, slipped it into the groove, winching back the cord. At first Eleanor couldn't understand until she heard it, a sound behind them. Someone was following them! Imogene moaned. Simeon immediately put a hand across her mouth. Theodore moved back, retracing their steps, then stopped.

161

'Who is it?' he called softy into the darkness. 'Come forward.' Three shapes emerged, cowled and cloaked. Eleanor caught the glint of eyes then straggling beards and moustaches. 'Come closer,' Theodore urged. 'Push back your cowls, lower your visors.' The three arrivals obeyed, pulling down the strip of cloth over their mouths. Eleanor closed her eyes. Jehan the Wolf and his two companions, Gargoyle and Babewyn! They had followed them from the camp.

'Well, friends,' Theodore said softly, 'how goes it? What are you doing here?'

'We could ask the same,' Jehan retorted impudently as he swaggered forward. 'You are deserting, aren't you? I saw the woman leave her tent and go to Count Bohemond's. I followed you there and then you came back. What mischief are you plotting, friend? Whatever you are doing, we will join you. We've had enough of rotting vegetables and hard biscuits. They say we'll be starving before the end of the month. We will come with you. You will vouch for us.'

'Of course I will.' Theodore lifted the crossbow and released the catch, and the bolt took Jehan full in the chest, sending him spinning back. The other two were so surprised they stayed stock still. Again Theodore moved, sword and dagger drawn in a hiss of steel. He attacked one, a swift thrust to the belly, and then the other, who was already trying to flee. Theodore's dagger caught him in the back and he stumbled deeper into the darkness. Theodore followed. Eleanor heard a faint moan, a slight scream abruptly cut off. Theodore came back and wiped his sword on Jehan's cloak. The Wolf was dead, but Gargoyle beside him was still

162

juddering on the ground, trying to rise. Theodore moved swiftly over, pulled back the man's head and cut his throat. Eleanor could only watch. Imogene swayed slightly on her feet. Simeon quietly vomited. Theodore resheathed his dagger, took his sword and neatly decapitated Jehan and then Gargoyle, before going back and doing the same to Babewyn in the darkness: an awful cutting sound followed by the drip of blood. Then he plucked up one of the cloaks, wrapped the three heads in it, tied the bundle with a belt taken from one of his victims and sauntered back as if he hadn't a care in the world. Simeon and Imogene had crouched down, holding each other, trying to control their tremors at the suddenness of the attack and Theodore's silent, bloody work in the dark.

'Why?' asked Eleanor, pointing at the heads wrapped in the cloak, the blood already dripping through.

'Why not?' Despite the dark, Eleanor sensed Theodore was laughing. 'What do you think would have happened? We would have entered Antioch and those three miscreants would have had us at their mercy. God knows what story they would have spun! They were treacherous. They were planning to desert, really desert. If Bohemond or Count Raymond had caught them, they would have been hanged.'

'And now?'

'Well, we can enter the gates of Antioch and show these heads as a guarantee. After all, Jehan did lead a company here. I'll say they tried to stop us so we killed them. It will make our story all the more convincing.' Theodore gestured towards the

163

shadowy walls of the city. 'They wait for us. Let's not tarry any further.' He brushed past Imogene and Simeon, who clambered to their feet. Eleanor followed, and they made their way down to the bridge. Behind them the noise of the camp receded, though she heard one shout of *'Deus vult!'* She closed her eyes. If God wished it she would come through this safely and rejoin her brother, but in the meantime she stared at those forbidding soaring walls, the lights along the battlements. Within a few hours, she would know her fate. Either they would be accepted or, sometime tonight or early tomorrow morning, they would be past all care. Theodore stopped and came back, clutching her by the wrist.

'Eleanor,' he tightened his grip, 'before we begin this, remember! Trust me because I love you.' And not waiting for an answer, he walked back into the darkness.

An arrow struck the earth, followed by a warning call; flames flashed as fire cressets fluttered. Yes, that was how it began, Eleanor reflected in her chronicle, their dangerous venture into Antioch. The arrow embedded deep in the ground before them was followed by a torch thrown to spread a pool of light. It happened so swiftly she had little time to reply, let alone reflect on what Theodore had just said. He now whispered at them to stop. He put down his baggage and grisly burden and walked slowly forward with Simeon. They both extended their hands in the sign of peace and shouted hoarsely in the lingua franca. A voice rang out, and Theodore answered.

'Deo Gracias,' he whispered and picked up his

bundles. 'At least they will accept us.'

They walked over the makeshift bridge of boats, stumbling on the wet surface, and slowly approached the main gate. They heard a creak and another torch was flung out. Again a voice shouted. Theodore ordered them to stop. In the flickering light Eleanor could make out the massive reinforced gates, the iron studs gleaming through the steel portcullis lowered in front of it. To the right and left of these rose fortified towers, lamps glowing at their arrow-slit windows. The night breeze was tinged with the smell of burning oil from the cauldrons ready on the battlements. At the base of each tower was a doorway, narrow and thin, its steps hacked away. The door to the right opened, and a voice shouted an order.

'One by one,' Theodore whispered.

They approached the door. Each had to hand over their baggage before being roughly grasped and hauled up inside. Eleanor, confused, staggered in the darkness, and a hand steadied her. A pitch torch flared, the shadows danced, a brazier crackled. Eleanor stared round the grim chamber with its rough walls and dirty floor. She glimpsed a dark bearded face, the glint of a spiked helmet, the flash of white head cloths. The sinister clatter of steel echoed. A hand stroked her breast. A rough voice barked with laughter, followed by a chatter of tongues. They were bundled into another room. Eleanor was concerned about Imogene, who looked confused and terrified. Little wonder: dragged from her tent, that grisly, violent meeting with Jehan and his two lieutenants, and now this.

The chamber they entered was ill-lit and cold. An officer, his head framed by a chain-mail coif, his damascened helmet on the table before him, shoulders draped by a dark blue cloak over an armoured breastplate, was warming his hands above a chafing dish. Around the room lounged men, crouching or lying down, playing knucklebones, whispering amongst themselves or half asleep. They rose as Theodore's party entered. One of them muttered a joke; a few laughed. Two of the soldiers drew their curved swords and daggers. The officer beckoned Theodore closer and spoke quickly in the lingua franca. Theodore replied. Now and again the officer's cold black eyes shifted to Eleanor, who caught her own name being mentioned. Theodore kept pointing to her, and with a flick of his finger dismissed Imogene and Simeon as mere nobodies. The conversation continued. All four were abruptly searched, and Theodore's weapons taken, as was the grisly bundle. When the three severed heads, eyes blindly staring, lips bloody and parted, rolled out across the floor, the officer gave a brief smile. He rose and kicked all three heads to one of his soldiers, who picked them up and put them in a reed basket. The officer returned, leaning against the table, arms crossed. He stared hard at Theodore and the questioning began again. Abruptly, the tension eased. The officer was laughing, poking Theodore in the chest, nodding; he even turned and smiled at Eleanor, then he gestured to the far corner. They went and squatted down, making themselves comfortable.

'Don't talk,' Theodore whispered in Latin. 'Except about what we are supposed to be, deserters from the Army of God.'

'I . . .' Imogene's eyes rounded as she tried to

Mr Wilson

6332 5000 2584 47

DAMAGED

http://mirror-uk-rb1.gallery.hd.org/_ex

speak.

'Trust me, Imogene,' Eleanor hissed. 'For God's sake hold your peace.'

'I know him.' Theodore smiled and gestured at the officer, who was now sitting at the table talking to one of his men. 'We fought in the same troop some years ago. In fact,' he clapped his hands and gestured around, 'I am sure they all know me.' Again he lapsed into Latin. 'Keep your peace, do exactly what I tell you. Don't talk unless I say.'

The officer shouted an order. A man left and came back with a bowl containing a mixture of meat and hot peppery sauce, as well as a jug of what smelt like curdling milk. They shared this out amongst themselves and had hardly finished when the officer strolled across. He snapped his fingers, gesturing at them to rise, and they followed him out of the chamber, down a narrow passageway and on to a slippery cobbled lane. A well of inky darkness, filled with slinking shapes and strange smells, greeted them. On both sides of the lane, the dusty walls of buildings reared up to the sky, so close they almost touched, leaving a narrow slit above them. With a clink of armour, the officer and his escort led them along this twisting byway. No glimmer of light showed from door or window, nothing except the lantern horns of their escort. A deathly silence held, as if they were crossing some City of the Dead. The lane descended more steeply. They stumbled down broken steps and across rough cobbles. On either side rose buildings with small windows high up in the decaying walls drenched with fetid-smelling liquids, the slimy moss, dirt and grime glittering in the light of the lanterns. Small doors were set deep in these walls,

167

murky openings leading down to gloomy cellars, the dwelling places of vermin. Out of these cellars billowed the stench of rotting garbage and decaying excrement. The smell of dead rats, an odour Eleanor was used to from the camp, hung heavy and foul. They turned a corner and were almost pushed into the downstairs room of what looked like a hostelry or tavern. The officer led them across this into a rear chamber. He gestured at Theodore, then left. The door was not locked. There was a cesspit outside, and more food—fruit, dried bread and brackish water—was brought. Theodore, whispering swiftly in Latin, made it very clear that they would be spied on: the chamber walls probably had eyelets and listening holes. He then dominated the conversation, talking loudly in the lingua franca about how pleased he was to be in Antioch, eager to sell his sword to his new masters. Eleanor, lying next to Imogene, pressed her lips against her companion's ear. She whispered in quick, short sentences how they had decided to flee the Army of God. They were now safe, and Imogene must not to do anything to alert suspicion. Imogene, of course, had a spate of questions, but Eleanor refused to answer, turning on her back to secure some sleep.

The following morning the officer returned. They were to be seen by Yaghi Siyan himself, the Governor of Antioch. Imogene was now openly resentful at what had happened, though she quickly realised that if she wished to survive she would have to comply. Nevertheless, the dark glances and the muttering under her breath clearly informed Eleanor that she no longer had a friend. The officer also returned their possessions, including Imogene's precious box and Theodore's weapons. The Turk was even friendlier than the previous evening, Theodore's desertion being regarded apparently as a glittering prize. He took them out into the streets. They had to shield their eyes for a while; the clouds had broken and the sun was strengthening. The officer was apparently under strict instructions to show these important deserters how strong Antioch was. The narrow streets he led them through teemed with men of many nationalities, all busy about their various affairs. They entered the great square, thronged with market stalls under their striped awnings offering bread, rice, meats already cooked and roasted in stews, together with pheasant and partridge, as well as fruit and vegetables including heaps of ripe watermelons. The officer bought slices of these and offered them round. The sweet juice tasted delicious, refreshing Eleanor's mouth and throat. Further on, stalls displayed silks, rubies, pearls, cloths and a wide range of spices. Deeper into the city they passed parks and paradises with graceful names such as 'the Sweet Green' and 'the Oasis of Fruitfulness'. In between these lay the trade quarters of the city: weavers, ironworkers, goldsmiths, potters, bowl-makers, tile-makers, craftsmen of every description.

The morning air was still cool, but already the din and clatter of the city was ringing out. People looked well fed and content. Eleanor's heart sank. The Army of God was apparently having little effect, a fact the officer loudly proclaimed as he gestured at the stalls piled high with produce. To achieve anything, Eleanor reflected, each of Antioch's gates had to be closely besieged. They

169

entered the wealthy quarter with its well-paved squares and streets. The fine buildings, decked in blue and gold tiles, overlooked elegant drinking fountains, richly decorated pools and elaborate bathhouses. High above all these loomed the minarets like watchful sentinels over the blue-domed mosques, their gleaming brickwork laced with elegant script done in turquoise and navy blue.

At last they reached the square stretching up to the ruler's palace, its buildings almost hidden by the luxurious greenness of its many orchards. Only here was the normal bustle of the city shattered by a gruesome scene. A spy, so the officer informed them, had been caught and was about to be executed. The unfortunate, bound hand and foot, was being dragged face down at the tail of a horse across the cobbled square, backwards and forwards until his body and face were torn to shreds. In places the blood swirled in puddles or congealed between the stones as the condemned man was reduced to nothing but a bloody rag bouncing behind the horse's hooves. The officer waited, eager to create a lasting impression upon his guests, before he crossed the square and led them through an ornamental gate with panels of mosaic faience and polished copper. Guards in brightly coloured quilted armour, soft boots on their feet, with turbans or spiked helmets over chain-mail coifs, patrolled every entrance. Others, Mamelukes in lamellar hauberks and breastplates, stood in recesses, armed with kite-shaped shields and wickedly pointed spears.

They went down cool, shimmering-white passageways, colonnades and porticoes brilliantly decorated in eye-catching floral patterns of blue, yellow, white and green. Scrolling vegetal decorations and elegant ochre calligraphy caught the eye. Some of the walls were decorated with glorious murals displaying green hexagons, or cranes, the birds of heaven, in full flight. Sunlight poured through fretted windows of coloured glass. Fountains splashed in bowls where red apples bobbed. Here and there, as Simeon later explained to Eleanor, were beautifully carved inscriptions to make the passers-by reflect, verses such as: 'The tomb is a door which everyone must enter', and 'The Prophet of God, peace upon him, said "Hurry with prayer before burial and hurry with repentance before death."'

Eleanor found the contrast with the dark, damp, evil-smelling Frankish camp almost breathtaking. Rooms were warmed by rotund copper drums filled with burning charcoal and crammed with pouches of herbs that burst in the heat to exude the fragrance of the most exotic garden. She was surprised, too. Old images, impressions, thoughts and ideas were being swiftly destroyed. The Turks were not barbarians. In many ways, they reminded her of the Byzantines of Constantinople: cultured, sophisticated and courteous. Certainly fearsome and bloodthirsty in battle, but, she reflected ruefully, so were Hugh, Godefroi and Theodore. Undoubtedly these chambers and halls represented the luxury of the great lords of Antioch, but they were a sharp contrast to the dirty, freezing-cold manors and castles of the Franks.

Eventually they were ushered towards the Halls of Audience, their walls decorated by a technique

171

known as thousand-leaves tracing, which secretly contained sacred names on tiles of turquoise within borders of navy blue. In the waiting chambers stood merchants bringing baskets of goods for the governor: nutmegs, cloves, mace, cinnamon and ginger. The sweet smell of these costly spices drifted everywhere. In other chambers traders waited to offer cloth, glass, metalwork, silk, taffeta, fur and ermine. Around the various doors clustered a horde of servants, cup-bearers, messengers, singers and zither players.

Yaghi Siyan held court in an inner chamber, its walls and floor an ivory colour; hence its name, the 'Hall of the Pearl'. The governor lounged on a small mattress stuffed with flock and covered with blue and silver embroidered cloth, which stretched along the dais. On either side of him squatted his leading officers, all dressed in open dark cloaks over dazzling white gowns. Some wore turbans; others let their hair hang free. At first glance, all looked powerful and forbidding, with their dark or olive-coloured faces, glittering eyes, black, grey and white moustaches and beards. Only Yaghi Siyan carried a weapon: a curved dagger in an exquisitely embroidered scabbard thrust through his waistband. Around the chamber stood his personal guards, clad in dark red turbans around silver damascened spiked helmets, glittering chain mail under blue cloaks, their hands resting on the hilts of drawn sabres. Theodore, Simeon and Eleanor were summoned to sit on cushions before the dais. Imogene knelt behind them.

Yaghi Siyan propped himself up against the blood-red cushions. He looked strange: a large-domed, balding head with protuberant ears, and a

172

white moustache and beard that straggled down to his waistband. He studied Eleanor closely, his popping eyes bright with interest, then turned back to Theodore to begin the questioning. Now and again he would turn and smile at Simeon. Eleanor wondered wildly if the scribe was what he claimed to be or, in truth, a Turkish spy deliberately placed in the Army of God. The interrogation was swift and intense, broken now and again by Yaghi Siyan raising his hand so that soft-footed mutes could serve goblets of ice sherbet and dishes of sugared almonds. Eleanor later discovered that once food had been offered and taken, no harm would befall them. Theodore also told her how Yaghi Siyan's inquisition was easy because he simply told the truth, whilst the governor's benevolence towards Simeon was due to the scribe's desertion being further evidence of the Franks' worsening situation.

Yaghi was keen to learn about the high councils of the Army of God. Theodore eagerly listed a litany of woes: the desertion of Count Baldwin to Edessa, the secret withdrawal of so many towards the coast, division amongst the leadership, the shortage of food, the depletion of livestock, especially horses and pack animals, the lack of an overall commander, the sickness of Count Raymond and the paucity of means to maintain a blockade against all the city gates. This proved delightful news to the Turks, Yaghi Siyan and his council nodding in gleeful appreciation.

Theodore also convinced them because he spoke passionately, describing things as they were rather than how he secretly hoped they might be. In addition, what the Greek said seemed to fit with what Yaghi Siyan had learnt or wished to believe. Theodore was very careful not to press the matter. He made no attempt to discover where the governor had gained his news. After all, that would not have been difficult to explain. Two of Antioch's main gates had been left unguarded so spies could enter and leave almost at will. Indeed, as Theodore had confided to Eleanor, the greatest danger facing them was that some spy in the Army of God might create suspicion about their desertion and pass this information along. In the end, however, Yaghi Siyan was satisfied.

'The Franks,' he declared, 'will be overwhelmed, drowned in a sea of destruction, consumed by the fire of perdition.'

The governor then made his greatest mistake. He committed Theodore and his party to the care of an Armenian noble named Firuz, who sat on his right: a tall, elegant man with deep-set eyes, a sharp pointed nose and full, rather protruding lips. Firuz wore a white turban and a sleeveless brocade coat over a dark cream gown. He rose at Yaghi Siyan's gesture and indicated to Theodore and his party to follow him. Yaghi Siyan, however, was not finished. He put his hand beneath a cushion and tossed Theodore a small purse of silver, which the mercenary deftly caught. This provoked laughter. The other councillors bowed towards Yaghi Siyan and rose to clasp Theodore's hand, Eleanor, Simeon and Imogene they simply ignored, though as a courtesy, Yaghi Siyan whispered compliments about Theodore's wife being 'pretty'.

They left the palace still escorted by the officer, who introduced himself as Baldur, a captain of Turcopoles. He was apparently on the most cordial terms with Firuz, who, as they made their way through the city, introduced himself as Armenian by birth and commander of two towers known as 'The Twin Sisters' to the south-east of Antioch on the slopes of Mount Silpius. Firuz led them there through the markets and bazaars, across squares where scholars squatted with their backs to a marble cistern as they disputed over matters of philosophy. They went along streets and alleyways, stepping aside for cavalcades of soldiers, men in armour, their ponies dark with sweat, foam bubbling on their bridles. Firuz, like Baldur, was determined to demonstrate the power of Antioch. He took them down market lanes reeking of hide and oils, where sallow-faced men clad in dark fur robes touted for business. Fires roared before the doors of shabby houses; quarters of mutton were being roasted and the traders' children offered wooden platters of the cooked meat piled high with rice and barley cakes. Customers could buy these and eat whilst they gathered round cotton booths where shadow puppets wiggled and strutted against lighted sheets.

Eventually they reached the city outskirts and climbed the trackway skirting Mount Silpius. On either side rose dark green poplars. Eleanor noticed how, apart from Baldur's two lieutenants, they now had no military escort. The Twin Sisters rose square before them, their turreted tops overlooking the curtain wall, the postern gate between them being bolted and barred, firmly blocked up. Firuz explained how it was of little use; Yaghi Siyan preferred to keep open the St George Gate for sallying out in sudden attack as well as receiving supplies.

175

Firuz and his wife lived in one tower, his kinsmen, servants and retainers in the other on the far side of the postern gate. The interior of the tower was very similar to those of Compiègne: rough, undressed stone with a spiral staircase leading to the upper floors. Nevertheless the chambers themselves were splendid. The walls, plastered and lime-washed, were hung with rose-coloured, silver-tasselled tapestries and brilliantly embroidered cloths, whilst woollen rugs lay strewn across the floors. All the windows on the inside were glass-filled; those on the outside, overlooking the walls, were covered with wooden shutters or strips of hardened horn. Candlesticks, spigots and lantern horns provided light, whilst copper braziers gave off perfumed warmth.

Asmaja, Firuz's wife, welcomed them with goblets of honey mead. She was truly beautiful: a close-fitting white veil framed a delicate, sensitive face, pale-skinned with lustrous eyes and rose-bud lips. Firuz clearly adored her. He immediately invited her and his new guests on to the dais of the main chamber. They sat on cushions around a low table. Servants brought platters of pitta bread, fruits, dried meats and delicious-tasting wines. Firuz, who was not a Muslim, openly rejoiced in feasting his guests; Baldur was more circumspect and frugal. Theodore acted the relieved man, happy at his reception by Yaghi Siyan. Simeon and Imogene remained silent; the latter, her precious box close to her, still looked sullen and petulant. Eleanor felt exhausted and dirty after the previous night's imprisonment. She was desperate for sleep but determined to remain vigilant.

Firuz, under the influence of the wine, explained

176

how Theodore would join him in securing the Twin Sisters tower and advising him on what siege machinery the Franks might bring up against them. Apparently his home was also to be their prison. Apologetically he explained how, for the time being, his guests, under pain of immediate death, were not allowed to leave the vicinity of the Twin Sisters for the city markets or bazaars, whilst they were certainly not to approach any of the main gates. Theodore, munching from his tray of diced lamb and vegetables, nodded understandingly and the conversation moved on. Eleanor, tired though she was, became distracted. At first she thought it was her own weariness, her bleary eyes, yet she was sure she caught a loving glance pass between Asmaja and Baldur. She lowered her head and mentally recited the Confiteor, an act of contrition for her sins and wayward thoughts. Yet as the meal continued, she glimpsed similar glances between the pair. Firuz, flushed with wine, remained totally oblivious, yet to Eleanor, his wife seemed deeply smitten with the handsome captain of Turcopoles.

The meal over, Firuz and Baldur wished to discuss things amongst themselves. Theodore, Eleanor and the rest were taken up to the highest floor of the tower, the staircase outside it leading through a narrow door on to the crenellated fighting platform. The chamber itself was comfortable, with pegs on the walls for their clothes, and chests and coffers for their other belongings. Servants busied themselves, and eventually four straw-filled palliasses lay about the room. Embroidered cloths hung against the walls, whilst rugs, shutters and bronze braziers kept out the cold. A wooden lavarium provided a bowl and water jug. Theodore, finger to his lips, indicated that they should remain silent whilst he loudly commented on how comfortable the chamber was and how, living at the top of tower, they would be more secure.

'And more easily guarded!' Eleanor whispered.

Once they had unpacked and made themselves comfortable, they went across to the basement of the other tower to wash and change their clothes. Afterwards they gathered in a circle in their own chamber. Theodore had inspected everything carefully, and had found no eyelets or peepholes in the wall, whilst the door was of thick, strong oak. They were safe. At first they had to listen to Imogene's hiss of hateful words, her fury at being taken away, her desire to return. Theodore calmed her, relaying what Yaghi Siyan had said whilst reminding her how fortunate she was. If Antioch fell to the Army of God, she would be safe. If the Army of God withdrew, they could all easily slip out amidst the joyful celebrations of the city. Moreover, if they had stayed in the camp, they could starve, die in the fighting or run the risk of even being ejected from the camp. Imogene seemed satisfied. Theodore pressed them all not to ask questions; their task was not to discover spies but to find a way for the Army of God to enter Antioch. Eleanor described what she had seen pass between Baldur and Asmaja. Theodore chewed on the corner of his lip, narrowed his eyes and told her to watch further. For the rest, he advised, they must only wait and see.

So, in that freezing January, the Year of Our Lord 1098, they settled down in the tower of the Twin Sisters in Antioch. Theodore joined the garrison, proving himself to be a skilled adviser, impressing everyone with his expertise. Eleanor and Imogene helped with household tasks. Theodore asked Simeon to tutor both himself and his 'wife' in chancery skills, declaring that he wished to extend his education. In many ways it was a halcyon existence compared with the horrors of the camp beyond Antioch. They were cut off from the siege but, through Firuz, discovered what was happening outside. Matters were turning from bad to worse in the Army of God. Rain beat through the fabric of the tents, rusting the armour, softening the bowstrings. The ground beneath became churned, the mud working its way up through the rugs and blankets on which the besiegers slept. Nature seemed to be against the Franks. One night the earth shook with a heart-chilling tremor. Pavilions toppled down. Men who ran out into the open were thrown off their feet. Fissures and cracks appeared in the earth. As the Franks gathered in groups to see what was happening, fresh horrors terrified them. In the northern sky plumes of flame shot up amongst the stars, the orange-red glow spreading out and changing to purple. The light rose higher, twisting and turning, brightening the sky until the Army of God could see the mud underfoot and the pale faces around them. Night turned to day; dawn broke even before the first cock crew. Surely it was a sign? The Army of God wondered about this, as did the people of Antioch. More news arrived at the Twin Sisters. Adhémar had declared that God was angry with the Franks so they must purify the army. All women had been forcibly driven beyond the camp down to Port St Simeon; now he ordered

179

a three-day fast with prayer. Sinners were rigorously punished. An adulterous couple, caught in their sin, were stripped naked and paraded through the camp to be beaten and humiliated. Theodore relayed this information while they were sitting at table with their hosts. Eleanor watched Asmaja's face blush lightly. Theodore swiftly moved the conversation on, praising Firuz and Asmaja for their food whilst pointing out that famine ruled amongst the Franks. Merchants were charging eight pieces of gold, a hundred and twenty silver dinars, for a donkey-load of provisions.

'Many are dying,' he declared. 'Even more deserting.'

Principal amongst the deserters were William the Carpenter and Peter the Hermit; neither could tolerate the deprivation any further and had fled into the night. Bohemond heard of this and sent Tancred in pursuit to bring them back. For an entire night William the Carpenter lay bound 'like some evil thing' in Bohemond's tent. The next day the Norman lord gave him a public lecture, calling him miserable, a shame and a dishonour to his own people, and making pointed reference to other betrayals when he had served in Iberia. William at least had the sense not to object. Other knights pleaded for him, and Bohemond finally agreed that he would not be punished providing he took an oath to remain. He did so, but a few nights later deserted for good. News of such betrayals spread joy in Antioch, especially when they heard that Tacticius, the Emperor's own representative, had decided to leave to report to his master. Tacticius took a solemn oath to Bohemond that all the castles and towns captured on the way would be his, and he left his tent and baggage as guarantee that he would return, but he never did. When Theodore heard this, he just shook his head.

'Foresworn he is,' he whispered. 'Foresworn he shall remain.'

At the end of January, Firuz called his household and guests together. Tonight they would celebrate, he declared, for wonderful news had arrived: Ridwan, Emir of Aleppo, was marching with twelve thousand men to raise the siege. The news had spread like wildfire through the city, and there were jubilations, dancing in the street, celebrations at the palace.

'We will crush them!' Firuz declared. 'We shall crush the infidels between Ridwan's army and the walls of Antioch.'

Theodore tried to put a brave face on it. Imogene had to leave the room, claiming she felt unwell. It seemed as if the Army of God was destined for destruction. Later that evening they gathered in their chamber. Theodore could offer no comfort.

'We can do nothing,' he whispered hoarsely, 'except pray.'

They waited. The days passed. At last news began to seep through. A miracle had occurred! Apparently the Army of God had decided to meet the foe out in the open. They put the command of the camp under Adhémar and Count Raymond, whilst Bohemond led out a thousand mounted men to meet an army of twelve thousand. He took up position near the Iron Bridge and camped on level ground about a mile long between a great lake and the marsh, which would defend his flanks.

He then organised his division into six cohorts and simply waited for Ridwan to approach. He did so swiftly, just after dawn. Scouts rode into the Frankish camp screaming how the enemy were almost upon them. Bohemond raged around, kicking men awake, urging them to don harness and saddle their horses. He ordered his cavalry out, five phalanxes lined up side by side; the sixth he kept in reserve.

Ridwan's army came on, thousands of them in two formations. The Turks expected the Franks to attack, but they did not, and the Turks had no choice but to come on, approaching at a trot. It was a grey day, so Eleanor later learned for her chronicle, and the battle was fought in a bleak place, a desperate struggle for survival. Turkish arrows whirred through the air, but still the Frankish line did not move. Saddles emptied, horses reared, plunged and panicked. The Franks just sang, verse after verse of the same psalm, as destruction fell on them. At last the Turks broke into a full charge and so did the Franks, long lances going down, shields up as they spurred their charges on. They ploughed into the Turks, sending the first line reeling back on to the second to cause utter confusion. Bohemond then committed his sixth phalanx, which circled the battlefield and tore into the right flank of the enemy. The swift horses of the Turks did not avail them. Bohemond surged on like a reaper through corn, first with his lance then his sword, his knights following, their crimson standards rippling in the breeze. The Frankish charge was relentless. Swords flashed, cutting through the enemy like a knife would cloth, dealing out death to the left and to the right. The

Turks broke, fleeing back. The Franks pursued. Confusion amongst Ridwan's forces spread like ripples of water merging into each other. In the end, Ridwan of Aleppo and his captains fled, leaving the field to Bohemond and his knights, who stormed the enemy camp and took possession of it. The black banners of anarchy were unfurled. No prisoners were taken. Wholesale executions were carried out. A day later, Bohemond arranged stakes along the ditch before Antioch. On each he placed a head so that the city garrison could stare out at the thousands of poles each bearing its gruesome trophy.

The news of Bohemond's victory spread gloom throughout Antioch, astonishing Yaghi Siyan and his council. Nevertheless, they still hoped that famine and pestilence would devastate the besiegers. The reports coming into the city were increasingly grim. The Franks were grubbing for roots and chewing on leather to stifle the ache of hunger. They gorged themselves on the sticky-sweet meat of dead camels and trapped rats and mice. Some of them turned to cannibalism and collected the carcasses of dead Turks, which they skinned and skewered, boiling chunks of flesh in their great cauldrons. Word of the ghastly feast spread through the camp and people came to watch. Once they had tasted human flesh, the perpetrators searched for more amongst the Muslim tombs outside the city.

Theodore confided to Eleanor how the Army of God had now shrunk to thirty thousand, yet they were still intent on victory, especially as help had arrived. Ships from England and Hainault docked in the port of St Simeon, bringing in engineers and wood to build siege engines. Yaghi Siyan heard about this and launched fierce raids, but they were driven back. The Franks had now decided that all gates to the city should be blockaded. They seized an abandoned mosque near Bridge Gate, beat off attackers, dug a double ditch and built a limestone wall with a tower which they nicknamed 'La Mahomeri', the old French for the Blessed Virgin Mary. Worse was to come. Tancred had taken up residence in the hills near the St George Gate. He attacked caravans and supply wagons, seizing horses and provisions before moving to occupy and fortify a disused monastery nearby.

As March turned into April, the city of Antioch realised that the Franks were still resolute in their aggression. Each gate was now controlled and blockaded, and despite sallies and forays, the Army of God held fast. In Antioch, fear and panic began to spread. No longer were the markets and bazaars full. The city teemed with people, and as the Franks tightened their belt around it, hunger soon made itself felt. Eleanor and the rest were no longer invited to banquets and feasts. Food grew scarce. Prices began to rise. The siege started to bite savagely. Yaghi Siyan turned to terror. He had prisoners taken up on to the walls. One knight, Reynold, captured in a foray, was ordered to renounce his faith but refused and was promptly executed on the battlements, his corpse tossed over into the ditch. Other prisoners were paraded. Again they were asked to renounce their faith but refused. Yaghi Siyan ordered brushwood to be gathered; the prisoners, men and women, were tied to stakes and the fires lit. The screams of the burning captives could be heard all over the

184

Frankish camp, but such barbarity only strengthened their resolve.

Inside Antioch, Theodore continued his deception. Eleanor reasoned that he must have communicated somehow with Bohemond, for the Poor Brethren of the Temple appeared in the rocky passes and culverts beneath the tower of the Twin Sisters. Theodore became busy advising Firuz on the mangonels, catapults and mantlets the Franks brought up. Eleanor felt she was in a waking dream. She was locked in the tower, acting as if this was her life, whilst a mere arrow-cast away, her beloved brother Hugh, Godefroi and the rest took up positions to shatter the world she sheltered in.

Life in the Twin Sisters was certainly changing. The blockade of Bridge Gate and the St George Gate, and the presence of the Franks in the foothills of Mount Silpius, had their effect. Food, supplies and provender were abruptly cut off. Markets closed. Bazaars emptied. Stallholders had nothing to offer as famine crept the streets. The effect of such strictures deepened. The Armenian population became restless; even Firuz began to rail at the harsh regime of Yaghi Siyan, arguing that his ruler should at least seek terms of surrender from the Army of God. Theodore, skilful and sly, noted this and cast about looking for an opportunity. Asmaja provided it.

Eleanor had volunteered to look after washing the clothes. These were piled into great tubs, soaked, squeezed and taken down to a nearby olive grove to be stretched out for the day. One morning early in May, taking advantage of the strengthening sun, she was laying out some garments when a flash of colour caught her eye. She left the baskets, moving silently as she had done when she and Hugh were children playing in the woods near their parents' manor at Compiègne. It was a beautiful day, the grass alive with crickets, birds singing in the branches above her, the scent of wild primrose heavy on the morning breeze. On the far side of the grove, she glimpsed Asmaja and Baldur, two lovers entwined, kissing and embracing, passionate in their desire for each other. Eleanor felt guilty, yet she stayed and observed even as Baldur took Asmaja deeper into the trees. She watched as they lay down, unaware of the sounds around her; only the flash of cloth kept her attention before she stole away. She felt guilty, disturbed at what she'd seen, but eventually she informed Theodore. During their stay in the tower, he'd kept his distance, acting the distracted husband, never intimate or personal. Now he took her hands in his and kissed her fingers gently.

'Eleanor, all you have done here,' he whispered, 'is to act the part as I have. I feel sorry for Asmaja, Firuz and Baldur, but I also pity my comrades rotting in the camp outside. What you have told me I must use.'

Over the next few days Theodore deftly wove a tapestry of subtle intrigue. Firuz learnt about his wife's infidelity, then witnessed it first hand. Publicly there were no confrontations or angry words. Baldur was summoned to the tower and dismissed, whilst Asmaja simply disappeared. Firuz informed Theodore that he had sent his wife back to her parents. Theodore, ever the good listener, counselled his new-found friend. Firuz appealed to

Yaghi Siyan for justice against the adulterer Baldur, but the ruler of Antioch had other matters on his mind and dismissed the plea out of hand. Firuz returned to the Twin Sisters deeply resentful, determined to drown his sorrows in goblets of wine. Theodore, like the serpent in Eden, wound his way round the man's soul. Firuz listened. Theodore pointed out how all the gates of Antioch were besieged, the city was locked and eventually would fall. He opened a way whereby Firuz could secure justice and vengeance, not only against his wife and Baldur, protected by Yaghi Siyan, but against the ruler of Antioch himself.

Within a week the web was woven and Firuz was trapped. He entered into secret pacts with Theodore and solemnly promised how, at a given time, he would deliver the Twin Sisters to Bohemond and the Army of God. The trap was closed. Firuz could not object. If he now revealed the plot to Yaghi Siyan, he, like Theodore and the others, would be executed as a traitor. It was only a matter of time, of waiting for the right opportunity.

Part 7

Antioch: The Feast of St Lawrence, 10 August 1098

Quo vulneratus insuper, mucorne diro lanceae.
(Where he was wounded by a thrust from the
sharp tip of that lance.)

Venantius Fortunatus, 'Hymn In Honour
of the Cross'

Full summer was now close. Water was plentiful in
the city but the markets remained empty. Firuz,
full of bitterness, had grown even more eager than
Theodore for the Army of God to act. The
situation in and around Antioch was worsening.
The army were digging up bodies to eat, and
cannibalism was rife in the camp, whilst in Antioch
the price of food soared so high that people lay out
in the streets begging for food. Violent clashes
occurred around Bridge Gate and that of St
George as Yaghi Siyan made a desperate attempt
to destroy the makeshift forts and redoubts that
had been thrown up, but still the Franks pressed
their siege. News filtered through. Khebogha,
Atabeg of the Caliph of Baghdad and Emir of
Mosul, was fast approaching the city with a huge
army, ready to crush the Franks. Such news
heartened Antioch. Bohemond and the others only
intensified their siege. Firuz made a fresh appeal
to Yaghi Siyan for justice, but Baldur was needed
to lead out sorties from Bridge Gate, and Yaghi

Siyan refused to do anything.

By the end of May both besieged and besieger were searching for a way to shatter each other. The Army of God, deluded by certain merchants of Antioch into thinking that the city would surrender, dispatched envoys through Bridge Gate under Walo, Constable of France. These were immediately surrounded and killed, their severed heads catapulted into the Frankish camp. The bloody incident increased tension. Theodore, fearful of Yaghi Siyan discovering his plot, believed Firuz was ready. On the Feast of the Blessed Virgin, the last day of May, the Year of Our Lord 1098, he and Firuz went out along the ramparts of the Twin Sisters. Theodore loosed an arrow carrying a message into the darkness below; a lantern flashed three times in reply, a sign that the message had been safely received and understood. The die was cast. The Twin Sisters were to be betrayed on the night of 2 June.

The hours in between were both fraught and frenetic. The city was bracing itself for more attacks and greater food shortages. News came through that Khebogha, the leader of tens and tens of thousands, was only a day's march away. The Army of God would be trapped before Antioch and utterly destroyed. Speed became the essence; the hours were passing. Early on the morning of 2 June, during the third watch of the night, Theodore roused Eleanor. Simeon was told to guard Imogene whilst she and Theodore followed Firuz up on to the fighting platform of the main Twin Sisters tower. The Armenian was quiet but resolute in what he intended to do, a man, according to Theodore, who had closed one door of his life and was prepared to open another.

Eleanor felt as if she was in a dream. She could hear nothing from the darkness below as a slight breeze cooled their sweaty faces. She stayed at the top of the steps just within the shadows of the doorway whilst Firuz and Theodore chattered to the guards, warming their hands over a brazier. Suddenly she heard the hiss of steel, the crack of an arbalest, followed by the sighs and moans of dying men. Her name was called and she hurried out. Corpses were strewn about the fighting platform; curls of blood coursed down the gulleys. Theodore was busy at the wall, leaning between the crenellations, letting down a tarred rope, whilst Firuz was tying the other end to an iron hook thrust into the wall. Eleanor ran across, peered over and glimpsed the dim glow of a lantern. On the strengthening breeze came the clink of armour. Men were massing below, desperate, hungry and eager for bloodshed. Theodore sighed loudly as he pulled up the rope; on its end hung an ox-hide ladder. Firuz secured this over the battlements. As Eleanor and Theodore waited in the shadows, an eternity seemed to pass. She heard gasps and moans from the blackness below, then Hugh appeared, stepping on to the fighting platform, Godefroi behind him. Theodore whistled, and they came over. In the poor light both looked like gaunt grey ghosts, chain-mail coifs pulled close over their heads, faces hidden by helmets with broad noseguards. Hugh embraced Eleanor in a gust of sweaty leather, stroked her gently on the back of the head, whispered something and disappeared into the tower. Godefroi kissed her full on the lips, winked and followed Hugh down the steps.

Theodore hastened after them as others poured over the crenellations. A short while later, across on the other tower, dark shapes bobbed and moved along the fighting platform. The faint clash of steel echoed; figures fell. Eleanor heard a scream.

'The ladder!' Firuz shouted. 'It's broken.'

Harassed, he threaded down the rope, and another ox-hide ladder was raised and secured. Eleanor kept to the shadows as Theodore had instructed her. More knights climbed over, pushing their way forward, eyes glazed with fear and anger. They were full of battle fury, torn between terror and the desire to wreak revenge on their enemy. Swords drawn, they hurried down the steps of the tower; Firuz followed. Eleanor heard a crashing and banging below. The knights were now trying to force the postern gates. Lights flared along the walls. The clatter of steel rang like a tocsin from the neighbouring towers. At last a resounding crash sent her hastening down the steps. Shadows fluttered. The narrow, winding steps reeked of sweat, leather, horse and the stench of the camp. A corpse swimming in blood lay across the threshold of the tower; the courtyard beyond milled with mailed men. The postern gate had been torn apart. A giant on a black war horse came clattering through. The blood-red banner he carried was unfurled to shouts and acclamations. Bohemond had arrived, standard in one hand, sword in the other; his great voice boomed through the darkness proclaiming the death knell of Antioch.

'*Deus vult! Deus vult!*' The cry was taken up. 'Antioch has fallen.'

Now the killing began in earnest. The Army of

191

God secured other gates before spreading like a turbulent river through the streets and across the squares. Turks, men, women and children, rushed out into the night only to be cut down until the paved areas looked like a bloody carpet. Horrible screams and heart-chilling yells broke the night, ringing out above the clash of steel and the thud of axe against wood. Bridge Gate was seized and pulled apart. Raymond of Toulouse and his Provençals poured in like a pack of ferocious wolves, fanning out down streets and alleyways. The army had rotted outside in the wind, rain and boiling heat. They'd eaten leaves and roots and drank water so muddy it stuck to their throats. Now, God's Day, the Day of Anger, the Day of Vengeance, had arrived. Blood would cleanse and purify the hardships they had endured. Antioch was to be put to the sword.

The Franks burst into mosques, expecting to discover all sorts of abominations, only to find peace and quiet, the sweet smell of candles and dawn's first light pouring through the fretted windows of coloured glass. The beauty of these places of prayer was savagely shattered. No mercy was shown to the imams and holy men turned devoutly towards Mecca; these met their death bravely enough as the prayer carpets on which they knelt became soaked in blood. The Franks stormed the palaces searching for gold, silver and precious stones. They looted hangings, tapestries, coverlets and cloths, wandering back into the streets dressed in their plundered finery. They smashed cabinets, coffers and chests. They seized women of the harem, beautiful Armenians and Circassians, violating them cruelly on the luxurious cushions and beautiful embroidered divans. Pale-skinned Greeks chanted prayers, made the sign of the cross and showed the crucifix in the hope of mercy at the hand of these killers sweeping through Antioch, their long swords cutting off life like the wind snuffs out a candle.

Turks were trapped and tortured; their stomachs ripped open, their entrails pulled out so that they could be burned or led around like dogs until they collapsed. The garrison retreated into the security of the citadel, where they displayed their green and white banners and waited for help. Bohemond immediately attacked the citadel, now commanded by one of Yaghi Siyan's sons, until an arrow took him in the leg and forced him to withdraw. Yaghi Siyan himself panicked and fled; drunk and frightened, he kept falling from his horse until his escort, desperate to flee, left him on the ground. An Armenian butcher came across the fallen ruler of Antioch, hacked off his head and took this and Yaghi Siyan's armour and harness to Bohemond for a reward.

Eleanor learnt all this as she sheltered in the Twin Sisters tower, exhausted and depleted. Theodore came to feed her, and Hugh and Godefroi returned, but Eleanor just sat, sprawled on cushions, staring into the distance. She quietly confessed to Theodore that she wanted to go home. He put it down to the tension she'd endured before the city fell. Eleanor, beside herself, just retreated deeper into the darkness of the tower, whilst outside the bloodshed gradually subsided. On 4 June, however, she was roused by Theodore, who breathlessly informed her that Turkish outriders and scouts had appeared in the foothills to the north of Antioch whilst those still holding the citadel had hoisted the black banner of war and threatened to push down into the city.

'You must come,' Theodore insisted. He hurriedly forced Eleanor to dress, collected her few possessions and pushed her through the door, down the steps and out of the tower. Hurrying along the dusty trackway, he warned her what to expect. They entered a city of the damned. Corpses still littered the streets. The white walls of houses and other buildings were now crimson with blood. The stench of corruption spread everywhere, polluting the air and sickening the stomach. Adhémar of Le Puy was doing his best to collect corpses in the squares and marketplaces; huge funeral pyres roared, their acrid black plumes blossoming like something evil against the white-blue sky. A new plundering was now taking place. The Army of God was locked in Antioch and there was little food to be had. Already Bohemond and other leaders, banners unfurled, were riding through the street, heralds scurrying before them, summoning men back to the standards. Eleanor felt as if she was crossing the wastelands of hell. Fires burned. Black smoke curled everywhere. Corpses, bloated and rotting, blocked her way. Only Theodore's arm around her shoulder provided protection against the feeling of utter hopelessness that hovered to engulf her, a night of gathering blackness that threatened to sweep her soul. One thought dominated her senses: Firuz! She did not know what had happened to him. Yet his personal pain was the cause of all this. He had been betrayed by Asmaja so he, in turn, had betrayed all. Yet, if he hadn't, what would have been the fate of Hugh, Godefroi and the rest? Was that life, she wondered, one door of betrayal leading to another? The priests preached hell; Eleanor felt as if she was buried there already. Was there salvation, or were she and the rest, Armenian, Greek and Turk, already judged and experiencing the horrors of eternal punishment? Eleanor babbled such thoughts as she was placed in the bedchamber of a Turkish merchant, its owner dead or fled. A leech was summoned who force-fed her a bitter-tasting drink that plunged her into a sweat-soaked sleep.

Over the next few days Eleanor, breaking through fitful dreams, became more aware of the gathering storm around the Army of God. Khebogha had arrived with an army, a moving mass of at least seventy thousand men against a Frankish force now reduced to thirty thousand, starving, still bereft of armour, horses, food and drink. The city was invested. A conflict, bloody and violent, began in earnest. The Mahomeri tower, the Castle of the Blessed Virgin, held by Robert of Flanders, was besieged. The Turks brought up mangonels and catapults to rain down sharpened death. Robert of Flanders burnt the castle and withdrew through Bridge Gate. Meanwhile, in the city, the Turks holding

the citadel went on the attack, launching fierce assaults. Bohemond organised the defence along a ridge opposite the citadel. Nevertheless a constant rain, a mass of missiles, arrows and stones, fell on the Army of God. Fighting lasted from dawn to dusk, so those who had bread did not have time to eat it and those who had water were not able to drink. Courage and chivalry were not lacking.

Robert of Barneville, with fifteen knights, charged a Turkish troops of horse only to be ambushed by even more. Robert turned, trying to flee back into the city, but his body was pierced by an arrow, his horse struck from under him. He was killed by a spear thrust through his head, which was later cut off and hoisted on a lance to taunt those watching on the battlements.

Bohemond emerged as the leader. He concentrated on the citadel, flying his blood-red banner, bandaging his wounded leg and driving back the Turks. He also fired the houses around, and the flames, whipped up by storm winds, ravaged the city but also drove out the Frankish deserters, whom Bohemond and his captains immediately marshalled against the enemy. Inside Antioch, Adhémar continued the grim task of cleaning the streets and burning the corpses. Churches were reopened and consecrated. The ancient patriarch, found hiding, was restored to his office. The Army of God still hoped for help from Emperor Alexius, but this hope was cruelly dashed. The stream of deserters grew; even Stephen of Blois and other leaders joined the 'rope-sliders', those who clambered down the walls of Antioch at night, evaded the Turkish patrols and fled to spread the widening tale of woe. They reached the port of St Simeon and warned off the sailors there. The Turks attacked the port and burned what was left, killing anyone unable to leave. Alexius also retreated, believing the Army of God, trapped in Antioch, would be annihilated, a conclusion even the Franks now faced. The outer forts were burned and abandoned, and the army fell back into Antioch, confronting a force over twice their number. Yet worse was to follow.

Starvation began to bite. Famine became commonplace. The Franks were forced to eat fig leaves, thistles, leather belts and even the dried hides of dead animals. A horse's head, without the tongue, sold for three gold pieces, the intestines of a goat for five and a live cockerel for ten. The knights were so desperate they drew the blood from their own horses and donkeys and drank it for sustenance. The Franks even opened negotiations with Khebogha, who demanded their total unconditional surrender and also that they renounce their religion. The Army of God truly faced annihilation. Hugh and Godefroi, however, vowed to fight to the death. They joined Eleanor in making their final confessions and returned to their plotting. God, they had decided, needed a helping hand.

One evening, a week after the fall of the city, Eleanor sat on the flat roof of the merchant's house with Hugh, Godefroi and Theodore. She watched a meteor score the heavens and fall in a fiery mess behind the Turkish camp. The Poor Brethren were joined by Count Raymond of Toulouse, who came to share a tun of special wine found in the cellars of an Armenian merchant. At first the conversation was desultory. They all agreed there was little hope of relief, so they sat enjoying the wine and the cool evening breeze, staring out at the pinpricks of light in the sprawling camp of Khebogha's advance guard. Eleanor drank slowly, half listening to the ranting of Peter Bartholomew the visionary, who was striding up and down the cobbled yard below. Peter's young, powerful voice rang out, quoting the psalms as he cursed the enemies of the Army of God.

> *He has sent divers swarms of flies amongst them which devoured them and frogs which destroyed them.*
> *He also gave their harvest to the caterpillar and the fruits of their vineyards to the locust.*
> *He has destroyed their vines with hail and their sycamore trees with frost.*
> *He has given their cattle to the hail and their flocks of sheep to hot thunderbolts.*
> *He has cast upon our enemy the fierceness of his anger, laughter and indignation by sending evil angels among them.*
> *He has made a way of anger.*
> *He has not spared their souls.*
> *He will give their lives over to the pestilence.*

Count Raymond drained his cup, his one good eye fixed on Hugh.

'It is only God we have left,' he declared. 'The Emperor will not help us. The Turks demand our surrender, or our heads, or possibly both. Our shepherds have deserted their flocks whilst the sheep starve.' He paused at fresh cries and shouts.

Eleanor stared up at the flashes of fire scoring the night sky. Broad blood-red flames lit the blackness. From the city rose shouts of *'Deus vult, Deus vult!* A sign, a sign!'

'They have asked for a sign; give them a sign!' Raymond leaned across and thrust his goblet into Hugh's hands. 'Give it soon.' He rose, cocking his head as if listening to Peter Bartholomew's fresh ranting, then made his farewells and left.

A short time later the Poor Brethren of the

Temple reassembled on the roof of the house. This time they were joined by Alberic and Norbert; they looked like brothers, cowls shrouding their cadaver-like faces, flesh shrunken from the depredations they'd suffered. Nevertheless, the eyes of both men were as bright and sharp as ever. They looked impatient, as if eager to begin some important enterprise. They were also joined by Beltran. He had openly rejoiced to find Imogene safe and well, delighted to be reunited with her though clearly bitter at the way he and his beloved had been deceived. Hugh had shrugged this off, dismissing Beltran's growing coolness by declaring that in order to succeed, Bohemond's plan had had to remain secret.

'Well, well,' Beltran murmured now, forcing a smile and glancing round. 'Will we escape this by treachery? By deceit, by cunning?'

'What shall be done?' Hugh retorted, his voice harsh at Beltran's jibes.

'What *can* be done?' Beltran's reply was almost a jeer.

'We must fight!' Theodore declared. 'We cannot withstand the siege. We grow weaker by the day. We have no choice but to leave Antioch and bring Khebogha to battle.'

'And be defeated?' Beltran asked.

'We are desperate!' Hugh broke in. 'We have no other choice. Theodore is correct. The army must be roused. They have seen the signs in the heavens. The Army of God must have a rallying point. We must be purified and purged.' His voice had risen; now it sank to a whisper. 'The count knows what I have discussed with him; God's will be done.' He and Godefroi rose and went down the steps. They

199

were joined a little later by Alberic and Norbert. Finally Beltran murmured his farewells and withdrew, leaving Theodore and Eleanor alone.

'You are well?'

She smiled thinly back at him. 'I am tired, hungry, dirty and . . .'

'Lost?' Theodore asked.

'Yes, lost.'

'We have all lost our way.'

Eleanor cocked her head. Peter Bartholomew was now silent. 'What does my brother plan, Theodore?'

'A sign.' He came over and sat on the cushions piled beside her. 'A sign from God.'

'With a little help from my brother?'

'Perhaps . . .' Theodore smiled. 'God helps those who look to Him for help.'

'And perhaps,' Eleanor murmured, 'those who are prepared to give Him a helping hand?'

'Precisely,' Theodore whispered. 'Eleanor, in Jerusalem lie the holy relics of Our Saviour. What if,' he stared up at the sky, 'such a relic could also be found here?'

The answer to Theodore's question came swiftly enough. Peter Bartholomew, who had mysteriously disappeared for a few days, re-emerged and presented himself before Count Raymond and Adhémar of Le Puy with the promise of a revelation. Peter's demand for an audience was like an answer to a prayer. In the city, panic was beginning to spread, people wondering what fate they could expect. The news of the impending revelation coursed like fire through stubble, and when Peter presented himself, the message delivered by his powerful voice was repeated

200

throughout the city. 'My lords,' he began, 'Andrew, the Apostle of God and of our Lord Jesus Christ, has recently admonished me for the fourth time. He has commanded me to give back to you, after this city was captured, the lance that opened the side of Our Saviour. I have not obeyed him. Today I went out of the city with the rest to do battle. I was caught between two horsemen. I was almost suffocated and sat down sadly on a certain rock, almost devoid of life. I was faint, exhausted from hunger, fear and grief. St Andrew came to me in a dream with a companion. He threatened me much unless I gave the news to you quickly . . .' At this, both the count and the bishop interrupted him, asking him to explain what he meant.

'Months ago, when the first earthquake shook Antioch, I said nothing, God help me. One night when I lay down, the earth shook again. My fear increased, and looking up, I suddenly saw two men standing before me in the brightest clothing. The first was older with red-white hair; his beard was wide and thick and he was of medium stature. His companion was younger and taller, handsome beyond any likeness of the children of men. The older man said to me: "What are you doing?" I was very frightened and I replied, "Who are you?" The man retorted, "Rise and do not be afraid and listen to what I am saying to you. I am Andrew the Apostle. Bring together the Bishop of Le Puy and Count Raymond of Toulouse and say these words to them: 'Why has the bishop neglected to preach and admonish the People of the cross, for it will profit them much?'" And he added, "Come, I will show you the lance of Our Lord Jesus Christ and you shall give it to Count Raymond, as God

201

intended for him to hold it ever since he was born."

'I rose therefore and followed St Andrew into the city dressed in nothing but my shirt. I passed unharmed through the streets of the Turks and he led me into the Church of St Peter the Apostle, which the Turks had turned into a mosque. Inside the church two lamps shed as much light as if the sun was pouring through. He told me to wait and commanded me to sit at the base of a pillar close to the steps leading to the altar. He went ahead of me and disappeared as if going down into the ground. He then emerged, bringing forth a lance, which he thrust into my hands. He said to me: "Behold the lance which opened His side from which the salvation of the whole world is come." I held it in my hands, weeping for joy. "Lord," I asked, "if it is Thy will, I shall take this and give it to the count." And he said to me, "Not now, for soon the city will be taken. Then come with twelve men and seek it from the same place I drew it from and where you shall find it again." And he put the lance back. After these things had happened, I was led back into the camp to my own tent. When I woke up, I reflected about the condition of my poverty, and I was too terrified to approach you. Anyway, it was the first day of Lent, around the of time of cockcrow, that St Andrew reappeared to me, in the same garb with the same companion, and a great brightness shone around them.

' "Are you awake?" St Andrew asked.

' "My Lord, I am not asleep."

' "Have you done what I have told you to do?"

'I replied, "Lord, I have prayed for you to send someone else to them. I am only a poor man, they will not believe me." He replied that God had

202

chosen Peter Bartholomew from amongst all men as a grain of wheat is gathered from chaff because he could see in me merit and favour.' Peter then explained how this message comforted him, though he had still remained silent, until now.

The news of Peter Bartholomew's vision spread through the city, as did his offer to test the truthfulness of his message by going to the Church of St Peter and searching for the lance. Other visionaries came forward recounting similar tales. Soothsayers and conjurors recalled the meteor that had fallen over Antioch, the earthquake, and how heavenly warriors had been seen amongst their ranks.

Eleanor listened with interest. She tried to entice Theodore into conversation but he simply pressed his finger against her lips and would not be drawn. Hugh and Godefroi acted likewise. They were now both desperate, urging the count to go to the newly converted Church of St Peter the Apostle and search for the lance.

'It is our only hope,' they whispered. 'If that is found, the great relic will be our rallying call.'

At last the count agreed. Accompanied by Theodore, Hugh, Godefroi, Peter Bartholomew and others, he went to the Church of St Peter; this was cleared of worshippers, though people gathered around the doors, the crowd increasing as word spread through the city. Paving stones were raised, and the spot the visionary had pointed out was feverishly searched, but nothing was found. Count Raymond left St Peter's to jeers. Hugh, Godefroi and Peter Bartholomew, however, continued to dig. Theodore told Eleanor what happened next. They had cleared the earth, digging deep, when Peter Bartholomew himself stepped into the pit wearing only his shirt. He knelt for a while offering solemn prayers to God, and a short while later, dislodging a rock in the wall of earth around him, put his hand in and drew out the spear head, the sacred point of the holy lance. He kissed this and held it up.

'A sign!' he cried. 'God wills it. We have God's approval.'

The news of the finding of the holy lance swept through the city. A sign had been granted! A miracle had taken place! The leaders immediately met in council and voted that Bohemond should take command of the entire army for the next fifteen days. Adhémar ordered three days of prayer and fasting as well as processions through the streets, invocations, litanies and masses. Exultation now replaced despair. The Franks believed the Angel of Death had withdrawn. The army roused itself and prepared to leave the city to meet Khebogha in full battle. Eleanor, shaken from her lethargy, tried to join in the celebrations, but she and Simeon were kept close in the merchant's house. Eleanor did not object, as she did not wish to become a burden on the rest. A way forward was now open. They would have to fight or die a lingering death.

Eleanor admired her brother's cunning, though as she confided to Theodore, she was growing increasingly alarmed by Peter Bartholomew's change of character as he was lionised and revered amongst the Army of God. He waxed full of fresh visions, becoming the virtual mouthpiece of the Almighty. The leaders accepted the sacred lance but became increasingly jealous of Peter

Bartholomew's insistence that Count Raymond had been specially chosen by God to carry it. Hugh and Godefroi realised that their newly enhanced prophet had to be curbed. Quiet words of advice were given, and the sacred relic was formally handed over to Bishop Adhémar in a public ceremony. The leaders were satisfied, though Bohemond, raging around the city like a ravenous lion, was dismissive of the lance, more concerned about organising the army for battle. The Franks now numbered about twenty-five thousand, but only three hundred horses were fit for battle. Nevertheless, Bohemond intended to gamble, using tactics similar to those employed against Ridwan of Aleppo. Five divisions were organised. Those knights who could not ride were organised into tight phalanxes of foot. They were given strict lectures on the tactics of the Turks, the importance of staying together and of following the directions of their respective leaders. At first Eleanor could not understand why Bohemond, his yellow hair now cropped close, face all fiery, those strange blue eyes gleaming, became a constant visitor to their house in the Street of Incense. Stranger still, he brought precious food, baskets of bread and bowls full of sweet delicacies. The house had its own stable, and three horses, fairly plump and strong, were also brought in and given the best fodder. Eleanor noticed how she, Theodore and Simeon became the principal recipients of the food, secretly served once darkness fell, away from prying eyes.

On the Feast of the Birth of St John the Baptist, Bohemond, garbed in a stinking, stained leather hauberk and dark blue leggings, his Spanish boots all worn and scuffed, came to join them at the evening meal. He loudly proclaimed how St John was his patron saint and that he would celebrate the feast day. He came blustering into the house, clasping Hugh and Godefroi's hands, patting Simeon on the shoulder, embracing Theodore and giving Eleanor a fierce hug that lifted her off the ground, his unshaven stubble prickling her face. He dropped her as he would a bundle of cloth, then scratched the sweat beads on his neck.

'Lord knows how I'd love a woman thrashing beneath me, but don't tell that to the bishop!' Bohemond spread his hands and roared with laughter at his own joke. Then he plumped down on the cushions and gestured at the others to join him. His great hands broke the unleavened bread, stubby fingers searched out olives from the bowl, great white teeth tore the cooked quail flesh. Every so often he would gulp from his goblet and thrust it out for Simeon to refill. He burped and winked at Eleanor, then licked his fingers, leaned across and thanked her for the deliverance of the Twin Sisters tower.

'And Firuz?' she asked.

'Dead.' Bohemond pulled his face all solemn, eyes mournful. 'He was killed by mistake in the first foray.'

Eleanor caught a shift in those light blue eyes and wondered if Firuz had been marked out as too untrustworthy to use any further.

At last the great giant declared himself satisfied and clambered up to inspect, as he put it, his 'lovely lads' who guarded doors and gateways against any spy or eavesdropper.

'Not only from the Turks,' Theodore murmured.

206

'There's growing bad blood between Raymond and Bohemond over who will hold Antioch.'

'I heard that.' Bohemond came back into the room. He patted Theodore on the back and sat down on the cushions.

'But first, before we sell the bearskin, let's kill the bear!' He dipped his finger into his wine cup and on a white napkin drew a crude map of Antioch. 'Here is the citadel on Mount Silpius, held by the Turks. They can communicate with the enemy outside by raising flags as well as by messenger. Each of the main gates, St George, Bridge Gate, Duke Gate and St Paul's, is now besieged by the Turks. Further to the north lies Khebogha's main camp. They have about eighty thousand men to our twenty-five thousand. They must have heard about this bloody . . .' Bohemond checked himself, 'our sacred lance but they certainly don't know that we'll fight! Out tactics will be simple. The Army of God will deploy in five divisions. The first will be led by Hugh of Paris. He will swiftly sally out and attack the enemy, driving them off, creating time and space for the rest to leave.'

'By which gate?' Hugh asked.

'The entire army will leave by Bridge Gate. The northern French, under Robert of Normandy and Robert of Flanders will follow Hugh of Paris. Next, Godfrey of Bouillon commanding the Germans, whilst Bishop Adhémar will lead the Provençals.' Bohemond shrugged. 'I understand Count Raymond has not yet recovered from an illness. Tancred and I will lead the fifth squadron. Once we leave the city, we will deploy in a semicircle and advance across the plain, keeping the Orontes on our right flank, to confront Khebogha. I need not tell you the dangers of such a plan.'

'As we deploy,' Hugh declared, 'those Turks besieging the gates will attack our flanks and rear.'

'Worse,' Godefroi added, 'if Khebogha advances swiftly towards us, we'll be encircled and crushed.'

'Very good, very good,' Bohemond breathed. 'Yes, that's what I thought you would say, but the enemy will not expect us. Tancred and I will take care of any attack from the rear. The Turks on the other gates have to cross the Orontes. They will be loose, scattered, easy to brush off, more of an irritant than anything else. The main threat is Khebogha, but he has made a great mistake. Too wide a gap divides his main camp from Antioch. If we can leave, deploy, brush aside the outposts and aim like an arrow for Khebogha's army, we might seize victory. Our men are desperate yet inspired. They now realise it is either fight and be victorious or face certain death!'

Eleanor felt her stomach pitch, and a cool ripple of fear crossed her back. She could see what Bohemond was plotting. His plan was crude, simple but very effective. The Army of God would pour out of the city across Bridge Gate and form up on the plain outside. They would advance north, their right flank protected by the river. Those Turks surrounding each gate might attack, but they'd be taken by surprise. They would have to ford the river and would be reluctant to take on the main Frankish host. Those in the citadel could do little; fearful of treachery or betrayal, they would stay there until the battle was decided. However, if Khebogha moved his massive army and marched, the Army of God would simply be surrounded, trapped and annihilated. She glanced up sharply. Hugh and Godefroi refused to meet her eye. Theodore was staring down at the crude map as Bohemond tapped his fingers against it. Beside her, Simeon was shivering slightly.

'You have to convince Khebogha not to move,' she said. Bohemond's ice-blue eyes held hers. 'You have already begun that, haven't you?'

He nodded imperceptibly.

'How?'

'Very easy. One of my commanders was killed in the fighting around the citadel. We made great play of trying to reclaim his corpse, but eventually we were driven off. He was a good soldier.' Bohemond narrowed his eyes. 'A fighting man; he loved the sun, the wine. He'd marched east to make himself a great lord. He vowed that he would serve me in life and death, and he certainly did. I deliberately left a letter on his corpse. The Turks in the citadel will have read it and passed it on to Khebogha. In that letter to the Emperor Alexius, I reveal that I have been made commander of the Army of God, and that I intend to desert Antioch and leave Count Raymond to meet his fate.' Bohemond smiled. 'After all, the animosity between us is well known, as is the fact that we plan to march back into the Emperor's dominions.'

'So Khebogha won't move.' Simeon spoke up. 'He'll stay in his camp, where there is a supply of fresh water, away from the contagion around the city. He knows all he has to do is just sit and wait. His garrisons at the city gates will inflict damage on you, perhaps weaken your army . . .'

'Precisely.' Bohemond tapped on the table. 'And by the time we reach Khebogha, we'll be depleted, burnt by the sun, starving and thirsty. We may surrender, we may put up some resistance, but . . .' he shrugged, 'why should Khebogha come looking for us when we will come to him? We'll have to tramp under the sun, through the dust clouds, and suffer attack. He thinks he is the hunter just waiting to spring his trap.'

'How do you know Khebogha has read your letter?'

'Very simple,' Bohemond mused. 'He hasn't moved. He knows from his spies, not to mention the watch in the citadel, that we are massing ready to leave. Nevertheless, he has not moved his camp or even strengthened his outposts around the city gates. No, I think the letter is there; he's waiting. What we have to do,' he pointed at Eleanor, 'what *you* have to do, is convince him by giving him the precise time, date and place of our departure.'

Eleanor felt her breath catch in her throat, her skin abruptly soaked in sweat. She glared accusingly at her brother and Godefroi. They just stared back, and in that moment, Eleanor realised how much things had changed. What was important to them was not any blood-tie, kinship or former memories, only the future, the vision: Jerusalem! Everything, including herself, was simply a way of achieving that. She stared at Theodore. He looked more composed, though she was sure Simeon's teeth were chattering.

'How is it to be done?' she asked quickly. 'Why me?'

'The same as before,' Bohemond continued evenly. 'You, Theodore and Simeon. During the afternoon of the twenty-seventh of June, the day before we leave, you'll escape and ride towards

Khebogha. The night before, Theodore will have shot an arrow into the enemy camp carrying a message informing the Turks that he will desert the next morning, bringing vital information for the Atabeg Khebogha. You will leave on those three horses specially stabled and cared for; that is why you have also been given food. I want Khebogha to realise that you have been hiding in the city and decided to escape.'

'But they'll know . . .' Eleanor stammered, 'that we betrayed the Twin Sisters through Firuz.'

'Listen,' Theodore broke in. 'We have been chosen precisely because of that. This is our story. We fled the Army of God and sheltered with Firuz, who quarrelled with Yaghi Siyan. Firuz was the traitor. He held the towers, not us. He was the one who betrayed them to the Franks, so we killed him in revenge.'

Bohemond clambered to his feet, left the chamber and came back carrying two leather sacks. He undid the cord of the first and drew out a severed head. The face was a deathly hue, the eyes closed, the blood-spattered lips half open. Firuz! The severed skin at the neck was clotted a dark red. In the other sack was a second severed head that Eleanor vaguely recognised.

'Firuz's brother,' Theodore explained, 'killed in the nearby tower, also judged a traitor.'

'But he wasn't. I know that,' Eleanor insisted. 'Firuz acted on his own; he was fearful of being betrayed.'

'Of course,' Hugh intervened. 'Firuz and his brother were killed by mistake in the first affray when the blood ran hot. It was difficult to distinguish between friend and foe. However, both

211

heads will be presented to Khebogha as the two traitors who delivered Antioch to the Franks.'

'And he will believe that?' Simeon's voice was almost a yelp. 'That we, well fed, with plump horses, could hide in Antioch for over three weeks, then ride out with the severed heads of two traitors?'

'Why not?' Theodore insisted. 'Remember, Antioch is a sprawling city with orchards, parks, houses, cellars and passageways. Turks still shelter in the city, well armed, well fed, with treasure and food. They must have heard about Khebogha's approach. They know the citadel is still being held. All they have to do is hide long enough and deliverance will come. We are three such people. We hid as long as we could, then decided to escape. It's happening every day; why shouldn't we flee? The Army of God is depleted and starving.'

'The information we bring?' Eleanor asked, trying to keep her throat wet to avoid any show of fear. 'How did we gain that?'

'Quite simply,' Theodore shrugged, 'we are in Antioch. Armenians and Turks mill about the streets, the blood lust is over, we mingled with this person or that. Let's look at it from Khebogha's point of view: why should we risk coming to him as traitors? No, no, our story will be believed. Eleanor, if you do not want to come, do not. The same for you, Simeon. However, it would be more logical, more convincing if all three of us were to explain how, after the Twin Sisters fell, we went into hiding, managed to survive, mingled with the Army of God, were discovered and fled. Count Bohemond is correct. Whatever happens, Khebogha must not move.'

The questioning continued. Eleanor tried to hide her own anxiety under Bohemond's powerful scrutiny. She fully understood the logic of his plan. She'd heard the rumours of how people were deserting, fleeing, so why shouldn't they? Their explanation was convincing enough. It was well known that Turks were hiding out in the woods, valleys, parks and orchards of the city, well armed and dangerous.

'You will leave by a postern gate near St George,' Bohemond explained. 'You will be pursued and shot at but you will successfully escape. Once you are in Turkish hands, you'll be safe. If they believe your story, so will Khebogha. Well?'

Eleanor glanced at Simeon, who sat, eyes closed, rocking himself backwards and forwards, silently mouthing a prayer.

'I will go,' Eleanor whispered, 'but the Lord knows it's dangerous. What if, and I say this, what if Firuz told someone else? What if some Turk knows we helped him betray the Twin Sisters and that Turk is now with Khebogha?'

'No!' Theodore used his fingers to emphasise his points. 'The Twin Sisters fell during the dark. Only Count Bohemond, Hugh and Godefroi knew of our involvement; everyone else believes it was Firuz alone. On the night the towers fell, Simeon and Imogene were kept close. You, as I told you to, stayed in the shadows; the men who passed you that night were battle-crazed. I disappeared immediately with Hugh and Godefroi . . .'

'Were you preparing for this?' Eleanor half laughed.

'No,' Theodore replied. 'Preparing for failure,

213

the prospect that the attack on Antioch might be repulsed. We would have had to concoct some story, very similar to this, that Firuz was the traitor whilst we were true adherents of Yaghi Siyan.'

'I will come to Imogene in a moment,' Hugh interrupted. 'But apart from her, and possibly Beltran, only the people in this chamber know the real truth about the betrayal of the Twin Sisters. Firuz and his men are dead and we shall now use that to our advantage.'

Eleanor recalled the corpse sprawled across the threshold of the tower, blood gushing out in the dim light. She wondered if that had been Firuz, an accident? Or had he and others been deliberately killed by these ruthless men? Eleanor felt cold, detached.

'What if,' Simeon retorted, 'a spy in Antioch tells them the truth?'

'Which is?' Bohemond asked.

'That when the city fell, we rejoined the Army of God, who accepted us for what we were, heroes!'

Again that calculating look from Bohemond. Hugh and Godefroi just sat, shoulders hunched. Hugh chewed the corner of his lip as if he had already reflected on what Simeon had said and knew the answer.

'Who knows that you've been accepted?' Godefroi replied. 'You've sheltered in this house for the last three weeks. How many people know? Nobody except a few trusted members of the Poor Brethren of the Temple.'

Eleanor now realised why she and Simeon had been kept so close. Few people understood what had truly happened at the Twin Sisters; that had been a closely guarded secret.

'There may be a traitor,' Hugh spoke up, 'amongst our brethren, that's what Count Raymond thinks. However, remember that only the people in this room, together with Imogene, and possibly Beltran, know your full role in Firuz's treachery. I swear to this, since Antioch fell, both Beltran and Imogene have been kept under the closest scrutiny.' He smiled. 'I think they know that. Moreover, you will flee Antioch late on the afternoon of the twenty-seventh of June; we leave by Bridge Gate on the morning of the twenty-eighth. No spy will have enough time to send a message to Khebogha, whilst you will carry those heads as proof of the story you will tell. Why shouldn't Khebogha believe you?'

'We will go,' Eleanor whispered. 'It is dangerous, but what we face here is equally perilous. We can at least try.' She pointed at Bohemond. 'But, God willing and we reach Jerusalem, you must swear that whatever I want, whatever I ask for will be given. If not from you, my lord Bohemond,' she turned to her brother and Godefroi, 'then from you and Count Raymond.' All three solemnly agreed. Theodore looked surprised. Simeon murmured something about his freedom, lamenting the danger, then the meeting ended.

Two days later Theodore was ushered up on to a lonely stretch of the battlements near St George Gate. Bohemond's men, who should have been on patrol, were secretly and abruptly withdrawn. An arrow was shot into one of the wooden pillars of the bridge. A Turk ran into the pool of light thrown by a cresset torch. The arrow was snapped off and the man disappeared into the darkness.

Late the following morning, Eleanor, Theodore and Simeon slipped through the stinking streets towards a large park that bordered on the Gate of the Goat, a needle-thin postern door about sixty yards from St George Gate. Eleanor, sweat-soaked with apprehension, carried a set of panniers stuffed with her paltry possessions. She felt very alert, aware of everything and everybody: a dog sniffing at a corpse lying in the mouth of a dark alleyway, two soldiers fighting over a basket of wild plants and herbs, a group of young men and boys bloated with hunger.

They hurried down a dark path that cut through the park, Bohemond's men stood on guard beneath the trees. A short distance away, along a rocky gulley, others were clearing away the rubbish and pulling off the beams across the postern gate. The three horses were saddled; Hugh and Godefroi in full armour stood guarding them. They helped Eleanor into the saddle, whispered their love and good wishes, then, like some dream in the night, Theodore urged his horse forward. Eleanor went next, followed by Simeon, and their horses gingerly picked their way down the narrow gulley of loose shale. The postern door creaked open. An officer beckoned to them, then they were through. Theodore urged his horse forward, and all three cantered out along the winding path, galloping furiously towards the narrow bridge across the Orontes. Immediately the make-believe pursuit began, led by Hugh and Godefroi; soldiers, swords drawn, stumbled out through the gate, screaming and waving their weapons. On the battlements archers loosed shafts that passed dangerously close. Eleanor was aware of her horse at full charge, its head bobbing, hooves clattering. The air reeked of that horrid sweet-sour stench of corruption, and corpses and pieces of armour and weapons littered the ground.

The shouts behind them faded. Eleanor's horse checked itself, then followed Theodore's, iron hooves pounding the wooden boards of the narrow bridge then on to rocky ground, the grass dry and sparse. As Theodore swerved to the right, galloping along the river bank, shouts and cries echoed from the battlements. Theodore slowed down as a group of Turkish horsemen, cloaks swirling, thundered towards them. He reined in, Eleanor and Simeon behind, and quickly raised his right hand, palm extended, shouting loudly, repeating the same gasping words. The Turks surrounded them, eyes gleaming in white-cowled dark faces. Theodore's sword and dagger were quickly plucked from his war belt. Eleanor waved at the cloud of dust threatening to block her eyes and throat. Another shout, and an officer in gleaming breastplate and damascened helmet, blue cloak flying, galloped up gesturing with his gloved hand that the riders pull apart. The tension was almost unbelievable. The Turks were undecided what to do. The only thing that had saved the deserters was that they had been pursued from the gate and galloped directly towards the Turkish outpost. The officer reined in, pulling a scrap of parchment from the cuff of his sleeve. He thrust this at Theodore, who nodded, pointed back at the gates and spoke quickly, urgently, repeating the name Khebogha several times. Theodore acted the part of a deserter with vital news which his new-found allies must know. He spoke excitedly, as if

217

he was the possessor of all the deepest secrets of Count Raymond and the rest. He patted the two leather sacks tied securely to his saddle horn. Firuz's name was mentioned. Theodore turned, hawked and spat into the dust. The officer, taken in by the high drama, was convinced. He shouted at his men, Theodore's weapons were returned, then the officer led them off at a furious gallop, a moving wall of dust across the Antiochene plain.

They must have ridden about five miles before they reached the picket lines of Khebogha's camp. They slowed down as they entered the main lane leading to its centre. Eleanor's heart sank. Khebogha's army was the great horde of Asia. Chieftains and emirs had responded to their caliph's call to annihilate the Frankish invaders. Masses of foot soldiers thronged in their body armour, heavy cavalry with their helmets and mail hauberks, all armed with spear, dagger and curving sword, and of course everywhere those deadly Turkish archers on their swift, nimble mounts. As far as Eleanor could see stretched a veritable forest of tents and pavilions of different colours and fabrics. The army seemed well provisioned, situated close to a river and lakes. The horse lines housed great herds, all plump, sleek and glossy-coated. Along the ground nearby ranged row upon row of the high-peaked saddles so favoured by the Turkish bowmen.

They were told to dismount, then led to the Atabeg's tent, a gorgeous purple pavilion with silver ropes and golden tassels. The pavilion and its surrounding tents were cordoned off from the rest of the camp by a palisade, its double-gated entrance guarded by splendidly attired warriors in

218

gleaming armour. Inside were planted the Atabeg's standards and banners, fixed into spigots driven into the ground. Eleanor glimpsed glossy horses being trotted around by grooms. Scribes sat under awnings, writing trays on their laps. At the entrance to one vermilion-coloured tent stood a group of beautiful maidens, long black hair hanging down free, their golden skin swathed in diaphanous gauze veils. The sound of music and laughter echoed. Eleanor took heart at this. Khebogha had decided not to advance. He was confident enough, apparently viewing the impending battle as already won.

Khebogha's personal guards took Theodore's weapons. They were searched and then, with a soldier on either side, escorted into the cool, fragrant-smelling pavilion. Khebogha sat on a pile of cushions. He was a young man with an imperious, arrogant face, small black eyes and a hawkish nose above thin lips. He wore a white turban and a loose embroidered robe. He seemed more concerned with the chess set before him, jewelled ivory pieces on a lacquered board. He spoke angrily to his opponent, an old white-bearded man, then turned to greet his three visitors, who were forced to kneel just inside the entrance. Either side of Khebogha squatted his emirs. In the poor light all Eleanor could see were dark faces, coloured turbans, a flash of white or the glitter of silver or gold thread.

At first Khebogha was openly hostile. He pushed away the chess board and squatted, hands hanging between his knees, as he questioned Theodore. Eleanor calmed herself. Khebogha was arrogant; Theodore was very clever. He told the

219

Atabeg exactly what he wanted to hear. How Count Raymond was ill, the leaders of the Franks divided; they were bereft of horses, starving, weak, desperate for home and openly mutinous. They intended to leave Antioch by Bridge Gate just after dawn the following day and march north, not to do battle but to negotiate their way through into Byzantine territory. It would be, Theodore concluded triumphantly, a matter for Khebogha to decide whether they lived or died. The Atabeg openly rejoiced at this. He nodded vigorously, turning to his colleagues, intent on demonstrating that what Theodore had described was precisely his own perception. They must not move but let their forces outside the gates of Antioch harass the Franks. The main Turkish force must sit, wait and spring the trap. Voices were raised in dissension but Khebogha ignored these. A shadow moved to Eleanor's right. One of the Turks leaned forward as he salaamed and gave his advice to Khebogha. Eleanor caught her breath. Baldur! The handsome captain, the seducer of Asmaja, the real cause for the fall of Antioch. Theodore and Simeon had also identified him but kept their poise. Baldur, whatever his private thoughts, was apparently desperate to hide his own role in the tragic events of the Twin Sisters' fall. He dared not voice his suspicions without laying himself open to serious accusation. Seduction of a fellow officer's wife would be as heinous amongst these pious Muslims as it would be with the leaders of the Army of God. Antioch had fallen because of Baldur's lust; that would be regarded as his death warrant.

Simeon later whispered how Baldur, instead of attacking or criticising Theodore, had insisted that

Khebogha question the Greek on his own credentials. Theodore, as Eleanor later discovered, complied adroitly. He gestured at Eleanor, describing her as his wife. He then described their desertion from the Army of God. How they had been accepted by Yaghi Siyan and entrusted to the care of the traitor Firuz at the Twin Sisters tower. How Firuz had betrayed his post for paltry gain and how Theodore, consumed with rage, had killed both Firuz and his brother. At this point he pushed forward the two leather sacks a servant had placed beside him. The severed heads were exposed to murmurs of appreciation followed by curses directed at these grisly trophies. At this juncture Khebogha clapped his hands. Ice sherbet and saffron cakes were served to his visitors, whom he now called his guests. Theodore, Simeon and Eleanor relaxed. Food and drink had been served; they were accepted.

Theodore now waxed lyrical. He described how he had cut one of the ox-hide ladders Firuz had lowered, a detail known to the Turks, then explained how they had hidden in Antioch, seizing food and horses whilst sheltering in the dense park close to the Gate of the Goat. How they had mixed with the Franks and learned their plans until they had been discovered. Suspicions had been raised so they had no choice but to flee. Theodore did not describe himself as a convert to Islam or even willing to serve Khebogha but as a simple mercenary who'd realised the Franks were finished and needed to flee. In the end Khebogha nodded, clapping his hands, looking around at his companions. The decision was made. Let the Franks emerge from Antioch. They would be harassed by his outposts and then destroyed by his main army. Theodore, Eleanor and Simeon were allowed to withdraw. They were given a small tent within the royal palisade and settled down to await events. Eleanor spent a tense day and night sleeping fitfully, disturbed by the sounds of the camp; only later did she discover exactly what had happened.

Bohemond left Antioch as predicted, though what Khebogha did not realise was that the Franks were intent on a fight to the death. Negotiation and surrender were now regarded as total anathema. The Army of God spilled out of Bridge Gate. Every type of horse had been gathered and fed with whatever fodder could be found. Hugh of Paris swept ahead to clear away any obstacle; his archers unleashed intense volleys at the Turks, who retreated in shock at the brutal and unexpected assault. The Norman French under the two Roberts, Flanders and Normandy, followed, then Godfrey of Bouillon with the Germans. Adhémar of Le Puy led the Provençals. Next to the war-like bishop his chaplain carried the sacred standard, the Holy Lance, which, the bishop had proclaimed, would bring them total victory. Behind all these thundered the fifth squadron under Bohemond's blood-red standards. The execution of Bohemond's plan was exceptional. The Army of God swiftly formed a rough semicircle about a mile wide, one flank on the foothills to the west, the other on the river Orontes. Those Turkish squadrons besieging the city gates moved to harass the Franks. Reinhard of Toul, with phalanxes of French and German knights, turned to meet them, but not to defend; instead they attacked like a pack of ravenous wild dogs.

In his camp Khebogha calmly organised his army into two broad divisions. Standards and banners were unfurled. The holy cry went up: 'Allah is God! There is no God but Allah!' The devout Muslims, once this prayer was finished, rose from their cloaks and makeshift prayer carpets and donned their battle harness. The Turks had been assured that they would spring a trap and easily destroy the Frankish army for good. Unbeknown to them, a mass of desperate soldiers, also trusting in God, were tramping through the dust towards them. Traders and farmers, garbed in rags and armed with rusty meathooks and axes, marched steadily behind their leaders; some even walked hand-in-hand with their young sons. Priests clothed in the vestments of the Mass chanted prayers as they grasped cudgels and clubs.

The Turkish advance guard attacked the Franks on their right flank, setting fire to the dry weeds along the river bank. The Army of God, behind their sacred standard, simply walked through the fire, beating at the flames with their cloaks. The smoke billowed. Turkish horsemen galloped through it like wraiths, fierce spectres armed with spears and rounded shields. They were met by a savage assault which brought down both horse and rider; lance, spear, axe and dagger whipped through the air, clubs rose and fell, swords hissed and hacked. The Army of God suffered casualties, men falling from every type of wound; these were left on the ground with grass or wild flowers thrust into their mouths as their host for the last sacrament. They whispered their dying confessions to the breeze and passed their weapons to the more able.

The Turkish cavalry charged, but the Frankish infantry still held firm. Again the Turks attacked, then recoiled in horror as mounted grey shadows thundered through the battle murk towards them. Mailed knights, lances couched, smashed into the Turkish line. More knights appeared, lances gone, drawing their long death-bearing swords. Turks fell, to be swept up by the Frankish foot now surging forward. The ground grew slippery with blood. Men staggered around screaming, with intestines pierced or tumbling out, their throbbing wounds pumping blood. Then the hammer blow. Bohemond's scarlet banner appeared! The mailed giant led his elite fighters deep into the Turkish squadrons. The Army of God surged forward like some huge boulder crashing down a mountainside. The Turks became nervous and panic-stricken. The air rang with screams of *'Deus vult! Deus vult!'* Mailed horsemen exultantly chanted hymns and psalms. Knights even took off their helmets and flung them at the enemy. Heavenly riders were glimpsed fighting on the Frankish side. The first Turkish line shattered completely, then broke and fled.

In Khebogha's camp, Theodore had already moved Eleanor and Simeon to safety. In the confusion they seized their horses and raced out to hide in the dense shrubbery around the nearby lake. Back in the Turkish camp, chaos rather than strategy prevailed. The Atabeg was confused. The reports he was receiving could not be true. His second line was marshalled. The main army was scarcely moving forward when the first squadrons of Turkish cavalry came hurtling back screaming their fear, pointing over their shoulders at the swirling dust and those demons on horseback. Bohemond's scarlet banner came fluttering towards them. The two Turkish hosts mingled. Confusion and panic spread. The ranks dissolved. Command collapsed. Banners and standards fell. Officers were unable to give orders. The Turks started to fight amongst themselves, desperate to flee. Panic turned to flight as the Army of God, horse and foot, smashed into Khebogha's disorganised force. The Turkish leaders galloped off; their army followed. The Frankish host poured into the camp, spearing women, looting the food supplies, pillaging the gilded pavilions, ransacking the cedarwood chests and coffers, plunging their filthy hands into mountains of pearls and precious stones, dragging away the tapestries, gorgeous hangings and carpets.

By the time Eleanor and Simeon returned to the camp, victory was certain, Khebogha's defeat total. Bohemond and the other leaders had already set up court in Khebogha's pavilion. Theodore and Eleanor, with Simeon trailing behind, were ushered in to receive the leaders' grateful thanks. Goblets of wine and sherbet were thrust into their hands, along with soft sweet bread and strips of cooked meat. Bohemond was bellowing that whatever they saw they could have. Eleanor simply rested on the cushions. Theodore delivered his report and, once again, received the giant Norman's thanks, then they were dismissed. Eleanor begged to be taken somewhere safe and quiet. Officers were already beginning to impose order amongst the troop when Theodore's name was shouted. They turned and walked back. A

225

group of German swordsmen had a prisoner manacled between them, Eleanor recognised Baldur, his finery all torn. The Germans gestured at their prisoner, and one of them lifted a sword, making a mock show of cutting off Baldur's head. Theodore spoke quietly to them, and the Germans lowered their swords respectfully. Theodore beckoned Baldur to approach as Eleanor came up behind him.

'What is it, brother?' Theodore asked.

Baldur licked dirty, blood-caked lips. 'My life, brother. I suspected the truth yet I did not betray you.'

'True.' Theodore nodded. 'You did not.' He turned to the German officer. 'Give this man some bread and water, his weapons and a horse. Let him go. Count Bohemond will stand guarantor for him.'

The German spat into the dust, shrugged and gave the order. Before they led Baldur off, the Turk turned and walked back. He took off his belt and thrust it into Theodore's hands.

'When you find your traitor,' he whispered, 'hang him with that.'

Part 8

Marrat: The Feast of St Hilary, 13 January 1099

Regnavit a ligno Deus.
(God reigns from a tree.)

Venantius Fortunatus,
'Hymn In Honour of the Cross'

'Babylon has become the habitation of demons and the house of every foul spirit and the cage of every unclean and hateful devil.' Peter Bartholomew's voice boomed out across the Army of God camped outside the town of Marrat in northern Syria.

'Not Babylon,' Eleanor whispered. 'No demons there! All the devils have come to Marrat.' She sipped at the goblet of watered wine, then passed it to Simeon, who looked anxiously at his mistress-sister. Over the last six months he had come to love this eccentric Frankish lady. Eleanor was amusing and brave, though full of ideas and notions that bordered on the childlike. Simeon could never understand why she suffered such bouts of spiritual darkness. Didn't she know how, in this world, wicked men constantly bustled about, busy with their evil deeds? Had they not often talked about that? How there was little difference between Frank and Turk?

'Is it ending, Simeon?' Eleanor stared out at the flames licking the night sky above the city of Marrat. The evening breeze carried the exultant

227

yells of the mob as they tore down the city walls.

'I don't think so. At least we are journeying to Jerusalem,' Simeon added mournfully. 'Your brother and Lord Godefroi have seen to that.'

'Yes, yes, they have! If we have changed, so have they.' Eleanor wiped the smoky dust off her face. 'Both men act like monks, as faithful to their rule as a Benedictine to his abbey.'

'And Lord Theodore?' Simeon teased gently. 'He is as passionate in his courting of you as ever?'

Eleanor blushed and glanced away. She picked up parchment and quill from the writing desk Simeon had looted from Khebogha's camp. The scribe smiled to himself. He suspected she would do that, to distract both herself and him. Yet she must, Simeon reflected, keep writing this chronicle. After all, so many others, including Raymond of Aguilers, chaplain to Count Raymond of Toulouse, were keeping theirs. Simeon hoped to win lasting fame through his account, or should it really be that of Eleanor de Payens? Ah well, he shrugged, the chronicle was the important thing.

'Lord Theodore?' he whispered, but instead of turning to the matter in hand, Eleanor continued to stare into the night. She and Simeon had composed their own secret riddle. According to this, mankind was divided not between Turk, Orthodox, Armenian and Byzantine but between those who were religious and those who were truly human. Those truly human might not be religious, whilst those who were religious might not be truly human. The first part of the hypothesis described Theodore: courteous, courageous and, if the truth be told, totally cynical about church religion, and even more so about the leaders of this so-called

228

Army of God. Eleanor also realised that Theodore loved her, and if only she could escape from this bloody mayhem, she would reflect on that as well as her own feelings for him. She breathed in deeply. She really must clear her mind! So much had happened since Khebogha's defeat. She turned to Simeon.

'Are you ready?'

'The great victory at Antioch,' Simeon murmured.

Ah yes, Eleanor reflected. If the Turks were overwhelmed by their utter defeat outside Antioch, so were the Franks by their miraculous success. The only explanation for their victory must be the presence of the Holy Lance, which had drawn down on to the Frankish side St George and the whole heavenly host. Hymns of praise were sung, battle psalms chanted, paeans of praise recited amidst the glorious words of the countless Masses offered in thanksgiving. Khebogha and all his might, both horse and rider, had been overthrown like Pharaoh and his chariots in the Red Sea. The season of want gave way to a season of plenty. Loot was collected, plunder piled, horses taken, food stocks replenished. Khebogha's camp was brutally stripped as bare as locusts would a vineyard or an orchard. Once they'd accomplished this, the Army of God moved triumphantly back to Antioch. The commander of the citadel surrendered to Count Raymond, who had been too ill for the battle but who recovered swiftly enough to send his banner into the citadel. Bohemond hastened back as if he suspected Count Raymond's secret plan to seize the entire city. The commander of the citadel promptly sent the Provençal's banner back, accepted Bohemond's and, at least publicly, converted to Christianity.

The Frankish victory at Antioch soon deepened internal divisions. The rivalry between Bohemond and Count Raymond intensified. Bohemond saw himself as the victor over Khebogha, but Count Raymond, to whom the Holy Lance had been entrusted, promoted himself as the real cause of the Atabeg's downfall. Bohemond, however, declared publicly that he didn't give a horse's turd about divine signs or holy lances. Khebogha had been defeated by his knights! He seized the citadel and other fortifications, whilst Count Raymond occupied the governor's palace and, most importantly, Bridge Gate, which commanded the road to the port of St Simeon and the sea. Neither was prepared to give way or concede an inch. A council was called but the two men were unable to agree, each reluctant to advance on Jerusalem until the ownership of Antioch was settled. A proclamation was issued covering up these differences, pointing out that the hot weather made any immediate march south impossible. The army would stay in Antioch until the Feast of All Saints, 1 November.

The Army of God, exhausted and depleted, accepted this, but as the weeks passed, resentment over the delay deepened. Bishop Adhémar, furious at such rancorous bickering, concentrated on purifying Antioch, as corpses still rotted in gulleys, alleyways, houses and cisterns. The Basilica of St Peter had to be reconsecrated and the Greek patriarch John IV formally installed. Nevertheless, God appeared to have turned his hand against his self-proclaimed army. A mysterious, virulent plague born out of the miasma and foul air from all the unattended corpses ravaged the city. An entire troop of German reinforcements, together with the crew of the ship on which they had sailed, arrived in Antioch only to be wiped out to a man. On 1 August, Adhémar himself died. According to a vision received by Peter Bartholomew, the revered bishop's remains were to be buried in St Peter's basilica where the Holy Lance had been found. Peter also proclaimed how Adhémar had personally appeared to him in a vision, full of remorse that he had once doubted the veracity of the Holy Lance. Indeed, Peter confided, Adhémar had only been saved from the fires of hell because of a candle he had lit as well as a donation he had made towards the Holy Lance. Peter's message was clear: his vision was a solemn warning from beyond the grave not to doubt the sanctity of the great relic or the fact that heaven's favour rested on its owner, Count Raymond of Toulouse.

The other leaders refused to be impressed and turned to their own affairs. Raymond Pilet, a leading Provençal noble, went foraging, as well as trying to impose the Christian faith through the sword on the terrified inhabitants of the surrounding countryside. Hugh of Paris journeyed to meet Emperor Alexius in order to ask for his assistance. Hugh, however, was exhausted, and decided to remain in Constantinople, later returning to France. Other leaders, with an eye to a quick profit, played upon the fears and jealousies of local Turkish rulers. The Frankish lords offered their soldiers and swords as mercenaries and left Antioch like hawks, hooded and eager for prey. Some were successful, others were not. Fulbert of

Bouillon, accompanied by his pretty young wife, journeyed to join Baldwin, who had seized Edessa. A squadron of Turks sent by the ruler of Arzen ambushed them, and Fulbert lost both his head and his wife, who was promptly married off to one of the Turkish leader's lieutenants. A great beauty, skilled in bed, Fulbert's lovely widow persuaded her new husband to convince his emir, Omer of Arzen, to call in Godfrey of Bouillon to check Ridwan of Aleppo, that old enemy of the Army of God. Godfrey hastened to comply, seized great riches, then deserted his new-found ally, to the murderous fury of Ridwan.

Eleanor, lodged in the comfortable merchant's house, could only watch and reflect as the Army of God began to fragment. Many of the Poor Brethren, and other contingents such as the Beggars' Company, were now dead or missing. The Beggars, who did not know the true fate of their leaders, merged with Tarfur, leader of the Ribalds' Company from Paris, a wild rabble always at the forefront of any excess. Hugh and Godfrey now hastened to mend bridges with the Beggars. They openly described the desertion of Jehan the Wolf and his two lieutenants as a blasphemy, whilst secretly ensuring that the remnants of that band of ruffians were always well provisioned with food and drink. Hugh's relationship with Count Raymond, on the other hand, cooled considerably. Hugh blamed the count for the Army of God's inaction and angrily criticised Peter Bartholomew's prophecies. He was also eager to tempt others to his side as leadership amongst the Franks disintegrated. Men began to leave one troop to join another. Hugh did his best to attract the best to himself. He believed passionately that the survival of both himself and Godefroi through all the horrors was a sure sign of God's approval for their plans and vision. He remained courteous and friendly towards Eleanor, highly appreciative of what she had done, but he was, as Theodore described, 'always looking towards tomorrow'. Hugh and Godefroi had both grown more distant and stern during the long campaign. They acted more like twins, the closest of blood brothers, already drawing up plans for when Jerusalem was taken.

Both knights kept well away from the women of the camp, including the beauties captured from the Turks. Theodore suspected the pair might even be monks, secretly sworn to vows of poverty and chastity in obedience to their vision. He often wondered if they had persuaded the Bishop of Orange, now the religious leader of the Army of God after Adhémar's death, to ordain them priests. They certainly remained warriors, fierce in battle, expert swordsmen highly skilled with lance and bow.

The Poor Brethren of the Temple, which had left Provence with such high hopes, was now more of a loosely knit contingent than a brotherhood. At Antioch it was replaced by a confraternity of knights whom Hugh and Godefroi attracted to their standards. They adopted a new banner fashioned out of an altar cloth displaying a red cross on a white background. They wore the same insignia on their left breast or the shoulder of their great cloaks. The knights who joined them accepted the published rule, though Eleanor was amused at a debate about whether they should shave their heads and faces or let their hair and beards grow. In the late autumn of 1098 the latter was accepted, though the unkempt appearance of the new brotherhood belied their military skills. They went on raids, tightly organised squadrons under the iron-hard discipline of Hugh. They took prisoners and treated them honourably. The violation of women captives was strictly forbidden. All possessions were to be held in common, every item of plunder handed over to the common treasury under Godefroi. They took over one of the small towers near Bridge Gate, which they renamed the Portal of the Temple, a name also shared by their brotherhood. Here they observed the horarium of the Benedictine order: morning Mass, celebrated by Alberic and Norbert, who acted as their chaplains, followed by the divine offices of Matins, Lauds and the rest. These knights also changed their attitude towards the leaders, distancing themselves from the rivalry of the Normans under Bohemond and the Provençals under Count Raymond and spending a considerable amount of time helping the poor amongst the Army of God. The Brotherhood of the Portal of the Temple set up a hospital as well as a common refectory serving food and drink to all comers. They even had their own exchequer for the distribution of money, an almonry for the weak and infirm, and an armoury for those bereft of weapons. They helped women, particularly widows or those on their own. They excluded these from the brotherhood, although they accepted able-bodied men as squires, pages and servants.

Hugh and Godefroi worked like men possessed, rarely returning to the house except late in the evening. Quite often they'd stay in the dormitories established in their own tower. They truly believed that God had a plan for them and that their secret vision had kept them safe. Tens of thousands had died, but they, Eleanor, Theodore, Alberic and Norbert were, apart from petty wounds and mild sicknesses, miraculously preserved, as were those on the edge of their company such as Imogene and Beltran, who were now living openly as man and wife. Moreover, the danger from the Magus, that sinister relic-hunter, and those fanatics the Fedawi appeared to have receded. Theodore agreed with this, arguing that perhaps all had been killed, either in battle or by sickness. Simeon thought differently. He was fascinated by the stories about the Fedawi being amongst them and found it difficult to accept that they would send emissaries so far away from their lonely hilltop fortress. However, he, Eleanor and Theodore were in agreement that Baldur's ripping off of his belt and throwing it in the dust with the words: 'hang your traitor with that' was truly puzzling, a possible reference to the fact that their secret opponent, or opponents, might only have disappeared for the time being.

In the late autumn of 1098 the harvest Hugh and Godefroi had sown began to sprout. A new faction or party emerged opposed to both Normans and Provençals, a movement that included the common mass, the poor of the Army of the God. They called themselves the 'Jerusalemites' and their message was stark and simple: enough time had been wasted in Antioch squabbling over plunder; the army should march on Jerusalem immediately. The surge of protests, managed skilfully by Hugh

235

and Godefroi, intensified. Peter the Hermit joined their ranks and became the Jerusalemites' eloquent mouthpiece throughout the city. Eventually they forced the leaders to return to Antioch from their various foraging campaigns. The army lined the streets and cheered as the Great Ones trooped back into the city, their carts piled high with plunder, followed by long columns of Turkish prisoners with the severed heads of their comrades tied around their necks. Nevertheless, the Jerusalemites soon forced the council of leaders to meet and Peter the Hermit stated their cause.

'Since the Lords are restrained by fear or other reasons, or by their promises to the Emperor, from leading us to Jerusalem, we, the people, shall elect from amongst us men-at-arms, people brave and faithful in the service of the Lord, with whom we will go on. Does it not trouble the princes,' Peter proclaimed, 'our lords, that we have delayed here for a year and that thousands of armed men have died here? Those who want to stay and gather gold, let them stay! Those who want Antioch, let them have it! We, however, shall set out on the road. Those who stay here will perish without doing any good, just like those who died here in the past. Indeed we have every day so many disputes in Antioch that we shall tear down its walls in order to restore the peace we had before the city was ever taken. Instead of being weakened by hunger and quarrelling, we ought to return to our pilgrimage.'

The lords of the council could not resist such a plea. The decision was made and a compromise reached. In November 1098 the army marched deeper into Syria, intent on taking Marrat en Numan a vital fortress controlling the routes further south. Marrat was a well-fortified town dominated by its blue-domed mosque on a great hill which stared out as the Army of God camped down amongst the olive groves beyond the city walls. The Franks set up their tents and bothies, covered with desiccated vine twine for protection, then watched and waited. Marrat was certainly well defended, with its formidable curtain wall, towers and deep dry moat. The Turks were not fearful; they had beaten off previous forays by the Franks and they thought this would be no different. The entire population of the city crowded along the battlements, cursing the Franks, railing at their cowardice and festooning inverted crosses over the walls. This provoked the desired response. The Army of God immediately attacked, bridging the dry moat and setting up flimsy ladders against the walls. These were easily destroyed, and the Franks withdrew and settled down to lay siege.

November gave way to December. Cold, hard rain rotted their tents, drenching depleted food stocks. The Franks, Eleanor included, were forced out into the fields, grubbing and scratching to find grains of wheat, barely, lentil or any other vegetable. Peter Bartholomew came into his own. Posing as a new John the Baptist, he accused the Army of God of countless filthy sins: murder, pillage, theft, rape and adultery; these, he argued, were the true cause of their present misfortunes. He urged that they purify their souls through the sacraments, prayer and the giving of alms. His comrades agreed, then swiftly turned to more practical matters.

The walls of Marrat were too thick to be battered, so the besiegers could either go over them or under. The Franks first tried the latter. They filled in part of the dry moat and their sappers crossed, only to be met by boulders, darts, bundles of fire, even pots of lime and hives full of angry bees. The sappers retreated and the Franks thought again. Raymond of Toulouse, assisted by the Portal of the Temple, ordered his troops into the nearby olive groves. Wood was swiftly hewed and a massive siege tower built which could be rolled forward on four great wheels. On the top Everard the Hunter, Raymond of Toulouse's chief verderer, armed with his horn, directed the knights who, in full armour, pushed the tower towards the wall. At its base sappers crept forward to tunnel under the wall to weaken that section. The Turks met this with catapult shots and sheets of fire. The knights on top of the tower responded by hurling lances, clubs and boulders as well as great hooks on iron chains to circle the battlements and so drag the tower closer. Behind them a long line of white-vestmented priests beseeched God to help the tower wreak bloody havoc on their enemies. Meanwhile, on the other side of the town, another phalanx of knights crossed the ditch, laid siege ladders against the walls and stormed up. The Turks panicked, drawing men away from the attacking tower. This edged closer, part of the wall collapsed and the Franks poured into the city just as darkness fell. The Frankish leaders ordered a pause, reluctant to engage in night fighting. The poor, however, starving and furious, led by Tarfur and his Ribalds, swept through Marrat pillaging and killing to their hearts' content. Bohemond,

238

who had also agreed to accompany Raymond, offered to accept the surrender of some of the city leaders, ordering them to assemble in a certain place for their own protection. However, as dawn broke and the leaders became aware that wholesale plundering had already begun, Bohemond had the Turkish leaders stripped of their possessions. Some were executed and the survivors hurried back to Antioch to be sold as slaves.

Marrat fell victim to general sack and pillage. No quarter was given. To walk the streets was to tread on a carpet of corpses. The Turks fled to caves beneath the ground but the Franks pursued them, pouring in sulphur and fire to kill them before going down themselves to search for any plunder. The Turks fought desperately, some even committing suicide rather than surrender. Marrat fell, and as Peter Bartholomew trumpeted, '*What a fall!*' Once again the Frankish leaders met to quarrel over who owned what. Meanwhile the rest of the army were reduced to desperate means as food supplies swiftly disappeared. The corpses of Turks had been ripped open to search for coins and gems they might have swallowed. Now rumours were rife that some Franks, tormented by the madness of starvation, were cutting pieces of flesh from the buttocks of these dead Turks which they cooked and ate, even devouring them in their frenzy before they were sufficiently roasted. Other rumours claimed that Turkish corpses, dumped in the nearby swamps, were being dragged out in order to satisfy the excruciating pangs of hunger. Yet still the leaders quarrelled. Eleanor, Simeon and Theodore survived on strips of tough goat flesh and thick soups concocted from various plants and seeds, whilst Hugh and Godefroi led out foraging parties though with little success.

On the Feast of the Epiphany 1099, Hugh showed his hand openly. Through his brethren, as he now called them, he organised a general assembly. The Army of God massed before the gates of Marrat surrounded by a ring of flaming bonfires. For an hour Hugh, his voice strident, harangued them, arguing that they should leave Marrat immediately for Jerusalem. The Bishop of Orange had recently died, and if there were no other leaders, he, Hugh de Payens, would take them south. However, he still wished their leaders to accompany them. If there was no Marrat, there would be no quarrelling, so they must destroy the city. The rank and file roared their approval and went on an orgy of destruction. Houses, mosques and temples were fired. The walls were weakened, the defences razed. Count Raymond hurried from his quarters to see the effects of such destruction. He had, at least publicly, a change of heart. Marrat, he promised, would be devastated and left deserted, whilst he, barefoot, clad only in a pilgrim's gown, would lead them south to Jerusalem.

Part 9

Arqa: The Feast of St Godric, 21 May 1099

Fulget crucis mysterium.
(The mystery of the cross blazes forth.)

Venantius Fortunatus,
'Hymn In Honour of the Cross'

'I have loved O Lord the beauty of thy house and the place where thy glory dwelleth.' The Army of God sang these verses as they poured down the hill past crumbling buildings towards the land of Christ's birth. The Christians of the locality, stirred up by Syrian monks from their small monastery around the Church of the Virgin, snatched up crucifixes and Ave beads to greet them. The Franks camped in a village only a few miles from Arqa. The army, now about twenty thousand souls, were jubilant, none more so, Eleanor wrote in her chronicle, than Hugh and Godefroi, who, once again, had forced the great lords to act. The Portal of the Temple, the leaders of the Jerusalemites, were now a power in the land. Jerusalem had to be taken swiftly. The Holy City had recently been seized by a new force dispatched by the Caliph of Cairo, the leader of the Fatimid sect of the Turks. He had sent his troops across Sinai to occupy Jerusalem, but the Army of God did not care. The Turks, whatever their name or origin, would be defeated. Jerusalem would be taken. They had to march swiftly. Now was the season when they could snatch crops from the ground, grain from the fields before the sun grew too hot and the earth became parched. Now was the time to march. Thousands of them had left Marrat, following the coast road. They went on foot, spears and packs on their shoulders, without baggage or carts; behind them trailed loaded camels and ox carts, but such things were not important. Jerusalem was their prize.

The hope of a swift march on the Holy City had been cherished by all when they left Marrat in February. At first Count Raymond and the other leaders seemed to have learned their lesson. Heaven now smiled on their venture. They entered southern Syria, part of ancient Canaan so the wise ones claimed, a land flowing with milk and honey especially during springtime. A countryside of deep purple hills and rolling grasslands, cut by ochre-coloured ploughland. Squat whitewashed cottages, with canvas and matting across their doorways and windows, nestled amongst black basalt rocks covered with golden-brown lichen. A land richly endowed with the plump silver-grey olive, shady tamarisk, blooming oleander, juniper and wild myrtle. Flowers of vivid hue caught the eye. Cloud shadows raced across the countryside where lavender-coloured rocks gave way to beds of primroses. Cool, fresh breezes ruffled the lush grass and brought the fragrance of cedar groves and dark pine, which also provided good shelter against the sun. At night the moon shone the pure yellow of primrose. At daybreak the sky became a festival of fast-changing colours. A rich land where cattle, sheep and goat browsed as thick as bees. A strange land too, dotted with ghost cities, ruins

242

from ancient times, their crumbling walls and vaulting gateways still guarded by evil-looking creatures carved out of stone. As they travelled further south, the Franks glimpsed the distant cap of the Mountain of Snow and stared wonderingly up at the lowering blue skies against which stretched the black stems of palm trees with their fan-like branches. Streams, springs and wells gushed in abundance. Water wheels clacked and the sweet smoke of cooking fires, rather than the acrid fumes of burning homes, teased nostrils and throats already pleased by the fragrance of acacia and azalea.

The inhabitants were friendly, eager to trade; many of them were Syrian Christians belonging to strange covens such as the Copts or Maronites. The news of the Army of God's great victories, the deeds of these ferocious iron men had preceded them; word of the defeats of Ridwan, Yaghi Siyan and Khebogha swept before the Army of God like a herald. Hugh, now speaking as vox populi, urged Count Raymond to treat with local rulers and show benevolence to all. Such diplomacy worked: the Emir of Shazir greeted them amicably, as did the ruler of Homs. On the Feast of the Purification of Mary, the army occupied the deserted town of Raphania, with its gardens full of vegetables and houses crammed with provisions. They rested there and took council. They could journey inland and lay siege to the sprawling city of Damascus, or continue to strike south-west along the coast. Hugh persuaded Count Raymond to adopt the latter course, arguing that the coastal route was easier, and they would also be able to maintain closer communication with cogs bearing provisions, which would accompany them on their march. Where possible, Hugh insisted, they must avoid battle and hardship. Count Raymond agreed. The Army of God marched down the coast of the Middle Sea. They faced some opposition. Turkish patrols from various isolated fortresses attacked the stragglers until the Portal of the Temple took action. They withdrew from the order of march and hid, watching the stragglers of the army go limping by. The Turks attacked, only to be furiously ambushed by Hugh's brotherhood, who circled them and utterly annihilated them.

Count Raymond continued his march. He seized certain hill forts and eventually decided to lay siege to the great fortress of Arqa. He hoped that if this fell it might attract back Bohemond, Godfrey of Bouillon and Robert of Flanders, who had not joined his march south. He believed Arqa could be taken easily. He was wrong. The Turkish defenders displayed superb bravery, engaging in ferocious forays against the Franks. Savage duels took place between the huge catapults of the city and those brought south by the Army of God. Pots of fire, bundles of flaming wood, pitch and brimstone were loosed to explode in a fiery blaze against the tents and huts of the besiegers. Raymond of Toulouse still believed the city could be taken and decided to teach the Turks of the area that he was to be feared. Hugh and Godefroi argued against this, but the count was adamant. He threatened the great ruler of nearby Tripoli by sending a raiding party to seize the neighbouring port of Tortosa. The ruler of Tripoli was suitably impressed and handed over a string of horses and ten thousand gold bezants. Godfrey of Bouillon and Robert of Flanders heard of this and hurried south to join Raymond, who had to use his new-found wealth not only to pay the warlike Tancred, who'd deserted his uncle Bohemond, but also to reward Godfrey and Robert.

One trouble followed another. Arqa refused to fall. News arrived that the Emperor Alexius had written instructing Count Raymond not to move any further south until he joined the army for the final march on Jerusalem. Peter Bartholomew, ever under Raymond's wing, emerged with more decrees as to how the Army of God should purge itself anew. Deep resentment festered. Fierce discussion took place. Representations were made that they had left Marrat with one aim, to march directly on Jerusalem, yet once again were delaying. Hugh and Godefroi discussed all this when they gathered for a special council meeting in Theodore's tent. Alberic and Norbert, gaunt-faced and zealous-eyed, later joined them, as did Beltran.

It was a balmy night, as Eleanor later reflected, one on which she and Theodore were accustomed to walk out of the camp to savour the thick, heavy smells of early summer away from the raw stench of camp fires, cooking pots, latrines, and the pervasive reek of filthy clothes on dirty bodies. Theodore was swiftly replacing Hugh as Eleanor's confidant. He did not lecture but persuaded her to talk, and she did, more frankly and honestly than in any shriving pew. Theodore encouraged her to discuss the past. Eleanor realised how the haunting death of her drunken, violent husband had receded during her journey. Sometimes weeks passed without her thinking of it. Now, however, as

245

Theodore paid court and they drew closer to Jerusalem after all the horrors of the campaign, Eleanor recalled the past. She spoke about the changes she'd undergone, the growing distance between herself and Hugh, the coolness of Godefroi, and how she had eventually found peace from her own scruples. She'd become firmly convinced that her husband had brought his own death on himself. If she was guilty in any way, then she had certainly purged such guilt. After all, how had she provoked her husband's raging fury, his foul mouth and violent ways? Moreover, what was his death compared to the thousands of innocents massacred on either side in this so-called Holy War? In the end, the journey east had not been what Eleanor had even remotely expected. Yet she was here because she was here and there was no turning back. True, the journey's end was in sight, but how would Jerusalem make her, or anybody else, more human or holy? If anything, she confessed to Theodore, the pilgrimage had purged her soul of so much rubbish. If they reached Jerusalem, if she survived, she would have no more part in the pursuit of visions; she would begin again, build her own world and shelter in it as securely as any nun would in her cell.

Theodore never disagreed. The pair of them took to riding away from the filth of the camp, the noise and rattle of the siege around Arqa. They'd gallop out into the countryside, searching for some whitewashed cottage with its animal pens, flower plots and vegetable gardens. Theodore would sit beside her on the grass and describe how his early life had been in such a place as this and how it had always been his dream to search it out again.

246

Eleanor listened as the door to her past shut tight behind her. There would be no return to Compiègne. No more agonising over the death of her husband or sharing some heavenly vision with Hugh and Godefroi. Once Jerusalem was taken—*if* Jerusalem was taken—her vow would be fulfilled and a new path waited to be followed.

Eleanor recalled her promise to herself when Hugh convened his meeting: her brother was now a power to be heard, a recognised leader, and he delivered his proclamation in authoritative, blunt words: Godfrey of Bouillon and Robert of Flanders had rejoined the Army of God, which was now a force about twenty thousand strong, at the very most. The siege of Arqa was draining resources and should be abandoned, whilst the Caliph of Cairo's great army was marching to Jerusalem's defence.

'How do you know that?' Beltran asked, blustering uninvited into the tent, Imogene trailing dolefully behind him. Eleanor studied her closely. Imogene was gaunt and thin-faced, not due to any deprivation, just because she and Beltran were now quarrelling incessantly, though over what, Eleanor could not discover.

'How do I know that?' Hugh retorted. 'By an act of God. One of my brothers went out hawking; his falcon attacked a pigeon and, wounded, it fell. My brother found the pigeon carried a message in a small cylinder attached just above one of its claws.'

'Never!' Beltran scoffed.

'It's true. I've heard the same,' Theodore intervened. 'The Turks have trained pigeons to carry messages over long distances.'

'And the news?' Alberic asked.

'What I've told you. The message came from one of the Caliph of Cairo's fortresses in the south,' Hugh replied. 'The Egyptians are sending a great army to defend Jerusalem.'

Only the crackling of the fire and the drifting sounds of the camp broke the silence.

'This nonsense must stop.' Godefroi clambered to his feet, hands outstretched. Eleanor hid her smile. Hugh had arranged this, even though he stood face all pious as any novice in his choir stall.

'Our allegiance is to Count Raymond,' Alberic offered.

'Only to take Jerusalem,' Norbert murmured.

'If he will not go,' Godefroi continued fiercely, 'then we'll withdraw our love and loyalty from him.'

This was greeted by cries of approval.

'But the lance,' Norbert declared, 'Count Raymond holds the Holy Lance and his prophet Peter Bartholomew sees that as a sign from heaven, direct approval by God of all Count Raymond does.'

'But who said Peter Bartholomew is a prophet in Israel?' Hugh asked menacingly. 'Heaven can withdraw its favour and God His approval. Is that not true?'

Over the next few days Hugh's question was answered as Peter Bartholomew made the situation much worse. He was now experiencing new visions of Christ, St Peter and St Andrew, and the story he proclaimed was chilling. The Lord had instructed him how too many sinners sheltered in the Army of God and that these must be ruthlessly rooted out. Count Raymond of Toulouse should

248

summon the entire army and have them lined up as if in battle. Peter Bartholomew would then miraculously discover the Franks arrayed in five ranks: those in the first three ranks would be the devoted followers of Christ, but the last two would include those polluted by the sins of adultery, fornication, pride, avarice and cowardice. Peter announced that the Lord had instructed him to oversee the immediate execution of all such sinners. Of course this was viewed as a direct threat. Count Raymond was already unpopular. The siege at Arqa was dragging on, the message from Alexius asked them to delay even further, and now this.

Rumours emerged, spreading fast and furious like fire amongst stubble. How Peter Bartholomew was a charlatan and the so-called Holy Lance no more than a Turkish spear head; Peter Bartholomew himself, probably with the connivance of Count Raymond, had planted it to be found. The Franks were tired of Peter's peering into the dark in the dead of night and relating his wondrous stories. It was time he was tested. Arnulf of Chocques, chaplain to the Duke of Normandy, led the opposition. He and others began to ask questions, and due to the influence of the Portal of the Temple, these questions were now chanted throughout the camp. Why was the Holy Lance discovered by Bartholomew himself, alone in a pit in the dark, instead of being revealed in the open light to many? Why did these visions come to Bartholomew, a former frequenter of taverns and possibly a deserter from the army? Moreover, how did the Holy Lance come to Antioch? When did Pontius Pilate and his soldiers ever visit that city?

Why did no one except Peter Bartholomew experience these visions and know where the Holy Lance was buried? Not even Adhémar of Le Puy had made such claims. Indeed, the saintly Adhémar had been highly suspicious of the sacred relic.

So the argument ran. Many began to regard the Holy Lance as no more than a piece of treachery. Arnulf kept up the attack, growing more and more insistent, until eventually he provoked Peter Bartholomew, who rose in full council to defend himself.

'Let a great fire be built!' Bartholomew exclaimed. 'And I will take the Holy Lance and pass safely through such a fire. If the lance be the Lord's sending, I shall come through unhurt; if not, I shall burn to death!'

The ordeal by fire seemed to be the only just solution. The day was chosen: Good Friday 1099. Peter fasted and prayed. On the appointed day, a level stretch of land was prepared. Wood was piled loosely in the centre for a distance of about five paces. Soldiers crowded the slopes around to watch the ordeal, the army turning out en masse to witness God's judgement. Near the centre of the cleared space stood a group of priests, the official witnesses; these were barefoot, clad only in their vestments. Eleanor and Theodore, mixing with Hugh's comrades, went down to watch. Peter Bartholomew was led out and stripped of his outer garments. The dried olive tree branches were set alight. The pile of burning brushwood now stretched for about fourteen feet, divided into two heaps each about four feet high. Between these two piles a space of about a foot had been left. The

250

fire roared up. Raymond of Aguilers, chaplain to Count Raymond of Toulouse, addressed the army, his powerful voice carrying.

'If the Almighty God has spoken to this man face to face and the Blessed Andrew revealed the lance to him, he will pass through this fire without harm. If it is otherwise, however, then he is a liar! Let him burn and the lance that he carries in his hands.' The entire army knelt and roared back, 'Amen!'

The fire leapt higher, the heat spreading out. Peter Bartholomew genuflected, took the blessing of a priest then shouted in a loud, strident voice that God be his witness, he had not lied. He also asked the army to pray for him. The priest took the lance, wrapped in a linen cloth, and placed it into Peter Bartholomew's hands. The prophet rose and went straight into the fire. A bird flew over the flames, the heat singed it and the bird plunged down. Peter, however, passed through the first pyre, paused for an instant and then continued through the second. The uproar that greeted his unscathed emergence rang to the skies. Peter held up the lance, still wrapped in linen; it too showed no sign of singeing. He ran towards the people, shouting how the Lord had proven he was no liar. Theodore withdrew Eleanor, as a riot now threatened. People crowded around Peter Bartholomew. Eleanor never really discovered the truth of what happened next. Whether it was adulation from the mob or the work of some enemy, Peter received more damage from his so-called supporters than from the fire: his legs were broken in two or three places, and serious damage was done to his back. In fact he would have been torn to pieces had not Count Raymond's henchmen broken into the crowd, freed him and hurried him off to the hut of Raymond Aguilers. The mob, however, believing they had witnessed a great miracle, now turned on the fire, gathering up the coals and ashes as sacred relics.

Immediately various stories began to circulate about how Peter had escaped being burned by the fire, and witnesses called to inspect his face and body vouched for this. Others, however, said he had collapsed because of the heat. Whatever, the day after the test, Holy Saturday, Peter Bartholomew died of his injuries and was buried in the very spot where the ordeal had taken place. If Count Raymond of Toulouse hoped the miracle would silence opposition, he was wrong. The stories were still rife: Peter Bartholomew was a charlatan, the Holy Lance a fake. Desperately, Raymond tried to hold on to his authority, but already Godfrey of Bouillon, Robert of Normandy and Robert of Flanders were determined to take over the leadership, a task made easier by the likes of Hugh and Godefroi. The Army of God were tired of Arqa. Jerusalem waited. An Egyptian army was approaching. They should seize the Holy City immediately! As if guided by some invisible force, the army struck their tents, burned their huts and, chanting hymns and singing psalms, set their faces towards Jerusalem. Raymond of Toulouse still insisted on having the last word. His failure at Arqa had made the ruler of Tripoli think again: were the Franks so weak they couldn't take a mere hill fort? He sent out raiding parties. Raymond retaliated ruthlessly. The raiding parties were ambushed and their corpses sent floating down an aqueduct back into Tripoli, decapitated cadavers and severed heads bubbling blood from their jagged wounds.

Part 10

Jerusalem: The Feast of St Mary Magdalen, 24 July 1099

Tam sancta membra tangere.
(Then to touch the sacred limbs.)

Venantius Fortunatus,
'Hymn In Honour of the Cross'

The Army of God advanced relentlessly on Jerusalem. The Franks sang hymns and chanted favourite lines from the psalms such as: 'One day in your court is worth a thousand elsewhere.' They certainly did not sing that about the land they were passing through. Summer in all its scorching, blasting heat hammered the army. Swirling dust clouds closed in as swarms of stinging gnats and flies tortured their skin. They kept to the coastal road, a narrow, perilous passage. Thankfully no enemy waited to ambush them, even when they had to pass round a rugged promontory that jutted out into the sea, a highly dangerous place the local inhabitants called 'the Face of God'. They warned the Franks that they would have to go round this fearsome place in single file, and so they did, but safely. Similar narrow passes were forced. The Dog river was crossed, Beirut circled. The Army of

253

God swarmed over the fallen marble of once great palaces and swept under the magnificent yet crumbling arches built by the Romans until they reached Sidon.

Here they rested and took sustenance near the watering places. They cut honey-sweet reeds known as sucra, greedily sucked the sweetness and moved on to gape at the former glories of Tyre. They were entertained and advised by the local Christian Maronites about the journey south: how the coastal roads had few water supplies and still more narrow perilous passes. The Army of God, however, kept to the coast road, all eyes turned inland, fearful of that flanking attack by Saracens and Turks that might drive them into the sea. Water was scarce, whilst the sandy rocks were infested with snakes and basilisks terrifying in their strikes. Men, women and children, delirious for water, grubbed greedily, Eleanor amongst them, only to be attacked by venomous snakes that turned their bodies into fiery, tormented tongues of pain. The bites, Eleanor wrote in her chronicle, made some so desperate for water that they plunged into the sea and gulped the salt-soaked waves, which only increased their thirst.

At last the Army of God broke free of the infested terrain and camped on the bed of a river that was nothing more than shallow pools along a shale-lined gulley. They followed the gulley inland on to a rocky, dirt-strewn plain dotted with fig trees and date palms. In the far distance they glimpsed the white-walled town of Ramleh, set in a forbidding dry landscape of hard-baked clay, jutting rock and wind-furrowed sand. Despite all the hardships and thirst, the army advanced cautiously, but the gates of Ramleh proved to be undefended. They passed within its walls and stared round the dingy, dirty town. Little greenery could be seen; nothing but arid dust clouds blowing through the streets and across desolate squares. The local Maronites crept cautiously out to greet them and showed the Franks the entrances to underground cisterns that fed the great bathhouses. The Franks crowded in, drank their fill and went on to the White Mosque. The cedar gates and heavy roof beams of the mosque were all black and charred, burned by the retreating Turks lest the Franks use the wood to build siege machinery. The Army of God knelt on the marble floor of the mosque as the townspeople whispered that beneath it lay the bones of one of their great patrons, the martyr St George. The Franks promptly turned the mosque into a church and elevated Robert of Rouen as its bishop. They would have dallied even longer, but Hugh, Godefroi and the Portal of the Temple continued their whispering campaign: this was not Jerusalem; they should move on.

Hugh and Godefroi had withdrawn from Raymond of Toulouse, being seen more and more in the company of the fiery Tancred. They also entertained their own visionary, a novice monk, Peter Desiderius, who constantly warned the Army of God to move towards its real destiny—Jerusalem. Tancred, however, needed little encouragement. He repeatedly voiced his demand that the army move quickly, and so, on 6 June, they reached the ancient town of Emmaus, only a few miles west of the Holy City, the very place where the Risen Christ had met two of his disciples journeying from Jerusalem. The Army of God, Peter Desiderius proclaimed, taking up the thread, must also meet the Risen Christ in Jerusalem. Tancred was determined to fulfil that vision.

In the middle of the night of 6 June, Theodore slipped into Eleanor's tent and shook her awake. One hand across her mouth, he signalled with the other that she remain quiet. In the poor light Eleanor gazed across at Imogene, now fast asleep after returning to sob quietly to herself.

'Listen,' Theodore whispered, 'Tancred has been approached by Maronites from Bethlehem. They fear the Turks might fire the town. He and a hundred knights, including Hugh, Godefroi and myself, are riding there. Do you wish to come?'

Eleanor pulled herself up.

'We will see Jerusalem,' Theodore added.

Eleanor needed no further urging. She quickly prepared herself and joined Theodore waiting outside. Darkness was beginning to fade, the sky lightening as they hastened towards the horse lines. Lantern horns glowed; wisps of smoke from the first fires drifted across. The yip, yip of a lonely jackal echoed, a strange contrast to the voices of the gathering men as they recited verses from the psalms.

Once they had finished their Matins, the knights donned their chain mail and helmets; girdles and belts were strapped on, long swords slipped into scabbards. Shields and lances were brought forward. No one objected to Eleanor's presence. Some of the men nodded at her as they pulled on their loose linen robes, sure protection for their mail against the sun and dust. The war horses, all harnessed and ready, were trotted forward. The knights swung themselves into the saddle, leaning down to grasp lance and shield. Theodore positioned Eleanor, riding a small but sturdy palfrey, in the middle of the group. Tancred unfurled his scarlet and gold banner and the troop broke into a gallop, swiftly clearing the camp, leaving the lights of their picket lines winking behind them.

They thundered through the night, reaching Bethlehem in that murky twilight before dawn, riding past crumbling huts of stone, blank walls and dark alleyways. Dogs barked, the only sound as they reined in before the basalt-paved square stretching up to the Basilica of the Virgin Mary. The troop fanned out behind Tancred. The hooves of their horses clipped the stones, leather harness creaked, the jingle of mail echoed, followed by the ominous slither of swords being drawn from scabbards. Tancred, tall and dark in the saddle, cloak flapping around him, his gorgeous banner ruffled by the chill morning breeze, advanced across the square. He paused halfway and rose in his stirrups brandishing the banner.

'*Deus vult!*' he bellowed. '*Deus vult!*' The cry was taken up by his escort, a triumphant chant of praise. As if in answer, the bells of the basilica began to peal their message. Lights appeared at windows. Doors were opened. People thronged into the square to view these dark angels on horseback who had brought deliverance to Christ's birthplace. The double gates of the basilica were pulled back and the ancient patriarch of the town, flanked by Maronite monks carrying candles, crosses and lighted tapers, processed out to greet them even as the bells increased their clanging peals.

Tancred led his knights across the square. Eleanor dismounted and, with Theodore's hand on her arm, followed the rest through the door into the cavernous cold nave smelling sweetly of incense and candle smoke. The Franks knelt as the dawn Mass was celebrated and then withdrew, though not before Tancred had hoisted his banner over the basilica. He also left ten knights to ensure it remained in place. Eleanor felt as if she was dreaming. The cold, hard ride and that long, gloomy nave with its tessellated floor, icons, mosaics and wall paintings. She had visited the town of Christ's birth, and now they were riding through a narrow ravine that cut through the shadow-shrouded foothills leading to Jerusalem. They reached a plateau as the sky lightened, galloping past clumps of olive groves, stretches of pasture and ploughland. On the edge of the plateau the horsemen dismounted, holding the reins of their animals as they whispered, 'Jerusalem! Jerusalem!' to each other. The morning sun was rising fast behind them. Theodore and Eleanor walked to the edge. The hill below fell steeply. At the bottom lay a small church and beyond that stretched a deep, desolate gorge. On the far side of the gorge reared towering walls that seemed to have no gate. A dome gleamed above the walls, and further down from that, a squat white building caught the light of the rising sun.

'Jerusalem!' Theodore whispered.

Eleanor stared. No gold, silver or precious stones! No angel trumpet blast! No heavenly chorus! Nothing but a mass of masonry. A voice cried out, making her jump. She turned to look where others were pointing. In the far distance, along the broad thoroughfare leading to the city, she saw the glint of armour, the glitter of weaponry, the flashing colour of banners. The advance guard of the Army of God! Hugh gave a cry of triumph. No doubt the Portal of the Temple led the advance. The army was about to besiege Jerusalem.

The Franks camped before the Holy City on 7 June, the Year of Our Lord 1099. Tancred and the Portal of the Temple immediately scoured the surrounding hills, whilst the other leaders decided on what to do. Fierce debate raged for days. Hugh and Godefroi relayed the discussions to their own followers. Eleanor, escorted by Theodore and a group of mounted men-at-arms, inspected the Holy City, which, to all appearances, lay calm and watchful. Jerusalem's Egyptian commander Iftikhar commanded a garrison of Turks and Saracens twenty thousand in number, with an elite corps of Ethiopian warriors and almost five hundred of Egypt's best cavalry. The city, so the Franks learnt from spies, was well provisioned, with many underground water cisterns. The Franks were not so fortunate. Iftikhar had torched the land around Jerusalem, seizing or killing livestock and emptying granaries. Worse, he had also poisoned or broken all wells, cisterns and springs outside the city. Summer was at its height, the sun already scorching the bleak surrounding countryside. The only source of good water was the pool of Siloam to the south of the city, near the entrance to the Kedron valley at the foot of Mount Sion. A small lake, Siloam was only fed every three days by a spring and lay within an easy bowshot of skilful archers on the city walls.

Eleanor, even on her ride around the city walls, experienced a deep desperation. The sun was relentless, whilst along the battlements flashed the glint of armour and the shiny iron-weighted cups of the catapults and ballistae. Black smoke billowed from the many pots and cauldrons whilst the acrid stench of sulphur, brimstone and hot oil drifted on the dusty breeze. Gates and postern doors were bricked up, every battlement fortified. Jerusalem was no heavenly city but a mighty grim fortress ready for battle.

Hugh's description, as Eleanor wrote in her chronicle, did nothing to reassure her. Once they had pitched tents, the Portal of the Temple gathered to the north of the city. They squatted under a makeshift awning facing a slab of sandstone; on this, using a piece of charcoal, Hugh scrawled a rough outline of the city defences.

'The walls,' he pushed back his cowl, 'are about three miles long, fifty feet high and in places nine feet thick.' He stilled their cries and exclamations. 'Think of Jerusalem as a twisted rectangle almost a mile across from west to east and about the same north to south.' He made a mark on the sandstone. 'We are camped here to the north-west. We can only attack the city from the west or the north. The eastern side is protected by a deep gorge or valley called Josaphat.' Hugh shook his head. 'It would be impossible to launch an attack from there. The only gate, the Josaphat postern in the north-east section of the walls, is completely bricked up. On the south-east of the city stretches the Kedron valley. On the south-west stands Mount Sion;

further along lies the valley of Hinnon.'

'You must understand.' Godefroi got to his feet, gesturing at the crude drawing. 'Jerusalem's walls are protected on its eastern, southern and south-western flank by hills that fall steeply into three valleys, the Kedron, Josaphat and Hinnon. Only the north and north-west provide flatter ground for attack: here the city defences are reinforced by an outer wall and a deep dry moat. This exposed part of the city is pierced by five gates, from Herod Gate in the north round the western wall to the Sion Gate in the south. Each of these five entrances, Herod, St Stephen, New Gate, Jaffa and Sion, is protected by a pair of soaring towers. Two fortified citadels offer further defence: in the north-west corner stands the Quadrangular Tower, and further down the western wall the Tower of David. Both,' Godefroi's voice grew stronger, 'are built of solid masonry, large stones sealed with mortar and lead. Godfrey of Bouillon, Robert of Normandy, Robert of Flanders and Tancred will lay siege from St Stephen Gate to the Quadrangular Tower. Count Raymond of Toulouse will camp opposite the Tower of David, though some claim he will soon move to Sion Gate.'

'It's like Antioch!' someone shouted. 'We cannot lay siege to the entire city, and where are our engines of war? There's no wood!'

'And where do we go?' Beltran asked jumping to his feet. 'North, south, east or west?' His question provoked guffaws of laughter.

'We wait!' Hugh shouted back. 'If these walls are breached, we as a company have one place to reach, the Dome of the Rock. No other . . .'

His words were drowned by the bray of horns, the shrill of trumpets, men shouting and running. Eleanor scrambled to her feet as a dust-covered herald brandishing a crudely fashioned crucifix, his symbol of office, came running up.

'We attack tomorrow,' he announced.

'Nonsense!' Hugh retorted. 'There are no—'

'Our leaders,' the man gasped, 'rode up to view the city from the Mount of Olives. A hermit sheltering in a cave came out to greet them. He prophesied that if they attack at first light tomorrow and fight to the ninth hour, victory will be ours.'

Hugh and Godefroi tried to restrain the enthusiasm of their own followers, pointing out that the leaders simply wished to test the city defences. Beltran agreed with them, shouting questions about the whereabouts of scaling ladders, battering rams and towers.

'Only one ladder is needed,' the herald gasped. *'Deus providebit*—God will provide.'

The rest of the day and subsequent night were taken up with searching for wood. Tancred claimed he'd miraculously found some in a nearby cave, though everyone knew he had suffered a painful attack of dysentery and gone into the cave to relieve himself. Whatever its source, the carpenters became busy, using the poor light of candles and lantern horns to piece together ladders out of palm stems, soft poplar, tamarisk and the twisted wood of olive trees. By dawn, Tancred's men were ready, massing directly between New Gate and St Stephen. Hugh and Godefroi, however, decided not to commit the Portal of the Temple but stood on the brow of a hill and watched the attack unfold.

The sun had almost risen, its glare lifting, as Tancred's men formed a testudo, shields locked above their heads, and advanced, going down into the moat and up to attack the outer wall. They were immediately met by a lashing storm of arrows and missiles from the battlements. Saracen and Turkish archers leaned over the ramparts, bows extended. Here and there one of these figures, hit by a Frankish missile, slipped and toppled over, arms and legs splayed, to bounce against the wall before crashing to the ground. Banners curled and flapped. Plumes of black smoke from cauldrons of oil, boiling water and sticky pitch hovered like dark wraiths across the battlements. The war cries of both Frank and Turk drifted on the air. Eleanor always found it strange that both sides could be so earnest in their beliefs, though Theodore had informed her that what united the various factions of Islam, Turk, Saracen and Egyptian was the firm belief among them all that Jerusalem was Al Kuds, the Holy Place. The defenders along the battlements were determined to fight just as passionately as the Franks in defence of their sacred sites.

The air became riven with the blood-chilling whoosh of catapults and mangonels. The testudo, however, was now close against the outer wall. Godefroi and Hugh were talking excitedly. The defenders, because of the huddle of buildings so close to the wall, were limited in moving their engines of war backwards and forwards. So cramped was the space that the engineers were unable to calculate the narrow distance between the attackers and themselves. Accordingly the rain of missiles did little damage to the Franks but smashed into the already crumbling outer wall. This was quickly breached, and an entire section collapsed, provoking a great roar of triumph from both the attackers and those watching from the camp. Eleanor and her companions now had a clear view of what was happening. Tancred's testudo reached the great inner wall only to be met by a hail of rocks, arrows, pots of fire and flaming bundles of pitch, an avalanche of deadly missiles. Nevertheless the testudo held firm. The great ladder was produced. Figures swiftly scaled its rungs, swords drawn, heads and faces protected by their great oval shields. For a few heartbeats Eleanor thought the walls would be stormed and taken. Black clouds of smoke swirled across, then, very faintly, the lonely sound of a hunting horn sounded the retreat. The testudo reformed, climbing back through the breach in the outer wall, the rearguard struggling to bring back their ladder.

'Heaven help them,' Simeon whispered to Eleanor. 'Look, mistress-sister, I know what that is!' The defenders were now hoisting up what looked like two great water pots on to the battlements. Instead of being tipped, however, these were carefully lowered and pointed at the struggling Franks retreating towards the outer wall. Black trails of smoke curled around the pots, which immediately spat out an arc of fire, an orangey-red sheet of flame that engulfed the retreating Franks, turning some of them into living torches. The screams were horrendous. Men ran back to help, only to be engulfed in more gushes of fire and a hail of missiles. Eleanor watched in horror as these figures jerked and danced until they collapsed. The horrid view was mercifully cloaked as Tancred's men, smoke and dust swirling about them, struggled back through the gap in the outer wall.

'Greek fire,' Simeon declared. 'Water and dirt cannot smother it; only vinegar.'

'What was that? What was that?' Hugh and Godefroi came bustling across, faces mirroring their conflicting moods: despair at the failure of Tancred's attack coupled with open relief that they had not committed their own company.

'Vinegar,' Simeon declared. 'Use vinegar and Greek fire can be doused.'

Theodore, overhearing this, agreed and joined in the vigorous discussion that ensued until Imogene's cry drew their gaze back to the battlements. She was pointing further down to the Quadrangular Tower, the turrets of which rose black against the light blue sky. Three figures, women, their grey hair streaming in the wind, stood between the crenellations, supported by people standing behind them. They had their arms raised, fingers splayed, and although they could not hear a word, Eleanor and her companions realised they were chanting incantations and shouting curses. The figures, stark images against the light, looked sinister and threatening. They were already attracting the attention of Frankish bowmen, who loosed shaft after shaft, but the height and distance were too great.

'Witches!' Beltran explained. 'They always accompany the Ethiopians. I'm surprised Iftikhar has used them.'

Eleanor stared at those grim figures, oblivious to the exclamations around her. Simeon tugged at her sleeve and indicated Tancred's men, now hurrying up the hill carrying their wounded. One of these, Raimbold Creton, had actually reached the wall only to have his hand severed; this now lay beside his body on a makeshift stretcher. Eleanor was to witness even more gruesome scenes as the Army of God settle down to its siege. No more assaults were to be launched until siege engines were built, yet there was little wood on that dry plain. The leaders eventually decided to send their cattle, horses and other livestock back thirteen miles to the wooded hills and pastures they'd journeyed through. Soldiers were dispatched to guard these as well as to fell timber for the Franks to build their assault weapons. Food also ran low, but the greatest hardship was the lack of water in those arid hills.

At Siloam, Eleanor, dirt-caked and thirsty, braved the whipping arrows of enemy archers above Sion Gate to fill their precious waterskins. Theodore went scouting through the Kedron valley, but the river bed was rock dry and the cisterns all smashed. As the availability of Siloam became known, a general panic to reach the pool ensued before the leaders could stop it. Men and livestock raced, desperate for water; others pressed in carrying their sick. These pushed the first arrivals into the water, churning up the mud, and throngs hastened after them, beating aside the half-maddened livestock. In a few moments the pool became the centre of an ever-increasing angry mob. Men struggled to enter the water, fighting those trying to leave. The banks caved in under the trampling and turned the pool into a muddy mire. The strongest men forced their way through to the pure water by the rocks at the mouth of the spring, whilst the sick and weak were only able to drink the polluted mess along its edges. Those unfortunate enough to gulp the muddy water swallowed leeches which, within a few hours, led to an agonising death. The leaders tried to intervene, imposing order and setting a guard as they furiously debated what to do next.

Eleanor could do nothing but shelter in her shabby tent, tongue swollen, lips cracked. Simeon relayed gossip about the growing desperation amongst the Army of God whilst continuing to insist that Eleanor write it all down in her chronicle. She was too exhausted to do anything but sprawl on her makeshift bed, one arm across her face, staring up at the stained goatskin covering. A hundred thousand had left the Frankish west; fewer than twenty thousand had reached this hideous plain before the grim, embattled walls of Jerusalem. Eleanor idly wondered about their first casualty, Robert the Reeve—what had truly happened there? And the Magus and the Fedawi? Had they all been swept away by the anger of God; were they, the remnant, to starve in full view of the Holy City or be crushed against its walls and massacred by the great host coming out of Egypt?

'Great news.' Theodore, covered in a fine sandy dust, wafting away the flies hovering in a black mass round his face, strode into the tent. He squatted down by the bed and grinned at her. Eleanor smiled back. Theodore, with his handsome face and persistent good humour whatever adversity threatened! Yet he'd also given Eleanor new fears, fresh terrors. She felt deeply for him and became highly anxious about news of any affray, ambush or sally. Would Theodore be hurt or, God forbid, even killed? And when those formidable city walls were stormed, would he survive the violent blood-letting? She often prayed that if Theodore were to die, she would die with him.

'Good news,' he repeated.

Eleanor apologised and drew herself up. Theodore cocked his head at the shouting and cheering that rang through the camp.

'That's the good news,' he declared. 'Twenty Genoese galleys put in at the ruined port of Jaffa and begged the Army of God for help. Of course our leaders were delighted. The fleet would provide a good supply of timber, perhaps more food and water. Two companies of knights and bowmen were dispatched down to the coast under Raymond Pilet. Enemy cavalry attacked them. Pilet and his men broke through and reached the ruined walls of Jaffa with enemy shields and cloaks draped over their saddles. The Genoese sailors greeted our men joyfully. They had been cruising up and down the coast for days, searching for any trace of the Army of God. Raymond told them about our hardships and the sailors immediately prepared a feast of bread, wine and cooked fish. Franks and Genoese sat down together to celebrate in the roofless hall of Jaffa Castle, lit by fires, candles and lantern horns. Platters were filled and emptied, goblets of wine passed round. They even brought in the watch from the ships to have their share of the feast.' Theodore shrugged. 'They celebrated too well. An Egyptian fleet far out at sea glimpsed the lights of their party and stole in to block the harbour mouth. When dawn broke, the Genoese hastened to their ships but found it futile to offer battle; all they could do was abandon their galleys and carry ashore a good part of their weapons and supplies. So that,' Theodore gestured with his head, 'is the good news. The Genoese have just entered the camp.'

At first Eleanor failed to see *how* it was good news. Matters continued to deteriorate. Each day when the sun rose the heat struck her tent, rousing her from a sweaty sleep after an uneasy night. Sharp winds gusted through the ravines and valleys, blowing clouds of dust from the deep hollows of the surrounding desert. Water continued to be scarce. Skins of foul water, brought in on camels, sold for high prices, whilst she and others had little release from the harsh grind of each day. Eyes were dust-reddened and throats silted, whilst the stench of dead animals hung heavy over the camp. Reports flowed in how the herds of livestock taken up into the hills were being attacked by Turks, who also hampered any efforts to find water. Men began to desert. They reached the river Jordan, bathed in it and gathered some reeds as a sign that they had completed their pilgrimage, yet where could they go? Turks roamed the countryside, and the port of Jaffa was firmly in their hands.

In the end Theodore's assurances proved right. By the end of June the first timbers came down from the hills, dragged or wheeled on carts by mules and camels or carried on the backs of men. Godfrey of Bouillon marshalled the Genoese to help cut timbers and plait ropes for the catapults, keeping them busy with the mallets, spikes, nails and axes they'd brought from their ships. Godfrey's engineer, Gaston de Béarn, was placed in overall command of the workmen, whilst the Genoese craftsman William Embriaco was assigned to Count Raymond of Toulouse. Everyone was given a task. Eleanor carried wood and prepared ropes. An array of dreadful siege weapons rose up in the camp like hideous creatures from the underworld. A massive battering ram with an iron head shielded by a wattle roof; huge catapults with twisting ropes and deep cups; numerous scaling ladders and a range of portable wattle screens behind which soldiers could approach the walls. Count Raymond moved his companies to the south opposite Sion Gate, and concentrated on filling the moat, announcing that if anyone brought three stones to cast into it they'd be given a penny. After three days and nights, a section of the moat was filled. More mantlets were organised. Each knight was to furnish two such screens and one ladder. The stone-throwers, powered by twisted ropes, were placed on wheels so they could be moved from point to point. Sows, or long sheds open at each end, were constructed so they could be pushed up to the wall to shield the sappers trying to break through.

The common consensus, however, was that the walls would have to be stormed rather than mined. The Franks placed their main hope in two fearsome siege towers built upon wheeled platforms that could be brought up against the walls. Each tower had three storeys. On the lowest were the men who pushed the tower forward; the middle storey, about as high as the level of the ramparts of Jerusalem, was for the armoured knights to cross to the wall; whilst on the upper level archers would cover the rush of the knights.

The defenders of Jerusalem watched intently and prepared their defences. They brought mangonels on to the walls to be in close firing range. They also took careful measures to protect those sections of the wall they thought would be threatened from bombardment by hanging over sacks of straw and ship ropes, thick and closely woven, to cushion the stone against attacks from the Frankish catapults. The Army of God, now fully intent on the capture of the city, demonstrated that no mercy would be shown. During one of their forays they captured a leading Muslim commander, treated him honourably but asked him to convert. When he refused, they took him out in front of the Tower of David, where he was decapitated by one of Godfrey's knights. A few days later the Franks caught a spy coming up out of Egypt. They decided that if he wanted to enter the city then he should. Still alive, he was fastened to a catapult. He was too heavily weighted down and was not hurled far, but fell on sharp stones near the wall and broke his neck instantly.

The mood in the Frankish camp changed imperceptibly. The machines were ready, the formidable towers rising up; food and water was organised. Hopes rose, only to be dashed when Hugh and Godefroi brought news that the leaders were beginning to quarrel amongst themselves again. Objections had been raised against Tancred for hoisting his standard above Bethlehem, whilst the leaders were also debating about what was to be done when Jerusalem was taken. The clergy became involved, pointing out that Jerusalem was the Holy City and should have no king but Christ. Other titles were put forward: governor or regent. Hugh and Godefroi listened and took council with their own company. It was time for another vision. Peter Desiderius came forward. In a dream, he proclaimed before the council, his words spreading quickly through the camp, the saintly Adhémar of Le Puy had visited him and warned him that the Lord was not pleased. The army needed to purify itself. They must confess their sins, purge their guilt and bring themselves to a state of unity and grace before the assault was launched. Once again this vision was accepted. The common people thronged around the tents and pavilions of their leaders, urging that this be so. An order went out. On 8 July 1099, priests and monks armed with crosses and the relics of saints would lead a procession of knights and every able-bodied man and woman before the walls of Jerusalem. Trumpets would be blown, standards brandished. Eleanor, Theodore and the rest marched with the Frankish host as it processed barefoot, singing hymns and raising crosses around the city. From the battlements the defenders mocked them, loosing stones and arrows, but the procession was completed. A fast was ordered and everyone went to a priest to have their sins shriven; even the great leaders clasped hands and swore eternal amity.

The attack would soon commence. To the south of the city Raymond of Toulouse moved his tower closer to the dry moat. In the north, Godfrey of Bouillon tried to mislead the defenders, who had been busy raising the level of the wall opposite the second soaring siege tower. Tancred, Hugh and

Godefroi were sent out to spy, and returned to report how that section of the fortifications was almost impregnable. A sharp discussion took place. Theodore was present and he later gave the information to Eleanor, who included it in her chronicle. Godfrey of Bouillon realised that their great attack must not fail, so when night fell, he gave secret orders for the tower to be dismantled timber by timber. The separate parts would be carried a mile further along the wall to where the fortifications were lower and the ground more level. The same applied to the mantlets and stone-throwers. Under the cloak of darkness the great siege tower was literally stripped, dismantled storey by storey, the beams passed down to waiting soldiers. Silence was ordered. No candles or lanterns were lit, nor did they make use of oxen-pulled sledges, as the garrison might hear these and sally out. Progress was slow, but by dawn, the defenders of the city realised that their preparations to protect that section of the wall had failed: Godfrey of Bouillon had moved his entire attack a mile further south. Nevertheless, the stone-throwers and tower had to be rebuilt. More days passed. On the evening of 13 July, however, everything was ready. The order was given. At dawn the following morning, the Army of God would launch its all-out assault on the city of Jerusalem.

*   *   *

'Days of Anger, Days of Fire, Days of Vengeance!' was the phrase Eleanor of Payens used in her chronicle to describe the furious final assault on the Holy City. A time of deep anguish, of bitter loss and sordid betrayal, yet she wanted to capture it all. She sent Simeon to collect stories and tales that she could then weave alongside her own about that season of blood, of ferocious courage on both sides, a savagery that must have made Satan and all his fallen angels weep. Everyone realised judgement was imminent. The bowl of God's fury was to be tipped out, but whom would it consume? On the evening of 13 July, the Year of Our Lord's Incarnation 1099, the Portal of the Temple gathered to break its last bread and share out wine. Norbert said grace. Alberic delivered a brief homily and Peter Desiderius provided one more rendering of his vision of Adhémar of Le Puy.

They had all gathered under a shabby awning to make their peace and prepare. Eleanor, sitting between Theodore and Simeon, did not care for visions. Simeon's teeth were chattering, as every able-bodied man and woman had been summoned to join the general muster and array at dawn the following morning. Theodore, on her right, sat cradling his sword. He'd given Eleanor a ring, slipping it from his finger on to hers, then pressing her hand close.

'A token,' he whispered. 'If I return, I will reclaim it. If I do not, remember me!'

Eleanor choked back the tears. Now was not the time for weeping. Across the camp fire sat Imogene, staring at her sadly as if regretting the distance that had grown up between them. Eleanor wanted to speak to Imogene one final time before the trumpet sounded and the battle began. Yet Imogene was still hand-fast to Beltran, who continued to act as Count Raymond's envoy, moving between the two great Frankish divisions bearing letters and messages; Imogene would stay with him that evening. The bread and wine were finished. Hugh cleared his throat, then spoke softly, eyes gleaming, describing how they would muster behind Tancred's new banner, a red cross on a white background. If Jerusalem was taken, they must avoid any general plundering but assemble around him and Godefroi and follow them, or Theodore if they fell, into the city. Only the chosen few knew what Hugh would be searching for, yet no one questioned him. All realised those walls had first to be stormed and taken.

The night was hot, the moon full, the stars low and intense. Tomorrow would be a different day, and how many of them would gather again? Reminiscences were voiced, memories evoked, stories retold. Eleanor gripped Theodore's hand as she recalled that cold nave at St Nectaire. Whatever happened tomorrow, she knew she would never return there.

Once Hugh had finished and Godefroi had answered any questions, the meeting broke up. Eleanor and Theodore walked through the camp and sat down on a small dusty hillock, staring out at the lights of the city. Against the starlit sky reared the great siege tower and mangonels. All was ready. The cries of sentries, the blowing of horns, the neighing of horses and the creak of badly oiled wheels fractured the silence. Smoke from camp fires hung in a haze as the last meals were cooked. Here and there hymns and psalms were sung or chanted. People still lined up in dark clusters for their sins to be shriven. As Eleanor stared across, she could make out in the far distance the faint outline of the Herod Gate and, closer to her, that of St Stephen. The attack would be launched against the section of wall between. She lifted Theodore's hand and kissed the back of it.

'Swear to me, Theodore, if we survive tomorrow . . .'

He turned, tipping her face back, and kissed her full on the brow.

'I swear,' he murmured. 'If we survive!'

As the first red light of dawn torched the sky, wood creaked and crashed, ropes wound and hissed as the long arms of the stone-throwers hurled their deadly missiles towards the sky. Great boulders soared to smash against the walls of Jerusalem. Crossbows snapped and clicked, their squat black bolts whirling up towards the ramparts. Beneath the horrid sound of battle came the crashing of the ram pounding against the foundations of the outer fortifications. Shouts and battle cries were drowned by the roar of falling masonry. Dust and lime hung in the air, drifting like some deadly snow over siege engines and men. Mailed figures, knights in full armour, clustered behind rows of mantlets and woven shields. Every so often they would edge closer, but progress was slow. Other men, helped by women and children, rolled boulders towards machines or carried quivers of arrows on their shoulders. Swabian axemen and German swordsmen thronged impatiently, shields on their arms, weapons at the ready. On a hill opposite the eastern wall of the city clustered the banners of the lords and their retinues, ladders ready on the ground beside them.

Men brushed the sweat from their eyes, peered through the dust and lifted hands against the glare of the sun. They listened to the crash and thud of battle before the barbican, the outer wall, trying to discover what progress was being made. Distant horns clamoured, trumpets rang out, messengers came and went with news that Count Raymond had also begun his assault against the southern wall opposite Mount Sion.

Eleanor listened to Simeon's gasping reports but she sensed the real battle would begin and end here between the Herod Gate and St Stephen's. The attackers were still clawing at the barbican. Stonework had been cut, gaps forced, and through these Eleanor and the rest could see the dark, shadowy figures of their enemies. Above them along the battlements thronged others. Now and again arrows flashed down, hitting the earth or piercing men struggling with picks and ropes to clear the debris of the outer wall so that the great tower could trundle forward and seize the advantage created by the ram still pounding away.

Eleanor, Imogene and the other women hurried backwards and forwards bringing skins of precious water for the men to wet their lips or clean the dust from their eyes. A great roar went up just as Eleanor returned with a pannier of water. The siege tower was moving forward. Slowly, great wheels creaking, it edged towards the filled-in moat, crawling towards the barbican. Almost sixty feet high, the tower sloped inwards on three sides. On the fourth side, towards the city, it rose sheer from the ground towards the drawbridge, that precious piece of wood and metal that would give them entry to the city. The tower slowed down.

Something had happened. Smoke swirled. The Turks and Saracens now used fire against both the tower and the great ram. Faggots of wood and straw, bound together with iron chains and soaked in oil, were hurled with great force. Balls of fire whirled through the air. Despite the scorching heat of the day, the Franks fought back with axes and wet hides, yet still the rain of missiles fell. Suddenly the tower stopped completely. A great sheet of fire was blazing around the barbican. Men came running back with the dreadful news that the great ram had been fired: drenched in sulphur, pitch and wax, it was now burning fiercely. It could not be pushed forward, but neither could it be pulled back to clear a path for the tower. Orders were issued. Eleanor was given a message and scrambled down towards the fighting line, where Theodore, Hugh, Godefroi and the rest were waiting behind mantlets ready for the wall to be stormed. She delivered her message, demanding that the captain of the ram leave the fighting to receive fresh instructions, then ran back up the hill to the safety of that line of banners.

A short while later a man blackened from head to toe came up beating at his charred clothes and shouting for water. He knelt at Godfrey of Bouillon's feet and talked tersely in gasping sentences. Godfrey crouched down beside him, feeding him the pannier of water Eleanor had placed there. The man nodded and hurried back. The ram was to be burnt, the attack called off. To the south of the city, Count Raymond's company had fared no better. They too had pushed their tower against the walls and a hellish battle had broken loose. Catapults on the battlements hurled

278

an avalanche of stones. Arrows pelted down like rain. The closer the Franks approached, the worse it became: stones, arrows, flaming wood and straw followed by mallets of wood wrapped in ignited pitch, wax and sulphur. These mallets were fastened with nails so they stuck in whatever they hit and continued to flare. Despite the intense heat and the ferocious defence, Count Raymond tried to edge his tower closer to the wall, but he too failed. The light began to fade, so the horns and trumpets sounded the retreat.

Eleanor, exhausted, black with smoke, her gown saturated with sweat, her hair charred, returned to her tent. She wrapped a couple of blankets around her and waited for the Portal of the Temple to emerge from the horrors only a short distance away. The attack had failed. All around drifted the shrieks and screams of men, women and children gruesomely injured by the fire. Keening and mourning echoed like some blood-chilling chant. Simeon came in with a wineskin and forced her to take hurried sips before he squatted down beside her and drank greedily. At last the others returned: Hugh, Godefroi, Theodore, Alberic and Beltran, blackened faces furrowed by lines of sweat, hands hardly able to grasp a cup. They tore off their armour, belts, straps and jerkins tossed to the ground, then threw themselves down, desperate for water and wine, anything to prise their lips free from the sticky dust, unclog their throats and bathe their eyes.

Eleanor did her best to help. Theodore, half asleep, murmured where she could find more wine and water, a secret cache buried in his tent. She hurried away and brought it back. For a while they sat drinking and tending to their minor wounds. Eleanor went to the edge of the tent and peered into the gathering dark. Norbert and Imogene were missing. She went back and questioned the rest, but they shook their heads and wearily conceded that they didn't know. Eleanor forgot her own exhaustion. She glimpsed the pinpricks of torchlight as others stole from the camp to look for their dead, or to plunder them. She tugged at Simeon's sleeve.

'Bring a crossbow, a sword and a dagger,' she whispered.

The scribe looked as if he was about to refuse.

'Imogene and Norbert,' she hissed. 'We cannot leave them out there.'

'They are dead,' he retorted.

'They might be wounded,' she whispered back. 'At night, Simeon, the prowlers, two-legged and four, will range the battlefield. Norbert and Imogene have fallen,' she continued, 'we feel fortunate to be alive. It's the least we can do. Anyway,' she picked up her cloak, 'I'll go.'

Eleanor left the tent. She'd scarcely gone a few paces when she heard Simeon cursing and groaning behind her. She stopped, took the battered arbalest and scuffed leather case of bolts from him and went down towards the place of blood. It was a hot, dry night. Nevertheless, even the fierce battle that had raged that day could not silence the constant chant of the crickets and other insects. A night bird shrieked. A dog howled in reply. Eleanor and Simeon approached their own picket lines, where groups of soldiers huddled around fires guarding the precious siege machinery, the mangonels, small rams and that

280

soaring battle tower still reeking of oil, sulphur and charred wood. In the distance a roll of drums echoed from the battlements. Eleanor glimpsed the flickering lights and tongues of flame shooting up above the cauldrons and pots along the ramparts, sure proof that the defenders were vigilant against a possible night attack. Their own picket guards let them pass. Other dark shapes were also sloping down towards the battleground. Eleanor recalled how both Imogene and Norbert had been helpers like herself, carrying water, arrows and messages to the fighters beyond the dry moat. She went back and begged a torch from a group of soldiers, who teased and jeered but handed one over, and she and Simeon entered that ghastly, gruesome field of the dead.

The stench was foul, reeking of blood, burning and that sickening sweet smell of corruption. Corpses littered the ground, sprawled in grotesque shapes. Some, with their eyes stark open, stared unseeingly up into the dark. Others crouched as if resting. Groans and cries shrilled into the night. A group of monks were already trying to drag the wounded away, disentangling them from the dead. The torchlight revealed grisly sights. A man squashed beneath a huge boulder. Corpses with heads, arms and legs severed. Faces with only the eyes intact. The parched earth was sticky with blood. The occasional bold jackal was already nosing at swollen stomachs; dark, dog-like shapes that fled swiftly at their approach. Eleanor stared despairingly around. The dead lay singly or in heaps. A monk came crawling over on all fours like some foulsome creature of the night, yet he proved friendly enough. A Frenchman, he gasped that he

281

was searching for the wounded as well as those who wanted a priest. He murmured a prayer but shook his head at Eleanor's descriptions of Imogene and Norbert.

Eleanor and Simeon continued their hunt. At times they had to cover both nose and mouth at the foul stench of dried blood, rotting entrails and the ever-pervasive reek of burning flesh. Charred corpses were common, nothing more than shrivelled black stumps of flesh. Simeon retched and vomited. Eleanor ignored his protests and moved on at a half-crouch. She tried to ignore the pallid faces, the eyes all caught in the shock of death. Only a few looked peaceful. They approached a cart burnt to cinders by an incendiary and found Norbert lying on his back, eyes staring glassily. At first Eleanor thought he was sleeping. She whispered to Simeon to bring the light closer, then covered her mouth at the horrid mess the sling shot had caused to the back of the monk's head, a congealed mass of shattered bone, dried brain and blood. She knelt, head down, making the sign of the cross and whispering the Requiem. Then she glanced around. If Norbert had been killed here, then perhaps Imogene wasn't far. She crawled across the ground.

'Imogene, Imogene!' she whispered hoarsely.

Nothing but silence. She was about to move away when she heard her name being called, a hoarse, dry whisper trailing out of the darkness in front of her. She crawled round the cart. Imogene lay by herself. She had turned on her side and was trying to drag herself forward. Eleanor caught her and cradled her carefully. Imogene sighed. Her hair was all dishevelled, her face sheet white, large

282

dark eyes gazing up, blood spluttering between her lips. She was trembling, trying to keep the veil pressed close to staunch the deep wound in her side.

'Eleanor,' Imogene panted, 'listen . . .'

'No . . .'

'No,' she gasped. 'Promise me, my parents' ashes?'

Eleanor nodded.

'You will bury them and say a prayer?' Imogene pleaded. 'Any prayer? If the city falls, do that, in sacred soil in the corner of some shaded garden. Do that, Eleanor, and my vow will be fulfilled. Promise?'

Eleanor tried to reassure her.

'No,' Imogene gasped, 'I'm dying, I know that. I will be glad to be gone. Too much pain, too much hurt! This wound . . . Beltran.' She spat the name out. 'He did this. He is not what he claims to be, what he pretends to be. He seduced me, Eleanor, not because he loved me but because of a conversation I had with him oh so long, long ago.' Imogene's eyelids fluttered. 'The night Robert the Reeve left the church and went into the dark, Beltran, I am sure, went after him. I kept silent about it then later teased him. He laughed it off even as he began to court me. You can't disguise everything, Eleanor, not for two years. Beltran has travelled far and wide. He betrayed himself in small things: knowledge of customs, petty mistakes; he too chattered in his sleep. On occasion he'd go missing and I began to wonder. He changed. The closer we came to Jerusalem, the more he wanted to enter the Portal of the Temple, draw closer to your brother. He wanted to be rid of

283

me, but without creating any suspicion.' Imogene coughed on the blood seeping between her lips.

Eleanor just stared down at her, a cold, gripping fear curdling her stomach as she recalled Imogene's questioning of her. Imogene had begun to suspect Beltran of imposture and falseness, and of course Beltran needed Imogene, who lodged with Eleanor. Imogene might learn so much about Hugh, Godefroi and their search for precious relics.

'Is he the Magus?' Eleanor asked.

Imogene shook her head in bewilderment. 'I don't know what you mean, but I am sure he was the horseman.' She gasped. 'I'm sure he was responsible for Anstritha's death, and for that of Robert the Reeve, who also suspected the truth. So hard, Eleanor,' she whispered, 'so callous. He wanted me dead. He had no need of me any more. In the battle today I saw Norbert being struck, I went to help him. Beltran slipped beside me, so swiftly . . .' She coughed violently, her body shook, her eyes fluttered, then she lay still. Eleanor let her go, placing her gently on the ground. Cries and shouts echoed from the walls. A bundle of fire, flames streaking, was launched from a catapult. It lighted the night sky then smashed into the ground in a burst of fiery sparks. Other sights and sounds came pressing in.

'Mistress-sister, what shall we do?'

'We must go back,' Eleanor declared. 'We must warn Hugh and Godefroi; we can collect the corpses tomorrow.' She blessed herself and stumbled back across the battlefield, trying to shut out the hideous images. She felt sick and exhausted. Slowly the two of them crept back towards the sloping ridge leading up to their watch fires. A shape moved abruptly to her right, fast like that of a loping wolf. She ignored it, but then halfway up the sandy, pebble-strewn hill, a shadow moved from behind a gorse bush to block her way. Exhausted, Eleanor sat down, peering through the darkness. Beltran, cloaked and cowled, squatted before her, grasping a Brabantine arbalest. In the juddering light of Simeon's torch, he looked sinister despite the smile, the casual way he kept the arbalest down, as if he was more surprised than suspicious.

'Eleanor, where have you been?'

'I found them,' she gasped. 'Norbert and Imogene.'

'Both dead?'

'Imogene was not!' Eleanor closed her eyes and groaned at Simeon's impulsive remark. 'You killed her!' the scribe continued hotly. Eleanor caught the passion in Simeon's voice and wondered if he too had been taken by the pretty Jewess. Beltran simply clicked his tongue.

'*Miserere mei*,' he replied. 'I thought the stupid bitch was dead. I suppose you shrived her, Eleanor, heard her last confession, but who'd care for a Jewess?'

'I do.' Eleanor let all pretence fall. 'I do. I did. I shall. God curse you, Beltran. She loved you, yet you murdered her because you didn't need her any more. The same callous way you murdered Anstritha and Robert the Reeve. Anstritha died because of a mysterious horseman: you. Robert the Reeve went stumbling out into the dark drunk, and you drowned him. You're a serpent in hell and you've made that hell worse. Now let me by!'

285

'I would love to,' he replied mockingly, 'but tomorrow we might all be in hell! Heaven forfend, the wheel does turn! You see, Eleanor, I need your priggish, murderous brother. I want to be with him if, or when, he finds that treasure hoard. True, I used Imogene like an eyelet into the chamber of your affairs. I thought she'd eventually tire of me but she stuck fast like a leech. She had to go.'

'And Count Raymond?'

'Oh, I joined his service easily enough. Men like the count always need men like me, obsequious, knowledgeable, ready to obey their every whim. Some serpents require little cunning. It's so easy to worm your way in.' He sighed noisily. 'Everything was upset by Urban's *Deus vult.*' Beltran laughed. 'All the Frankish west roused to march on Jerusalem! The treasures of the east would be seized. My commercial affairs would be harmed. First my stupid sister Anstritha went looking for protection, then your brother and his coven with their vision of this and that. Robert the Reeve suspected I was the horseman, that I was not what I claimed to be. He became curious about my affairs, so I killed him.'

'You are the Magus? You pretended to be the Fedawi?'

'I sell relics to those stupid enough to buy them, and yes, I had to protect my interests! Seize back my stupid sister's map. I left it too late. Your brother had it.' Beltran shrugged. 'He'd have made copies.'

'And a spy?'

'I have no faith, no allegiance, no lord. I move among men. I bustle busily to earn a crust. I tell this person that, that person this. I'm just a

286

merchant in a marketplace.' He waved a hand. 'Look at these fools. I am here for gold, the real possibility of making myself rich with a king's ransom. Such business always carries risks. But the likes of your brother? Dreaming of marvels, myths and make-believe! No reward in this life, and after death? Not the light he or you hope for, just a darkness more profound, the darkness of nothingness.'

Eleanor heard a sound behind Beltran. She calmed herself. She must delay him, hold him whilst looking for any opportunity.

'You're a spy,' she rasped. 'You sell information, be it to the Byzantines or the Turks. So easy, certainly before Antioch, to ride out and meet enemy scouts, and give them information. Baldur, oh yes, you know him? He certainly knew of you! He played a game with your name. He tossed his belt on the ground and told Theodore to hang you with it. A belt for Beltran, a clever conceit but true! You will hang!'

'I do not think so.'

'You're the horseman, the Magus, the Fedawi,' Eleanor continued desperately. 'You used the confusion of battle to slip here and there, disguised as this or that. You used your position with Count Raymond to hint that the spy was a member of my brother's company.' She laughed sharply. 'For once you told the truth: there was a spy—you, though Count Raymond never suspected that!'

'A merchant moves from one place to another . . .'

'You're a killer!'

'*Negotium auri*, Eleanor, the business of gold.'

'And now?'

287

'I heard you leave. I did wonder if Imogene was dead. I could take no chances.' Beltran knelt, bringing up the arbalest. 'Your stupid scribe has brought your deaths on you.'

'Beltran?' The whisper hissed through the darkness.

Beltran turned. The whirr of a crossbow bolt cut the air and struck him deep in the face, its barbed shaft shredding skin and bone. A blood-spattered mess, gruesome in the poor light. A shadow sped forward. A knife glinted as it drove deep into the side of Beltran's neck. Beltran gave a loud, gargling sigh and pitched forward on to his face. Theodore stepped into the pool of light. He knelt, grasped Beltran by the hair, pulled up his head then let it fall.

'I heard you whispering in the tent.' Theodore went down on one knee, staring at Eleanor. 'Then you both left.' He gave a lopsided grin. 'Simeon, you grumble like an old sow. I thought of accompanying you, but I was exhausted. I was making myself comfortable for sleep when he . . .' Theodore gestured at the corpse sprawled in an ever-spreading pool of blood, 'moved too quickly for a supposedly tired man. I smelled mischief.'

'Did you always suspect him?' Eleanor rose clumsily to her feet.

'Yes and no,' Theodore murmured. 'Beltran was an enigma. He made mistakes, small ones, inconsistencies. Like the other day he seemed to know more about the Governor of Jerusalem and Ethiopian troops than he should have done. He was so eager to join the Portal of the Temple, but Hugh and Godefroi objected to his relationship with Imogene. A spy?' The Greek shrugged.

'Perhaps! Until the Battle of Antioch, any one of us, as we know,' he smiled, 'could move from one army to another. Then there was the Fedawi.' Theodore rested the arbalest against his shoulder. 'I found it difficult to accept that they were amongst us, so far from their castle fastness, so close to us.' He shook his head and extended a hand. 'Come, leave the dead to bury the dead. Tomorrow, God knows, we might join them!'

*   *   *

At daybreak on 15 July, the Year of Our Lord 1099, Godfrey of Bouillon and Raymond of Toulouse flung their armies at the walls of Jerusalem. A beautiful dawn, as Eleanor de Payens wrote in her chronicle, its serenity soon shattered by the creak of twisted ropes, the curses of men, the screech of wheels and the blood-chilling whine of fiery missiles, stones, arrows and blazing bundles. Crashing and thudding swept the air as the terrifying din of battle increased. Godfrey of Bouillon, his gold cross standard openly displayed, ordered his great tower forward. The defenders of Jerusalem brought up their slings and mangonels, loosing firebrands dipped in oil and grease at the attackers. A deadly race ensued; that was how Eleanor de Payens described it in her chronicle: the Franks desperate to bring up their tower, the Turks and Saracens eager to burn it before the besiegers ever reached the walls. A thick pall of smoke ringed the tower, penetrated only by missiles. At one time Godfrey of Bouillon himself was nearly killed. A stone hurled randomly struck a squire standing close to him; the man's skull was

289

shattered, his neck broken, and he died instantly. Godfrey, having narrowly missed such sudden death, fought back fiercely using his crossbow to bring down defenders.

The tower crept forward through the breach of the outer wall, closer and closer to the main defences. The top of the tower threatened to overlook the battlements of Jerusalem. Frankish archers and slingers released a deadly storm of stones and arrows. Fire was hurled back, but the tower was protected by mantlets and wattle screens covered with slippery skins. The firebrands and burning coals struck these only to slip down to the ground. The defenders brought up tubes of Greek fire, which belched out greedily, but the outside of the tower had been doused in vinegar whilst wineskins hung in the tower held more. The tower inched its way forward. On either side of it thronged archers who loosed shafts wrapped in flaming cotton; these struck the wooden defences, the sacks of straw and oiled ropes the Saracens and Turks had arranged along the wall to protect it against the rams, and they burst into flame, forcing the defenders from the parapets. Scaling ladders were hurriedly brought forward, whilst Tancred took a force of knights to pound at St Stephen's Gate.

The defenders were now confused by the fires billowing along the battlements; curling smoke and acrid fumes blocked their view and confused their actions. The Portal of the Temple put up its scaling ladder, and one of their company, Lethold of Touraine, clambered up over the walls, the first knight to enter Jerusalem. The tower edged closer. Godfrey of Bouillon glimpsed two great beams thrust out by the Turks to hold it off. He swiftly cut the ropes of one of the ox-hide-covered mantlets, which fell across the beams to provide a makeshift drawbridge. Godfrey hurried across, his men pouring after him, their long swords hissing and cutting, fighting like demons through the black smoke. The breach was stormed and held. The tower crept closer. Further along the wall the three witches and the slaves supporting them were deluged by a hail of stones that pulped them into a bloody mess. The tower now leaned over the walls of Jerusalem. Its drawbridge fell. Scores of knights ran across on to the battlements to join Godfrey. The defenders panicked and ran. The collapse spread. The garrisons at the Herod Gate, St Stephen's and further along at Mount Sion simply fled. Entrances were forced and the Franks poured like a river of revenge through the city, spilling out along every thoroughfare, street and alleyway. No quarter! No mercy was to be offered, nothing but the sword for men, women and children.

The Franks fanned out like reapers gathering some bloody harvest. Groups of Turks and Saracens made one final stand, archers still loosed arrows from rooftops, but it was all over. The governor and remnants of his Egyptian cavalry fled to the Tower of David and locked themselves in. The Franks simply passed through, living incarnations of the Angel of Death, a black cloud of murderous fury. Streets, squares, houses and gardens became thickly strewn with the corpses of men, women and children. Axes and swords fell until the fountains splashed red and the white walls became drenched in blood. Some hoped to gain sanctuary in the mosques; none was given. The

Franks reached the courtyard of the Holy Sepulchre, where more people were huddled. They advanced, sword and axe at the ready, but their intended victims hurriedly knelt, crossing themselves, and croaked the prayer of mercy from the Mass: *'Kyrie Eleison, Christe Eleison'*—Lord have mercy, Christ have mercy. The Franks sheathed their weapons, touched the heads of these Armenian Christians and went searching for other prey. They burst into the great Temple enclosure where Turks and Saracens clustered to surrender. None was accepted. By the time the slaughter was ended, men waded through blood that lapped beneath their knees and stained the harness of their horses.

At sunset the Franks put an end to their killing. They had, like wolves snuffling through the scrub, glutted themselves on gore and blood; now they doffed their armour, put on gowns and walked barefoot to the Church of the Holy Sepulchre to give thanks. They passed mounds of severed heads, arms and feet. They crossed a mat of corpses as they reverently chanted their psalms and hymns. They made their devotions and retired for the night.

Meanwhile the Portal of the Temple were hurrying down into the warren of gloomy passageways beneath the Dome of the Rock. Hugh de Payens and Godefroi of St Omer had survived and were zealous in their quest. The Fedawi had either fled or died in the massacre, so they hacked down doors and lifted rusting iron-plated traps until they found their treasures. They moved quickly and orderly all through that night and the next day, when the slaughter in the city began once again. No mercy was to be shown. This was God's work, the Franks argued: their enemies had mocked, humiliated and used all manner of wickedness against them; this could only be purged by blood. Some survivors climbed on to the flat roof of the Aksa Mosque; Tancred offered them protection, even handing over his own stand-ard, but the killers ignored this, storming on to the roof and massacring all three hundred survivors.

As smoke hung like a black cloud above a city stinking of slaughter, in the narrow passageways beneath the Dome of the Rock, Hugh and Godefroi ransacked the secret treasure hoards hidden away in chambers where the great Solomon had once stabled his horses. In the light of candles and lantern horns they rolled out the sacred cloth that once covered the Lord's face. They knelt in adoration of it and repeated their solemn vows: kingdoms, princes and powers could trample through the streets of the Holy City. They would come and go, nothing more than a watch in the night, but the Portal of the Temple, the House of the Temple, the Templars would take root and grow as magnificent as the cedar of Lebanon . . .

*   *   *

Under the awning of her shabby tent on a hillside overlooking Jerusalem, Eleanor de Payens made herself comfortable on a faldstool, threading battered Ave beads through her filthy fingers. Theodore, blood-stained and smelling of fire and wood smoke, squatted before her. He had taken off his hauberk and leather leggings, and cradling a wineskin, he toasted Eleanor before taking a drink.

'The City of Jerusalem has fallen.' Theodore wiped his mouth on the back of his hand. 'Your brother, using the maps he had gathered, has found his treasure trove. Relics, Eleanor, linen sheets containing imprints of our Saviour, documents, artefacts, precious stones, silver and gold. He and Godefroi—'

'They are well?'

'As strong as lions! They lost some of their company.'

'Were they involved in the massacre?'

'Mistress!' Simeon, sitting behind Eleanor, leaned forward. 'Mistress-sister,' he whispered, 'leave that.'

'Oh yes, I will!' she retorted harshly.

'Will you go into the city?' Theodore asked. 'Hugh and Godefroi are waiting. They've given thanks to God, they . . .' His voice trailed off at the look on Eleanor's face. 'I told them about Beltran.'

'And?'

Theodore spread his hands. 'They saw him as a troublesome wretch, nothing more. Eleanor, will you come?'

'I have travelled thousands of miles,' she murmured, closing her eyes then opening them. 'I thought I would dance under the gateway of Jerusalem, but now I am here, I do not want to go into the Holy City. I do not want to see any more severed heads or blood-spotted walls.' She stared out at the black plumes of smoke rising above the city. 'Here, Theodore,' she tapped her breast, 'here is Jerusalem. Here,' she leaned forward and caressed his cheek, 'is the Face of Christ. Here,' she pressed her hand against his chest, 'is true religion. There,' she gestured with her hand, 'some

294

whitewashed cottage, with the honeysuckle climbing up the walls, is paradise.' She put away the Ave beads, wrapped her cloak tight about her and got to her feet. 'And Alberic?'

'He fought like a warrior, wounded but well.'

Eleanor smiled and extended her hand. 'Come, let us search out Norbert and Imogene and give them honourable burial.' She gestured at the finely carved box lying next to her stool, the one Imogene had so treasured. 'For the love of God, Theodore, and for love of me, take this into the city. Bury it deep in the black soil beneath some cypress tree.' She smiled. 'Then come back to me, and we shall find our own Jerusalem.'

Author's Commentary

The Templar is based solely on eye-witness accounts that can be read in translation in a splendid book: *The First Crusade. The Accounts of Eye Witnesses and Participants*, ed. A. C. Krey (Princeton, 1921). A good modern account can be found in Christopher Tyerman's *God's War* (Allen Lane, 2006). The perspective of the Byzantines is clearly reflected in *The Alexiad of Anna Comnena*, trans. E. R. A. Sewter (Penguin, 1979), and that of Islam in *The Damascus Chronicle of the Crusade*, ed. H. A. R. Gibb (Dover Publications, 2002). As regards the theft of sacred relics and the exploits of men like the Magus, please see *Furta Sancta, Thefts of relics in the Central Middle Ages* by Patrick Geary (Princeton, 1978). The relics of Christ's Passion have been the subject of many books, but I do recommend Ian Wilson's *The Blood and the Shroud* (Weidenfeld & Nicolson, 1998).

The First Crusade was a phenomenon still debated today. Pope Urban's speech comes to us second hand, but its effect through Europe was electrifying. The composition of the Crusade is faithfully reflected in this novel. There were as many reasons for going as there were participants, the idealistic to the depraved and cruel. However, what is fascinating is the incredible courage and stamina of those involved. The ferocity of the battles and the massacres that followed clearly did away with any theory of a just or holy war. In a sense the Crusades were total war, where no prisoners were taken and the absolute destruction of the enemy was a military objective. Of course, certain mysteries still persist. There are no clear reasons why the Byzantines attacked Raymond of Toulouse's army near Radosto, but bearing in mind the rapacity of certain of his followers, the reason given in this book is probably as valid as any other. The Magus and the Fedawi do figure in history, whilst the finding of the Holy Lance and its psychological impact on the Frankish army is, in my opinion, one of the most brilliant propaganda coups in the history of warfare. Firuz was involved in the betrayal of Antioch and some chronicles do mention that it arose due to grievances over a woman. Firuz apparently disappears from history, but his brother was killed in the first blood-letting. Khebogha's advance on Antioch is as I have described it. In my view he was tricked. According to many accounts he was still playing chess when the Frankish army deployed!

Finally—the Templars. The origin of the Templars, according to all accounts, was linked with Hugh de Payens and Godefroi of St Omer (in some accounts he is called Geoffrey). The Order was founded some years after the taking of Jerusalem, and became a great power in western Europe until its destruction by Philip IV of France between 1307 and 1314. One of the earliest accounts is that of William of Tyre in his *Historia* who talks of them being 'devoted to God'. In my view William is referring to the Order in its early stages. In many ways the Templars were enlightened. They had a strict code and it is interesting that in their First Rule, confirmed at the Council of Troyes, there is an explicit reference in section 53 to 'no further acceptance of sisters'. Proof enough that at one time, in its early history, women were accepted as members of that mysterious Order.

Paul Doherty,
April 2007
Website: www.paulcdoherty.com